CONAN THE REBEL

by

POUL ANDERSON

ROBERT HALE · LONDON

© Conan Properties, Inc 1980

First published in Great Britain by Sphere Books Ltd 1984

This edition 1984

ISBN 0 7090 1545 3

01860653

Robert Hale Limited
Clerkenwell House
Clerkenwell Green
London EC1R 0HT

18413814

Printed in Great Britain by
Photobooks (Bristol) Ltd
and bound by
W.B.C. Bookbinders Ltd.

CONAN THE REBEL

Continuing the sword-clashing saga of the mighty Conan, first seen in *Conan The Barbarian* and now a bestselling screen figure.

Against the reptile god of the evil sorcerer of Khemi the fearless Conan rises. With the raven-haired beauty Belit and her crew of savage pirates he braves the dreaded land of Stygia—where cold air sighs up from the crypts and crocodiles drag themselves across the mudbanks. He storms the walls in hot-blooded fury to free her kin from the overseer's lash and the chains of eternal darkness.

Also published by Robert Hale Limited

Conan the Barbarian
  by L. Sprague de Camp & Lin Carter

CONTENTS

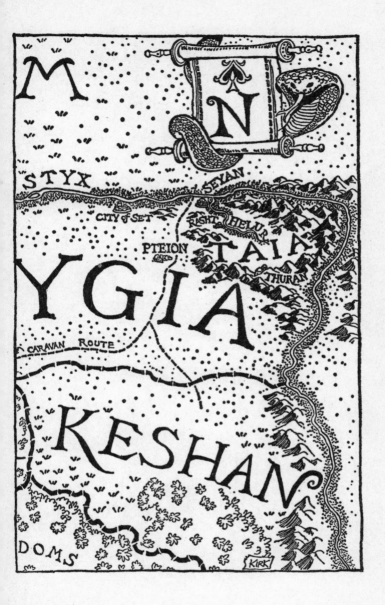

1

THE VISION OF THE AX

Night lay heavy on Stygia. Where the great river emptied into its bay, no whisper of wind came off the ocean beyond. The sky was hazed, so that only a few stars glimmered in sight above Khemi, and it was as if they were embers of that furnace heat which the stones of the city still radiated after day had long departed. Outer walls lifted sheer to hold off any coolness the sea might have sent, even as they held off the world from the secret doings within. Around those iron-gated cliffs, watchtowers reared higher yet, their battlements like teeth bared at heaven. The streets beneath were guts of blackness, silent, deserted, save where a sacred python rustled scales dryly over the paving in search of prey, or footfalls padded of someone from whom it slithered back with a hiss of alarm.

The air was otherwise where the magician Tothapis slept. In a crypt among those carved deep out of bedrock, slaves toiled at a giant wheel driving fan blades in a shaft. The breath they sent aloft lent its chill to the sultriness and incense of their lord's bedchamber. The whir made an undertone for the slumber-music of a carillon played by that same machinery. Though his mattress was hard, as became a man of austerity, it was stuffed with the tresses of sacrificial maidens, while his gown and sheets were of silk, ebon-hued, so fine that the fabric might have been spun by spiders.

Nevertheless, on this night he slept ill, tossing and muttering. Abruptly he woke, sat up, gasped. Four sable candles at the corners of his bed, man-tall, mounted in the legbones of behemoths, flared high and went out.

Such a sign had not come to him before in his centuries of life, but he knew what it portended. He scrambled free of the top sheet with which he had been struggling and sought the floor. There he prostrated himself, kissed the carpet, writhed serpentine. *'Iao, Setesh!'* he shrilled. *'Anet neter aa, neb keku fentut amon!'*

Only then did he dare raise his head and stare before him. Amidst the blindness now prevailing, he saw a pale yellow glow; amidst the deafness, he heard a susurration that came out of no human mouth. The glow strengthened, grew, became the image of a huge golden-colored snake coiled in a circle from floor to high ceiling. By its light he could dimly see the hieroglyphs on every free surface in the room. The sibilance became a monstrous rushing noise, like that of the River Styx in its cataracts far to the southeast. Tothapis groveled again and adored his god.

The noise formed language: 'Speak, man. Declare who I am.'

'You are Set,' the wizard intoned, 'lord of the universe, whom the Stygians worship before all others.'

'Declare how you yourself do serve me.'

Words torrented forth: 'In every way that man may serve That which was before he was, and will be when he is no more. I am a priest in your temple, and if I am not its chief hierophant, the reason is that I can further your cause the better in the Black Ring of magicians whereof I am head. My spells confound the infidels who acknowledge you not, my counsel strengthens the hand of the king against them. Soon, soon they will learn from us how terrible is your wrath, O Set. True, my service is but the least and humblest of tributes to your darkling glory. You have made my days and my nights long in the world; you have given me power over both men and demons; foremost of what you have granted has been an ever more profound understanding of those mysteries that are of your essence. And tonight you have revealed yourself to your slave. What else dare I ask? What else dare I offer in return, O Set?'

'Rise, man. Behold me. Hearken.'

Tothapis got to his feet and stood rigid, arms held straight out, palms down. The reptile head gaped before him, tongue aflicker between fangs, but the lidless eyes unmoving in their stare. 'Heed me well,' he heard. 'You have called me lord of the universe, but you know how many and diverse are the gods of earth, sea, sky, and underworld. You know how few of them own me their master, how few of their peoples look on me as aught but a devil. Mightiest of my rivals is Mitra of the Sun, who would fain tread me underfoot.'

'Cursed be Mitra and the Hyborians that follow him,' Tothapis mumbled.

'Cursed indeed,' answered the apparition. 'Yet through chronicles and through more arcane lore you know its strength from of old. I send this sending unto you to warn of a new danger. It menaces yourself, your king, your nation, and your very god. This day a man and a woman have joined. Never will any child come of their union; but already, all unwitting, they have begotten a destiny. Can it not be slain in womb or cradle, it will fast grow gigantic, and in its hands will be a war ax that hews down many – that will at last, in years to come, strike at the pillars of mine own sanctuary.'

Tothapis, who had gazed with calm upon hellish things, shuddered. If Set could not smite down a pair of mortals, but must instead call for mortal help, then unimaginable Powers were at strife in the world beyond the world.

'Sorcerer, fear not,' hissed the voice. 'What is to happen must happen on earth alone, for if the great gods intervened, that could bring on the Last Strife. Yet I, who am Stealth-in-the-Night, bear to you the foreknowledge you will need; and you will have your wonted cunning, your magic and monsters and demons, at your beck, against a foe who remains ignorant of what he himself portends. He is but flesh and blood, however powerful the flesh and fiery the blood. Were it not for this chance encounter with the woman, he would live and die an obscure rover – as you can still make him die.

'Watch, and learn well.'

Within the circle of the serpent's coil, an image came to being. It was as if Tothapis winged out through the dome of his house to a mile above Khemi. He saw the city hunched by the gleam of river and bay and ocean, he saw cultivated hinterlands like a gray tapestry silver-threaded by canals and spotted with humble villages. Upward his view receded, until Stygia lay stretched immense along the stream that was its northern boundary. Beyond reached the farmlands and grasslands of Shem, southward desert,

3

and then the jungles and veldts of Kush. At this height he discerned no trace of man's works.

Dizzyingly swift, his vision swept down the Kushite seaboard. Rain forests brooded over surf; swamps and rivers sheened; as the view descended, he glimpsed open spaces where the black primitives had burnt off woods for their plantings. Hawklike, sight swooped westward across the water.

Tothapis saw a ship. She was a fighting craft, a lean black galley with a raised deck from stem to stern. Below were benches, and below them a main deck covering the hold. At her prow gleamed a gilt image, the snarling head of a tiger. Shields hung on the low rails. The forty oars were inboard, for a wind bellied out her single square sail and drove her north in long, feline bounds across whitecaps. Most of the crew were at rest, their sleeping bags laid on decks or benches. As his sight drew close, Tothapis saw that they were Negroes, strong young men who wore little clothing or none but who showed battle scars and kept weapons ready at hand.

His view ranged astern. A small poop deck formed the roof of what must be the captain's cabin. On it stood a white man and woman. The man's right hand grasped the tiller of a steering oar, his left arm lay around her waist, and she caressed him in her turn. They were easy to see, for here the sky was altogether clear, thronged by stars and girdled by a brilliant Milky Way, while phosphorescence went swirling over the waves.

Tothapis was celibate, lest he lose energy to the ordinary things on earth. But as he looked upon this woman, the air whistled between his teeth. She was young, thinly clad though the sea wind must be cold, a dirk at her hip and a silver headband her sole accessories of dress. Raven-dark hair blew loose, well-nigh down to her waist. Somehow the starlit vision of Tothapis showed colors; he saw that her eyes were big and lustrous brown beneath level brows, her complexion olive, her lips full and vivid. That, together with the finely sculptured curve of nose and the high cheekbones, proclaimed her a Shemite. She was taller than was usual for her race, and never had he beheld such a figure – large yet firm bosom, slim-waisted, long-limbed, no trace of softness underlying those curves. When she moved, she moved like a panther.

'Here is Bêlit,' the voice of Set told him. 'Female, she has nonetheless turned her savages into the most fearsome pirate crew that ever harried the Black Coast; and now they are beating north to Stygia. This day she attacked a vessel whereon Conan of Cimmeria was traveling. She took it at heavy cost, since he fought against her. As he did, love flamed between them across the swordblades, and they made peace; but together they would make red war ... Take your heed off her, you fool! Observe Conan.'

Tothapis hastened to obey. The helmsman was also young, albeit at first glance he seemed older. In height and bulk he overtopped most men. The play of muscles in an arm that effortlessly handled the heavy, bucking oar bespoke strength to match his size. However, he was no less agile and supple than his mate. A square-cut black mane fell to his shoulders. The clean-shaven countenance was handsome in a massive fashion. Its sternness had eased into lines of laughter, and the blue eyes sparkled where formerly they had often smoldered. A tunic he had slipped on when he and Bêlit decided to go topside for a while was rather too small for him. Thus the watcher glimpsed skin the sun had not bronzed; its whiteness proclaimed a man of the far North – a barbarian.

The sibilance ended. In its place Tothapis heard rush of waters, creak of timbers, thrum of rigging. He could almost feel the deck pitch and sway underfoot, or taste salt blown on wind. Bêlit spoke, her husky voice gone soft. 'The stars rejoice with us, beloved.'

She used the nautical lingua franca. Conan's bass replied in the same tongue, his Cimmerian accent musical enough to surprise a Stygian who had read few and vague accounts of that remote warrior folk. 'Well they might, seeing they look on you.' He chuckled and hugged her closer. 'But they will miss you at your most beautiful, when we go below again.'

'Soon?' she purred.

'Quite soon. I told you I just wanted a breath of air, and thought I might as well get some practice at seamanship, if we are to adventure as corsairs. Yes, I'll call N'Yano and Mukatu back to this tiller in a few more pulsebeats.' Conan grinned. 'And back to their envy, no doubt.'

'Fear no envy or treachery from our crew,' Bê lit assured him. 'They are my own dear men of the Suba, who have given me their blood oath. Never once while we fared has any laid untoward hand on me, or offered me the least insult.'

'Woe betide whoever did,' Conan said, only half in jest. 'But – hm – I suppose we had better give them a romp somewhere before long.'

'They know they can have that whenever we put into a port safe for us. We carry loot aplenty to pay for it. But revenge is a more urgent wish, in them as in me. First we harry Stygia.'

Conan frowned. 'What? Oh, we can strike here and there, but why? The more so when today's fight cost you a number of your lads.'

'Fear not that the others hate you on that account. No, they are glad to have you as my lover and fellow captain. And I am overjoyed.' Bêlit kissed him. 'The Suba think a man who dies in battle goes to dwell forever among the gods in riotous happiness. You gave some of their comrades that gift, without harming any women or children of theirs. Now your strength and skill are on our side, to further our vengeance. You more than make up for what we lost. Aye, you are very welcome aboard, Conan!'

'We share feuds, Bêlit, as we do all else.' The Cimmerian hesitated. 'However, I know nothing of what yours may be, nor of how a single ship can do much against one of the mightiest realms on earth.'

The woman winced. 'Let me give you the reason later, most dear,' she said unevenly. 'Tonight should be for us two alone.'

Conan consoled her. After a while she stood back and said, with the silver band agleam on a head again lifted in pride: 'As for now we can make the Stygians grieve for what they did –'

Tothapis leaned avidly forward.

Across the coil of the serpent and the scene that it enclosed, smote downward the vision of a great battle ax. Darkness filled the circle, and the scaled shape writhed. 'Mitra!' he heard fading away. 'You found me. But the game is not ended, Mitra ... no, we have scarcely begun ...'

Murk and silence entombed Tothapis.

In a far corner of his own mind, it seemed strange that he did not fall delirious to the floor, after what he had witnessed. Had a part of Set's reptile spirit entered him, this night or during the centuries of his necromancy? He did not immediately know or care. What mattered was that he could await no further miracles from his god, nothing but what he himself could contrive. Yet, before some supernatural balance of power cut it off, he had received a fragment of a prophecy. He had been given a mission.

Tothapis groped his way to the door. Lamps glimmered along the hall beyond. Still trembling, but on resolute feet, he hurried toward the centrum of his stronghold. There he could find that which he needed to cast his questing spells. Given the clues he already had, a certain dead man could tell him who among the living had more information about Bêlit and Conan, and point a way to their destruction.

II

A GATHERING OF
SORCERERS

The sun rose, tinging the Styx bloody. Fowl clamored on high, out
of the reed marshes along it; vultures took station, crocodiles
dragged themselves onto the sandbars and mudbanks that were
theirs by antique law. High in stem and stern, slant of sail, boats
plied the stream; from cargo barges resounded the gongs that set
time for slave oarsmen. Across intensely green vastness, serfs came
out of their villages, naked or in loincloths, to begin the day's toil.

At the bay into which the river emptied, limestone heights
started the northward climb of the land toward Shem. Here the
latter country was not visible, for the uppermost branch of the
delta marked the border. In these parts, that border was scarcely a
frontier; the Shemitish city-states nearby were tributary to Stygia.
As if to weight down this fact forever, on the southern side the
Grand Pyramid bulked close to the northeast corner of Khemi,
overtopping walls and towers. Untold centuries of weather had
pitted and scarred its facings, so that they did not glow mellow but
ochrous. Otherwise it remained inviolate, dominating those of its
kind that could be seen in the distance or within the city. Below it
and the ceremonial road around it, the terrain fell in a chaos of
tombs, abandoned quarries, and one pit where men still dug stone
beneath the overseer's lash.

The sun climbed on, until it scorched the last darkness from the
streets of Khemi. They filled with laden camels, oxcarts,
horsemen, pedestrians, crowds in the bazaars. The traffic was less
thick than might have been awaited in a metropolis, less lively,
infinitely less cosmopolitan. Stygia allowed no more foreigners in
than it must. Even Luxur, the royal capital far upriver, saw fewer
than did most mercantile towns abroad. Khemi, the religious

8

capital, was closed to all who did not have passes – Stygians among them; and its masters gave out passes grudgingly. If admitted, an outsider found that almost no dweller dared converse with him, except for whatever persons his business required him to meet. Those were few and closely watched.

The sun trudged and glowered through the day. Afternoon heat drove folk indoors to rest. A part of them sought palaces where fountains splashed in shady gardens; most went to apartments of a room or two in high, dingy tenements. None lacked a roof of some kind, for the hierarchy wanted everyone's whereabouts and doings known.

Toward evening, when a measure of coolness returned, they came forth again and took up their affairs. These generally ended about dusk. The shops must by law be closed. Several inns in the poor sections furtively received patrons for a while, but they would not stay open late. Though there was little crime in Khemi, the streets after sunset held their special perils. Under orders or necessity, or in boldness, various kinds of people did fare about by torchlight – soldiers, messengers, porters, harlots, tradesmen in curious wares, now and then a robed and masked priest. Hardly a one would remain out long.

Night never left the mansion of Tothapis. Sheathed in white bone, its walls lifted sheer on the Avenue of the Asps, their blankness broken only by doors and airslits. Around the dome on top, a roof garden held not the usual blossoms and bowers, but beds of black and purple lotus, and things more exotic. Within, light was from lamps and candles. The central chamber received never a sign of the world outside, apart from the cold air sighing up from the crypts.

During the day, the wizard's minions had been busy. As the sun descended crimson, a pair whom they had summoned arrived singly, and were conducted by tongueless slaves to the centrum. A third soon appeared. But he came in chains, under guard, and his party was taken to a different room and bidden to wait.

Tothapis received his visitors with aloof courtesy. He was a tall man, gaunt in a plain black robe, shaven-headed as became a priest of Set. On him, the typical hatchet features of a Stygian aristocrat

9

were scimitarlike, and the gullied skin dark ivory rather than light brown. The irises of his deep-set eyes might have been polished obsidian. A ruby glittered on his left hand, carved and incised to represent the terrestrial globe, held between the jaws of a golden snake that formed the ring. A talisman more potent still, in its nameless way, was the articulated skull of a viper, hung on a chain about his neck.

'Be seated,' he told the newcomers when formalities were done, and took his own chair. The back of it was carved in the form of a cobra, whose outspread hood made a canopy. Elsewhere, vague in the gloom, stood or hung objects less recognizable. A nine-branched candlestick on an altar block gave dim light. The time-blurred glyphs chiseled in the stone were of Acheron, which had perished three thousand years before.

'We are met on a grave and urgent matter,' Tothapis continued. 'Set himself,' he drew a sign, 'has vouchsafed me a vision of it. That was interrupted by an apparition I believe was from accursed Mitra, for it had the form of an ax –'

'The Ax of Varanghi?' exclaimed Ramwas. He remembered whom he confronted. 'I servilely beg my lord's pardon. I was startled.'

Tothapis' gaze sharpened upon him. 'What know you about the Ax of Varanghi?' the magician demanded.

What he saw in the chair before him was a sturdy, middle-aged person, square-visaged, prow-nosed, tan-skinned, clean-shaven. The hair that fell in severe outline down past his ears was grizzling. Outer garment doffed, Ramwas wore a plain white tunic and leather sandals. He had also, of course, left in the vestibule the shortsword which he, as a military officer, was entitled to bear. In addition he was a minor nobleman and large landholder.

'Hardly more than what you hear in Taia, my lord,' he said uneasily. 'I was stationed there years ago. The natives claim it is a relic from Mitra, hidden away somewhere, and someday a leader will bear it again and set them free of us.' He shrugged. 'The usual kind of superstition.'

'Except,' Nehekba murmured, 'that now Taia is once again in rebellion. And Our Master of Night appears to know this is no ordinary uprising for a few regiments and executioners to quell.'

'Quite so,' Tothapis agreed. 'He Who Is did not bespeak Taia as such. Perhaps he would have later. The spells I cast afterward concerned chiefly a certain female pirate named Bêlit –'

Ramwas started.

'– and her present companion, a barbarian from the Northlands,' Tothapis continued. 'About him I could learn virtually nothing, though it is him rather than her that I was warned against. She, however, has been in these parts erenow. As always, the stones and the ghosts remember. Thus I got your name, Ramwas. My mundane agents learned more about you, and that fortunately you were at present in Khemi, inspecting your property nearby. They tell me you are an able and reliable man.'

Ramwas bowed his head over folded hands.

'Perhaps, my lord,' Nehekba suggested, 'you could begin by describing your vision to us.'

Tothapis gave her a look more whetted than he cast on the officer. The high priestess of Derketa was subordinate to the hierarchy of Set. Nevertheless this goddess of carnality, who was also a goddess of the dead, and believed to lead them through the sky on midnight winds, was no minor deity. Her cult reached far beyond Stygia; and in that kingdom, the common people probably invoked her oftener, more fervently, than they did remote and terrible Set. As mistress of her mysteries, the high priestess in Khemi was always an accomplished witch, and the sole woman who sat in the Council of Sacerdotes.

'Have a care, Nehekba,' Tothapis said low. 'You and I have worked together before, yes, but you are apt to skirt insolence.'

'I pray pardon, lord.' Her tone was unrepentant. 'I thought we should not dawdle in the business of the Serpent.'

His gaze lingered a moment longer. Ramwas' did, too. Nehekba had come to office young, amidst rumors of poison, by insinuating herself with the right faction in one of Khemi's hidden struggles for power. She retained the beauty of her youth. Slightly taller than most Stygian noblewomen, she had their slenderness, but she made it altogether sensual. Her countenance was an oval, bearing straight nose, exquisitely molded lips, huge eyes of lustrous bronze

11

hue beneath high-arched brows. Flawless, her skin was the color of smoky amber. Strings of faience beads confined the jet flow of her hair, down to just above bosom and shoulder blades. At present she wore her crown, shaped like an unfolding lotus, and a gauzy white undergown; she had left her robe outside. The rings that glittered on her fingers and the pectoral on her breast were mere ornament. Her amulet was a tiny mirror on a silver chain at her throat.

'Well,' Tothapis said. 'I will relate that with which Our Master of Night favored me.'

His account was straightforward, simply omitting mention of any terror he might have felt. He finished: 'We can do nothing about winds until that ship is much closer, and then very little. But to judge from her present location, she will take a fortnight to work this far north; the current being against her, she must needs stands well out to sea if she would make any real speed. Thus we have time to think and prepare.'

'What can a lone buccaneer vessel mean, lord?' Ramwas wondered. 'Seaborne commerce is not vital to the wealth of Stygia – supposing our warcraft cannot hunt her down.'

Tothapis stared into shadow. 'He who has come aboard her is, in some unknown way, a torch that fate may kindle.'

The soldier shivered and signed himself.

'If this be true,' Nehekba reminded, 'then our actions to thwart him could prove to be the very sparks that light the flame.'

Tothapis nodded. 'Indeed. But if we sit passive, then surely something else will set it ablaze; and we shall not be near to seize it and quench it in the Styx. He Who Is would not reveal himself to me in vain.'

He addressed Ramwas: 'Hear why I have sent for you. The necromancy disclosed your name, enough else about you that my servants could readily learn more, and the fact that you have formerly had to do with Bêlit, and still keep what can lure her. This ought to give us a hold on Conan.' Contempt twisted his mouth. 'I saw how lost in her he already is. A half month's cruise will utterly besot him.'

Nehekba drooped long lashes. 'He sounds interesting, though,' she breathed. 'Could you describe him more closely, my lord?'

12

'And Bêlit, I beg you,' Ramwas added.

Tothapis did. When he had finished, the nobleman tugged his chin and said slowly, 'Aye, no mistake, no forgetting her. She is a former slave of mine, captured with her brother and a load of tribesmen in a blackbirding expedition to the south that I commissioned about three years ago. I sold most of the Negroes, but kept those two whites, and lived to regret it. Hell-spawn she was, and before long escaped, leaving good servants of mine dead behind her. The brother is no better.'

'Yes, the spell told me a little of him, wherefore I ordered you to have him led here,' Tothapis answered. 'Now tell me more.'

Ramwas shrugged. 'He is a Shemite, the name, um-m, Jehanan. Strong, intelligent, and intractable – the dangerous kind. He kept trying to break loose himself, but in his case he failed. Repeated lashings and stays in the Black Box wrought no cure. When at last, bare-handed, he killed an overseer who was punishing him, I decided he would never be of use on any farm of mine. I had him clubbed before the eyes of his fellow slaves by an expert who knows how to do it so the pain will last a lifetime. Then I rented him out to the quarrymaster below the Pyramid. They are accustomed to hard cases there.'

Nehekba stroked her cheek. 'Could we bring him here for an interview?' she asked.

'Pointless, my lady,' Ramwas assured her. 'By report, not even the endless pain has tamed him. He works steadily these days, but simply because chains are never off quarry slaves. I have a notion he would enjoy resisting us, no matter how he was tortured.'

'Torture would be stupid in any event,' the priestess said impatiently. 'I want to know him.'

'That is why I sent for my lady of Derketa,' Tothapis explained. 'She has arts no male will ever attain. Still, no need to bring a stinking stonechopper to this place. I will give you a sight of him where he is, Nehekba.'

He traced a symbol and muttered a few words. In the gloom of the corner, an invisible door seemed to open, and the three looked into a guardroom. Armed men lounged at ease, talking or dicing. Yet they were never entirely relaxed, and two of them stayed afoot,

13

pikes grounded, free hands near shortswords.

He of whom they were wary sat on a bench under a decorated wall. Lamplight showed a young man of medium height but huge breadth of shoulder and depth of chest, the muscles in limbs and belly like ship's cables. He wore nothing but a dirty loincloth, his bonds, crusted grime and sweat-salt. The Stygian sun had burned his skin leathery. His matted hair and beard were brown, but filth blackened them, too. A smashed nose sprawled across a once comely face now turned into lumps and jaggednesses; numerous teeth were missing; scars crisscrossed the entire body, a broken left collarbone had been deliberately misset. Nonetheless his eyes, almost golden, were akin to a hawk's.

Sound came through the portal, click of dice, grumble of a warder: 'How long must we stay here? I go on duty at dawn, I do.'

'Hush,' cautioned another. 'We serve great lords tonight.'

'On his account, plain to see,' the first guard snapped, and jerked a thumb at the slave. 'Hey-ah, why couldn't you have died before, fellow? Most don't last as long as you have.' He spat on his charge's bare foot.

Jehanan sprang erect. The links clanked between his ankles. He swung his arms up, as if to bring their fetters down on the skull of his tormentor. Pikepoints were instantly at his throat. Snarling, he eased his stance. 'The revenge I will take, when my hour comes, keeps me alive,' he said, in harshly accented Stygian, through ragged gulps of air. 'But *you* are not worth spitting back at.'

He turned. The fresco behind him depicted Set receiving a sacrificial procession. He spat on the god.

A gasp of horror broke from the keepers and from Ramwas. 'Hold!' Nehekba cried. 'They will kill him if you don't stop them, Tothapis.'

'He blasphemed,' said the magician shakily.

'There are worse punishments than death,' Nehekba reminded, 'and first we need him, for the Lord of the World Below.'

Tothapis gave a stiff nod, made a further gesture, and rapped a command: 'Desist! Let him be! He is fated!' The guards heard. In awe, they retreated from Jehanan, who grinned defiance at them. Tothapis terminated the view.

'What shall we make of him?' he asked after a silence.

14

Nehekba stirred out of thoughtfulness and smiled a slow sleepy smile. '*I* will make him what we need, my lord.'

'How?'

'Not by scourging or locking in a coffin under the sun or aught like that. No, let him be conveyed to the Keep of the Manticore. Let him be bathed, anointed, well clad, well dined and wined. Let him have a soft bed in a beautiful room where the air is cool and fragrant. When he has rested, I will seek him out. Presently we shall know much more.'

Tothapis' own hard mouth quirked briefly upward. 'I am not surprised, Nehekba. So be it.'

Again he turned to Ramwas. 'You are a trusty man,' he said. His voice dropped. 'I hope you are.'

The other shrank back the least bit. 'I strive to be, my lord,' he replied, not quite steadily.

Tothapis nodded. 'Good. Though the penalty for failure is unbounded, the reward for success can be high. This must remain a very secret matter, at least until we understand better what it portends. Else we could find ourselves entangled at cross-purposes with many an ambitious official, not to speak of a civil service which has grown over the state like coral. The business is too urgent and too deadly for that.

'Therefore, Ramwas, you must become an agent of mine.' He lifted a hand against the man's alarm. 'Fear not. You will not have to deal with magic – much. It is only that, in this time of crisis, I require men who are competent to meet emergencies as they arise. I have none such in Luxur whom I think is advisable to make privy to this affair. But I may well need one – the more so when the Taian revolt is perhaps linked to Conan's destiny that we must abort. You have been there often, you know the city and people, you have authority. A word from me to the Grand General will get you posted to Luxur on a "special mission". You will organize a corps of men to keep watch on every suspicious place there.'

'But – but my lord,' stammered Ramwas, 'it is hundreds of miles upriver. Killing horses along the way, I could hardly arrive before that pirate ship reaches our coasts. And then, the fastest carrier pigeons could never –'

Tothapis cut him off. 'Be still and hearken. You will travel aboard the sacred wingboat. Of it you may not have heard; but it will bear you thither in a night and a day and a night. With you will go a homunculus that can relay your words to me, and mine to you, across the leagues between at the speed of thought.'

Ramwas, who had hunted lions and men, could not repress a shudder.

Tothapis saw and told him soothingly: 'You will have time to set your own concerns here in order if you are diligent. You will also have time to prepare yourself in Luxur. First, of course, you and I must speak further, more than once. And ... never forget, Ramwas, the hour of trouble is the hour of the bold. They come to power, and the ages afterward revere their names. Would you not like that, Ramwas?'

Nehekba curled serpentine in her chair and smiled to herself.

III
THE WOMAN AVENGER

'For me,' Bêlit said, 'happiness died when a black sail hove above the sea-rim.'

She stood beside Conan on the upper deck, at the prow, next to the figurehead. Its gilt flashed brilliant under a cloudless heaven. Sunlight glittered off waves where they rushed blue, green, white-maned. A stiff and bracing breeze filled the sail and sent *Tigress* northward at a pace that had foam hissing around her cutwater. The galley plunged like a living beast; cordage sang; land had dropped from sight, but gulls yet trailed her, purity and grace on the wind. Below, crewmen laughed and jested in their native tongue as they went about their duties.

Yet the soul of Bêlit was afar, in a terrible place. She stared from the storm-wrack of her unbound hair, out across leagues and years. When Conan laid an arm around her, she did not flow to him as erstwhile. Her monotone went on:

'Belike I should start at the beginning, however much pain is in memory raised from its grave. My father was Hoiakim, a man of Dan-marcah on the northern coast of Shem, near the Argossean border. The city is not large, but she is tributary to none. The forests of her hinterland give timber for many ships that fare widely in trade; foreigners make lively her taverns and crooked streets; serenity dwells in the temples of her gods.

'Hoiakim wed Shaaphi and brought her south. A treaty had lately been concluded with the Suba tribe on the Black Coast, for a trading post among them. It was a rare opportunity for a young man. The Suba were fishers, farmers, and hunters in the jungle. They also dealt with peoples inland. Thus they had abundant goods – hides, gems, gold dust, hardwoods, curious animals and birds. In return they wanted iron tools and weapons, fabrics,

17

spices, medicines, and the like. My father became the factor.

'Soon he was mighty among them. Not only was he strong of arm, tireless in the chase, a peerless archer, but he was wise and just. The natives came to him for counsel about most things and for judging of their disputes. In bad times – hurricane, flood, murrain, drought, war – he took over leadership in all but name. The chief did not resent this, for he, like the rest, thought that great magic lived in Bangulu. So they called my father, Bangulu, the High One. Nor did the witch doctor mind that my mother Shaaphi went among the folk as an angel, healing, midwifing, consoling, teaching women and children arts – gardening, weaving, preserving, cleanliness, music – that bettered their lives.

'There Jehanan was born and, two years later, I. There we grew up, friends of the Suba, rangers of woods and streams and sea, learning their wild skills and alien lore. At the same time, we did not become savages. Our parents saw to our education as proper Shemites. They had many scrolls and instruments for us as well as themselves. We accompanied them on their visits home. Besides, ships came to bring new trade goods and carry back what we had gathered. Foreign vessels, bartering or exploring, would put in too, for exchange of information and for merriment. No, we were not isolated. Life was good to us.

'The bud of my happiness broke into flower when –' Bêlit gripped the rail hard –'when I wedded.

'That was on the last voyage I made back to Dan-marcah. Jehanan was in no haste to marry; native girls were ever eager to please him. But I – I was a maiden still, and ardent. For my parents' part, they wished grandchildren, and a helper, since the post and its business had grown. In the city they engaged a marriage broker, who presently found a suitable youth. Neither pair of elders needed much persuasion for Aliel and me; we tumbled into love.

'My bridegroom returned with us. He proved an able assistant, and was soon well liked by the tribe. My happiness bore fruit next year, when a son was born unto us, our own little Kedron.

'Three months later, the black sail hove above the sea-rim.'

*

18

At first there was joy ashore. Visitors were always welcome. Warriors did hasten to take up spear, bow, knobkerrie, shield, and form a line on the beach. A few times the sight of them had caused a vessel to sheer off, revealing her as a pirate or a slaver.

Bêlit left Kedron in his cradle and hurried outside to join Aliel. The sight before her, around her, was magnificent. At her back, beyond cultivated fields, the jungle rose intensely green under a blue dazzle of sky. A stream flowed thence, bright through the millet and yams, past rail-fenced paddocks where cattle grazed, to the sea. Beside it, on the edge of the beach, the kraal stood. Grass roofs, weathered golden, showed above palisades which honeysuckle made verdant, snowy, perfumed, bee-murmurous. The trading post lay by itself half a mile off, a long building of rammed earth, whitewashed and thatched, amidst a riot of oleander colors. The beach was quartz sand, blinding bright. The brook emptied into a cove which gave safe approach and anchorage. Elsewhere, surf creamed and thundered in the van of sapphire waters. A fresh west wind bore heat away. A flight of parrots went by, noisy rainbows.

The warriors of Suba were poised tall along the shore. Naked save for grass skirts, plumed headdresses, bangles, beads, their sepia bodies gleamed as if oiled. From the stockade poured lithe women, fleet children, grave elders, the chief in a leopard skin. Chatter and laughter blew across to Bêlit. A drum throbbed in gladness.

Hoiakim and Shaaphi were already outside. The older man stroked his gray-shot beard and rumbled, 'What do you make of yonder craft, Aliel?'

His son-in-law squinted into glare. The ship was now hull up and nearing. She was big, her sides high and round, the few oar ports clearly meant for no more than close-in maneuverings. From strakes to sail, she was unrelieved sable; but a scarlet pennon fluttered at the masthead. Large objects of some kind were mounted at bow and stern. Light winked off metal as numerous men moved about her decks.

'Stygian, from the lines and paint,' Aliel decided. 'I wager they have others along, though; Stygians are no great seafarers. What

19

venture might they be on, this far from home?'

Unease touched Bêlit. She had heard too many ugly tales about Stygia. Aliel sensed it, squeezed her hand, smiled at her. She gave him back the gesture, cheered and grateful.

'Perhaps they seek knowledge,' Shaaphi suggested in her gentle fashion. 'They are said to be a nation of philosophers.'

Hoiakim patted her shoulder affectionately and forebore to dispute.

As the ship drew in, Bêlit saw that Aliel's guess had been right. The majority of the crew were swarthy Stygians, but she identified Shemites among them, and men more fair who were probably Argosseans. But why were they armed and armored – edged steel, helmets, breast-plates, shields? Surely everybody knew by now that the kraal of the Suba and her father's trading post offered treachery to no guest. The warriors on the strand felt the same doubt and closed ranks. Other people edged back toward the stockade.

A leadsman called warning. Anchor cables and sail rattled downward. The ship lay at rest in the cove, broadside to.

A trumpet sounded aboard. Men sprang to the objects on deck. They were great jars of glazed clay, on iron grills above trays where charcoal fires glowed to heat them. Their mouths were tightly fitted into long, flexible tubes of leather. Stygians pointed these shoreward and, careful to stay upwind, drew out the stoppers that closed them.

From either one billowed forth a murky cloud. Men caught at their throats, staggered, dropped their weapons, slumped to the sand. A faint whiff reached Bêlit and whirled her into a dizziness that passed when the breeze shifted.

'Ishtar aid us,' Hoiakim cried. 'They must be slavers, with some drug borne on the air to break our defense!' He drew his shortsword. 'Aliel, get the women and the child to safety.' He ran from his kindred. 'To me, men of the Suba!' he roared. 'To me, and do battle!'

The jars emptied, the cloud rapidly dispersed. A gangplank splashed from the bulwark. Down it swarmed the invaders, waded ashore, sprang into formation, and charged. No resistance was left on the strand, only men who lay unconscious or weakly stirring, unable to rise. The Stygians and their allies moved toward the kraal.

Through nightmare, Bêlit saw her father dash about, bellow his war cry, seek to rally whatever fighters had escaped the narcotic. She even heard him yell at the chief, 'Ungedu, get the people back inside, close the gate, for Adonis' sake!'

Jehanan burst into sight. He had been fishing up-stream, and sped the whole way hither afoot. 'No!' Bêlit shouted to the brother she adored. 'Get away!' He did not hear, he plunged to join Hoiakim.

The remaining hale men of the Suba began to do likewise.

Bêlit saw an Argossean bowman stand forth from the ranks of his comrades. With ghastly deliberation, he nocked an arrow, drew string, took aim. Did she catch the twang? She did see the arrow smite, and Hoiakim fall. Briefly, he tugged at the shaft in his breast; then he was still.

Jehanan howled. Maddened, he dashed straight at the Stygians. They surrounded him. Bêlit saw pike butts lift and crash down.

Dismayed, most Negro fighting men gave way before the onslaught of a disciplined squadron. It reached the stockade ere the gate could be shut. Leaving a few men to hold that position, trapping those within, the marauders spread out in pursuit of the majority who were outside and fleeing.

'Father,' Bêlit sobbed. 'Jehanan.'

Aliel shook her. 'We must escape,' her husband said between locked teeth. 'That was the last charge he laid on me.'

A far part of her remembered that they, the Shemites, ought to be immune by treaty to slavers. But what use were treaties? If they were caught, who would make complaint? 'Kedron,' she gasped.

Shaaphi came from the house, grandchild in arms. Her own tears laved the infant, but she said levelly, 'Yes, let us be off to the jungle and hide, before we are noticed. Many will take the same way. We can join them here . . . afterward.'

In the bosom of Bêlit, love for these three was like soft rain falling into a white-hot cauldron – of hate for the slayers of her father, the captors of her brother, the destroyers of every

21

happiness. She darted back inside, snatched a spear off the wall, and came back to the rest.

They struck off across the fields. A haroo snapped Bêlit's glance rearward. The heart froze in her. Four raiders had seen her and were in chase.

Shaaphi stopped. Bêlit did also, as if helpless, while Aliel raged at them to be on. Shaaphi raised her gray head. 'I cannot outrun them, at my age,' she said, 'nor should Hoiakim stand alone before Ishtar.' She gave the wailing infant to Bêlit, who took him numbly. 'Go,' she said. From her girdle she unsheathed her knife. 'Fare always well, my darlings.' The blade flashed. Blood spouted, unbelievably red. She knelt down among the grainstalks and sang her death prayer in a voice that soon died out.

'I will do that for you, beloved, if I must,' Aliel vowed to his wife. 'Now come!'

They fled onward. Young, hardy, they could have distanced their mail-burdened pursuers. But no mortal goes faster than a lead ball from a sling. Abruptly there came a shattering sound, and Aliel went down. The back of his skull was no more. The kindly grain rustled to and fro to hide that sight from Bêlit.

She held Kedron in her left arm. Her right hand gripped the spear. She ran.

Anguish exploded in her left thigh. A second ball had struck. She stumbled, recovered, tried to go on, and knew she was lamed. With great care, she dropped her weapon, uncovered a milk-heavy breast, brought her son close and gave him that gift for a moment. Then she laid him on the ground, took the spear again, and gave him freedom.

Thereafter she waited at bay.

'I killed one of them, and wounded two more,' Bêlit told Conan. 'A mistake. I should have done as my mother did. They overcame me.'

He held her to him.

'No need of relating what happened next,' she went on in a while. She had not wept. 'They did leave me alone on the voyage back to Stygia, and let me heal in flesh if not spirit. After all, I was now valuable merchandise. So were Jehanan and such of our friends as they had caught, but I was kept apart and saw little of them. I heard that no few took sick and died in the foul hold where they were chained.'

Her voice was dry. 'It turned out that this was a one-time venture. A Stygian aristocrat and enterpriser named Ramwas had learned enough about the Suba and our post that he decided a raid would be worthwhile, for plunder as well as slaves. It would require special equipment, though, to break our defense.'

Conan frowned. No matter pity for Bêlit, his barbarian practicality had come to the fore. 'Why is that mist of sleep not seen in war?' he asked.

'It is too costly, in too short a supply,' she answered. 'Certain swampdwellers in Zembabwei brew it from a poisonous fruit found nowhere else. The agents of Ramwas could only collect enough for this single task, at a price to make it worthwhile, because it chanced they had wormed out a shameful secret from the chief's past and threatened to spread it abroad. At that, the preparation of such an amount took months.'

'How do you know this?'

'Ramwas told me once, when he was in his cups and boastful,' she sighed. 'He put most of the captives on the auction block, but Jehanan and me he kept for himself. Jehanan was to be a plantation laborer. We hugged each other, in a single heartbeat, before we were parted. I – Ramwas had me brought to his harem.

'First – he did not want inconveniences – he gave me into the hands of a witch, who cast a spell that made me barren. What was done left no mark on my skin, but – Oh, Conan, the pain of that day I can put behind me, but never the pain that I cannot bear your child!'

Muscles bunched in the Cimmerian's jaws. He wanted to smash something. Instead, he held Bêlit very gently to him, though he shivered.

She laughed a little, as a she-wolf might yelp. 'He got small joy of me,' she said. 'I almost raked his eyeballs out. He barely escaped, yammering. Since whips leave scars, he – well, he had the juice of

23

purple lotus forced between my lips, which paralyzes the body for hours. But not often.'

'And in hope, I think,' Conan whispered. 'You are so lovely.'

Bêlit shrugged. 'Perhaps. Be that as it may, I began to see that I did wrong to yearn for death. What revenge can the poor dead take? No, I must use my wits, so that Hoiakim, Shaaphi, Aliel, and Kedron may have many slaves to attend them.'

A flaw of wind made the ship lurch and the sail crack.

'Ramwas had business in Khemi,' Bêlit said. 'I never pretended aught but hatred for him. I could not bring myself to anything else. I could, though, I could be mild enough about it that he brought me along. For Khemi is a seaport –'

The new moon sank in a greenish west, the glimmer of the old in her arms. Silence brimmed the street beneath ogive windows through which coolness entered. Their grillwork filled with violet and the evenstar.

In a chamber of red velvet, Bêlit left the couch where she had been waiting. Nearby stood a glass vase full of lilies. She ripped the blossoms out and cast them on the floor. A blow against the tabletop shattered the bowl of the vase. Jagged neck in her fist, she glided to the door.

Her other fist smote the panel, again and again. 'Open!' she moaned. 'Open, let me out, send for a physician, I perish!'

The bolt clicked, the barrier swung wide. Lamplight in the corridor beyond revealed, gigantic, the guardian eunuch. He touched his sword, but his face was unsuspicious as he asked, 'What do you want, woman?'

Bêlit grinned wide. 'This,' she said, and drove the broken glass past his jowls, into his throat.

She twisted her weapon. He reeled back but could not scream, only gurgle, because she kept after him, thrusting and twisting. He sank to his knees, to his belly. His blood spurted across walls and floor.

'Would you had been Ramwas,' she said when he lay slack. But time was scant. She plucked his Zamboulan scimitar from its scabbard and padded off to the stairwell. Lamps flickered in

24

brackets along it; shadows moved monstrous. Bêlit hurried downward.

At the bottom, where a door gave on the world, a second sentinel was posted. He was an entire man, burly, blue-cheeked, in helmet, cuirass, leather kilt, and greaves. A pike stood in his grasp, a blade was sheathed at his hip. 'Hold!' he exclaimed. The walls of the antechamber flung that word back in echoes.

Bêlit kept the scimitar behind her. She gave him the smile she used to give Aliel. 'Hold?' she murmured. 'Why, yes, in greatest pleasure, if you wish to be held, soldier. A girl grows weary of the harem.'

Half perturbed, half allured, wholly confounded, he retreated from her. She whipped her weapon forward and attacked.

Almost, she killed him. He sprang back, eluded the whistling edge, brought his pikeshaft up to block its second cut. Bêlit slewed her blade around and sliced into his thigh.

He yelled for help. She closed in, under his guard, smiting right and left. He dropped the pike. Had he kept his wits, he might have used it well against her – but a woman pressing in on him, laughing, reckless of life, roused terror. Bêlit had learned swordplay from her father; she had killed buffalo and lions in Kush.

'Witch, witch!' he screamed, and snatched after his own blade. Bêlit's stroke caught his wrist on the way, and made it useless. He gaped. Bêlit hewed at his neck.

'I went out,' she told Conan. 'What cared I about what might prowl around? Night fell swiftly, to cover me.

'I sought the harbor. There I slew a watchman and stole a felucca. By then there was an ebb tide to bear me off.

'Understand, I cherished no hopes, except for revenge. I expected my death in battle, and felt surprised when it came not. Well – I am become a harp that Derketa plays on, to call men to her queendom.

'For a few hours I did let a dream flicker in me, of regaining Dan-marcah. Soon, though, the gods told me otherwise. The current southward is strong; unless granted favorable winds, which I was not, I could never single-hand a boat against it. Yet

25

ample food and water were aboard – a destiny?

'So I made my way back to the Black Coast, at last to my Suba.

'The survivors among them had returned after the ship departed. Diminished, they were prey for neighbor tribes, who came looting and slave-catching. As the daughter of Bangulu, I helped them regain some strength.

'Yet clear was to see, the Suba would not soon be great again. And I ... I had my score yet to pay.

'A vessel from Shem came in on the chance of trade. With what ivory, apes, and peacocks we could muster, I sent back a commission for a warcraft to be built and outfitted. Soon she arrived, this beautiful, vengeful *Tigress* of mine – of ours, Conan. My Suba fishermen needed but little exercise to learn the use of her. They are warriors as well, and have death-debts of their own. Moreover, the booty they bring home buys their tribe a new beginning.

'I am the daughter of Bangulu. They follow me wherever I lead. Now they will follow you too, Conan.'

The calm that had been upon Bêlit broke. She grabbed the rail harder still, arched her back, and screamed at the sky, 'Stygia, Argos, yes, many in Shem and Kush, what you have done! I curse you, I, Hoiakim's and Shaaphi's daughter, Jehanan's sister, Aliel's wife, Kedron's mother! Fire be upon you forever!'

Conan gathered her to him. 'Beloved,' he said shakenly, 'you are hurt, beloved, and would that my sword had been there to defend you. At least it is here for your revenge.'

Bêlit cast herself against his breast and wept. Later she raised her eyes to his, gold-brown against ice-blue, and said low: 'Conan, I have been with no man since I escaped, until you. In you, my joy and my hope are reborn.'

'And mine in you,' he murmured.

Her fingers ruffled his hair. 'Vengeance, yes. But afterward, Conan, a life together. If the jealous gods allow.'

26

IV

A DAUGHTER OF
THE FREE FOLK

Where the Styx, flowing north from unknown sources, bent west on its long journey to the sea, was the northeastern corner of the Stygian kingdom. South of this rose ever steeper highlands, which finally crested and descended again toward the primitive but powerful realm of Keshan. Those hills and mountains formed the province of Taia.

Shuat of Stygia, commanding the governor's militia against rebellious natives, led a detachment up the Helu. That river ran swiftly through its vale, eastward until it joined the Styx, creating a strip more fertile than most of the region. Here the Taians, who elsewhere were mainly herdsmen, dwelt in farming villages; here was the main artery of trade for the province, and of civilization. Or so it had been. Now, at his back, smoke from the thatch of mud huts rose to stain heaven, date palms and orange groves lay hewn down, vultures descended on corpses, lines of captives stumbled in chains on their way to the slave market at Luxur. As yet the right bank was untouched; but its turn would come.

Shuat, a big, hard-faced man, rode at the head of his force. On his left, a standard-bearer held on high the snake pennon of his rank. Immediately behind him, amongst his personal guards, came his chariot. Thereafter, in a cloud of dust, boom of drums, tramp of feet and hooves, creak of wheels, the regiment followed. Ahead of him the riverside road lifted sharply with the terrain, and the valley narrowed into a gorge. Its sides were red rock, vivid against a sky where the sun blazed fierce. There the stream dashed white and loud.

His adjutant trotted up to join the commander on the right, slowed his own horse, and reported, 'Sir, Captain Menemhet

27

requests orders as to where we shall camp for the night.'

'What, when it is scarcely past noon?' Shuat snapped.

The adjutant pointed. 'My lord knows well that that defile is a long one. We cannot get through it, out onto open ground, before dark. May I respectfully suggest that it is no good place for us to be attacked?'

'I hope we shall be.' Noting the officer's surprise, Shuat deigned to speak on: 'Have you considered why we are ravaging the valley, instead of merely garrisoning it as was done in past uprisings? After all, it yielded more taxes than the entire rest of this wretched domain. Well, it has been even more important to the highlanders, both for what it produces and because of what it once meant in their history. Were it left intact, they would get supplies smuggled to them by their kinfolk here, and we might spend years chasing down their last insurgent bands. This way, outrage and a sense of desperation should provoke them to headlong tactics. A troop that has seemingly boxed itself in a ravine can tempt those of them who are nearby into an immediate assault.

'If that happens, fear not. I am not so foolish as to try pushing on. We will repulse them and then make an orderly withdrawal. Our men are well equipped, they are used to fighting in close ranks, they will inflict far heavier casualties than they suffer. That is my objective.'

'It is not for me to question my lord's widsom,' said the adjutant dubiously.

Shuat gave a dour chuckle. 'Nevertheless you do. I agree, this seems much more expensive in every way than simply wearing the clansmen down as aforetime. But I have my orders. The rebellion *must* be crushed soon, regardless of price. I have laid my plans accordingly, and Governor Wenamon has approved them. He dared not do otherwise.'

'Sir?'

Shuat grew somber. 'Those orders came lately from Khemi, countersigned on their way here by the king in Luxur. They were borne in a magical boat which made the journey in some three days. That I know from the date on the document, and from the priest-magician Hakketh who was aboard and now waits at Seyan for my report on this expedition.' He made a sign. 'I did not ask why the matter is so urgent. Before the hierophants of the Great Lord Set, one does not ask for reasons. One prostrates oneself and obeys.'

Despite the heat and brilliance of the day, the adjutant shivered.

Above the gorge, land rolled rugged, immense, to mountains which made a distance-purpled wall on its southern horizon. Save for scattered tamarisks and acacias, it was treeless, begrown with tawny grass and thorny shrubs. The largest of the boulders that lay strewn about had long since been piled into dolmens, where ancient heroes slept. Antelope grazed among those graves. They had drifted back here after folk drove cattle and goats to the safety of higher ground.

They bounded off as a troop of warriors approached. These were Taians, taller, more slender, darker of skin than Stygians. They tended to be handsome, their features broad-nosed, full-lipped, but regular, hair blue-black and straight, beards generally shaved off. Most wore little besides a kilt dyed to show the owner's clan, a part of it draped over the left shoulder; at night it became a blanket rolled around the person. Their chief arms were dirk, spear, sling, bow, ax, though some possessed Stygian shortswords or curved blades from the East. Many bore rectangular hide shields, reaching from knee to chin, and on many of these, the bright paint included a solar disc.

Ausar, their chieftain, led them at the long stride of a mountaineer. His hair was gray and his face furrowed, but time had done little else to his body. That countenance was sharper than common in these parts, its complexion lighter. His garb was a lion skin, and on a headband shone the Sun symbol, in gold. Besides a dagger, he carried a battle ax – three-foot haft, steel head tapered at the rear to a point.

Reaching the brink, he signaled his followers to hold back and crouched for a look unseen from below. Noise and gleam of the river came to him out of shadows filling the ravine. When he peered downstream, he caught a different sound and glitter that made him nod in grim satisfaction.

He rose and returned to the men. Several hundred strong, they stood close enough together that all could hear him. 'Aye,' he told them, 'the scout spoke truly. The Stygians did indeed go on, and are now making camp just where I deemed they would. It appears as desirable a site as can be found hereabouts, the bank wider between cliff and stream than at most places. However, they are still perforce strung out in a long line. And because the Helu is narrower at this point, it is also deeper and swifter. An armored Stygian, merely pushed into that water, would not come back out of it.' He lifted his ax. 'No cheers yet, lest they be warned. But we will strike them!'

Weapons shook aloft to catch the red beams of a sun sunken nearly under the mountaintops.

'Here is my plan,' Ausar went on. 'They outnumber us, but we will come on them behind the head of the snake that they are, chop it off, and kill those men. Mitra grant their commander be among them! Meanwhile certain of us will form a row across the bank and hold off the rest. There is no time to talk further, so I bestow that honor on those of Clan Yaro who are present. After dark, we will retreat back up the steeps – yon blundering flatlanders will never dare pursue – and tomorrow see how next we can harass them. For Mitra and Taia – now onward!'

He started off parallel to the verge. His youngest daughter Daris increased her pace to join him. Unwed women often hunted beside their brethren in this country, and fought in time of war. Though he had been unhappy about her wish to fare along in his roving force, he could not well deny it, when her sisters had infants to care for and her brothers were off on forays of their own.

'Stay behind,' he urged. 'You send a wicked arrow, but this will be fighting at close quarters, and some of the foe will not yet have doffed armor.'

A dirk slid forth in her grasp. 'I am nimble enough to make good use of this, Father,' she answered.

He sighed. 'Mitra ward you, then. Your mother was dear to me while she lived, and you are much like her.'

Daris loped on. Her rangy height did not lack curves to bespeak her a woman. Her features were still more straight and finely chiseled than his, her hue still lighter, golden rather than brown. Great dark eyes looked from between wings of shoulder-length

30

midnight hair. She too wore a small Sun disc on her brow. Otherwise her garb was a cuirass of boiled cowhide over a brief tunic, and a leather skirt studded with brass. On her back she had slung a bow, quiver, and packet of dried meat such as Taians were wont to carry when traveling.

'Remember,' she said, 'I vowed before Derketa that I would see dead Stygians to the number of the Farazis. It is for me to bring down as many of them as the Sable Queen will grant.'

Ausar's lips drew taut. When Clan Farazi protested a redoubled tax on livestock, Governor Wenamon invited them to Seyan for a feast of reconciliation and parley. About half came. His militia seized them for hostages. That latest act of Stygian misrule brought most of the highlanders up in arms. When the governor then slew his prisoners, instead of terrified submission he got rebellion ablaze throughout the province.

Daris fell silent, for her father had turned toward the defile. Quickly he scanned over its edge, nodded, raised his ax for a sign, and started down. Few people in the world could readily have crossed a slope so steep, gullied, and twilit, but these mountaineers were agile as goats, quiet as leopards. Below and ahead, the Stygians were blots of gloom, glints of metal, beside the roaring Helu. Campfires twinkled to life through the length of their host; a breath of smoke drifted with the coolness breathed from the water.

Not until talus rattled beneath calloused feet did anybody notice the Taians. A shout lifted, trumpets blared, horses whinnied in alarm, iron clanged. 'Forward!' Ausar cried, and sped to battle.

Helmet, breastplate, greaves, shield of a sentry sheened in the dusk before him. The Stygian drew blade, stood his ground, sought to stab his oncoming foe. Ausar dodged. His ax flickered sideways. Barely did the soldier withdraw his sword arm in time. The axhead edge clashed on his shield. Again Ausar hewed, and again, to bring the greater mass of his weapon in battering and leverage on the defense. The shield slipped just enough aside, and his ax bit into the Stygian's thigh. Blood jetted. The soldier howled and stumbled. His face was unguarded. Ausar sent the point through a temple, leaped over the corpse, and plunged on. Around him raged a wave of his men.

Daris danced about, crouched low, seeking her chances in the

31

tumult. A mailed Stygian fought a Taian who wielded a scimitar. Unarmored, the highlander could not stand before his opponent. Already slashed in a dozen places, he gave way step by step; at his back was a line of the enemy. Abruptly he saw an opening, yelled, and sprang closer, while his sword whirred downward. A skillful feint had caught him. The shield tilted back to intercept, while the soldier trod forward. He sheathed his blade in the native's belly, and ripped. Then Daris had an arm under his chin from behind. Her dirk made a single deep slash across his throat. He fell, gurgled, flopped, and lay still beside the Taian man. Daris was already elsewhere.

A horseman forced his way through the struggle. From above, he chopped down right and left on rebels as they combatted Stygian infantry. Daris wove her way amidst violence. Heedless of danger from hooves or aught else, she glided under the horse. It screamed and reared as she hamstrung it, fell heavily, thrashed about. Daris was on the rider like a cat. Before he could recover himself, the lifeblood was pumping out of a forearm laid open on the inner side from elbow to wrist.

Daris rolled and scrambled to her feet. Seeming chaos ramped on the riverbank. But – Armor! Lines! Horses! She gasped in dismay as she realized. The Stygians had kept themselves fully ready to fight, well-nigh every last man of them. The Taian assault had only thrown them back a little, then they rallied in disciplined ranks. The confusion was among Ausar's band, suddenly made to recoil. And now torches flared out of campfires, to light this ground for the king's troopers. Now trumpets sounded triumphant, cavalry thrust in close formation, chariots rumbled forward on sword-hubbed wheels. The Stygian standards advanced from both east and west; the defenders of Clan Yaro had gone down under weight of mail, horses, vehicles; the attackers were trapped.

'No! she dimly heard her father shout through the clamor and clangor. Above the heads of men who surged back and forth, seeking to win out of the press, she saw Ausar. He had cut his way back to the talus slope. Instead of fleeing at once, he stood, ax raised high, in flickery torchlight, under the first stars, for a sign and a rallying point. Stygian arrows buzzed around him, but he heeded them not, and they missed him in the dusk. 'Here, men of Taia, here to me!' he bugled.

His warriors had not penetrated the foe so deeply that they were boxed in beyond escape. Pantherish cries lifted from them. They hurled themselves toward him with terrifying vigor. Comrade aided comrade as they charged. The soldiers did not harvest many of them before they had reached the wall of the gorge and bounded off, unfollowable, starward into the night.

Daris glimpsed that much while she struggled for her own freedom. She had been headed out of the battle when its tides swept her against two Stygian infantrymen. They seized her by the arms. She fought them in hissing fury. Once she tripped the left-hand man and all three went down in a heap. She managed to sink her teeth in his neck. Horrified, he slackened his grip. She tore loose of him and twisted about, to bring the heel of her hand under the nose of his companion. That could have been lethal, but he ducked in time and the nose was merely broken. The first man was upon her again. His fist slugged at her jaw. She took the blow on her cheekbone instead. Yet it dazed her momentarily. He took hold of her throat and squeezed. The other Stygian hampered her resistance till she sank into blackness.

Little remained of Thuran. In the course of conquering Taia, the Stygians had besieged and largely destroyed its capital, while devastating the hinterland. Afterward, five hundred years of neglect and weather gnawed at what had survived. Terraces crumbled, walls collapsed, canals and reservoirs silted, soil eroded, rich farmland became gaunt wilderness. When at last men returned, it was as pastoralists. They bore off the toppled stones of the city to make shelters, miles apart. Mostly they lived in skin tents, carried on oxback, in the cycle of their wanderings. This was bad country for horse, camel, or wheel; its dwellers perforce grew deep-chested and fleet-footed.

Nevertheless Thuran-on-the-Heights was holy to them. Varanghi had founded it when he led the ancestors hither, and had consecrated it to Mitra. Here a long succession of kings reigned gloriously, a civilization flowered. Here was still the olden temple of the Sun god, half in ruins but housing a few priests who still

33

practised the pure rites and conserved something of ancient relics and lore. Here the clan chiefs and their households gathered each winter solstice for sacrifice, deliberations, trying of lawsuits, and business more worldly. Here folk made pilgrimage to cleanse themselves of guilt, swear the most sacred oaths, to find solace in the mysteries of Mitra.

Here Ausar brought his men after their defeat on the Helu. It was a natural place for all to meet who fain would join his army. The Stygians would not soon come this far; if nothing else, supply lines were too easily cut in the arid, tumbled uplands. He could hope to find new recruits waiting for him.

'But scant hope have I else,' he told Parasan.

'You do wrong to despair this early, my son,' the high priest counseled him. 'Perhaps you lost a battle, but the war is young.'

'I lost a beloved daughter,' Ausar mourned.

Parasan reached out a frail hand to clasp the leader's shoulder. 'She fell valiantly, in a just cause. Mitra, himself a warrior, has taken her home to him.'

'Aye. If she did perish – O Sun Lord, grant that she perished, that she is not captive!'

For a while there was silence. The two men sat in the priest's quarters inside the temple. Sunlight slanted through windows to reveal a pair of stone chambers, austerely furnished. Dimmed by time, a mural above a small altar depicted a youth riding a bull, between whose horns glowed the Sun disc. Elsewhere stood shelves of equally aged scrolls, tomes, bits of philosophical apparatus, graceful figurines salvaged from the ruins. Patient in his blue robe, Parasan waited.

Ausar mastered himself and said, dry-voiced: 'Can unwisdom ever be righteous? I did not imagine we could drive the Stygians altogether out of Taia. But I thought perhaps our warfare would make it too costly for them to send their tax collectors and judges through the hills; that in due course we would be left alone, and even reach an accommodation with them. Instead, they have scorched the Helu Valley to impoverish us further. I see no reason for supposing they will let it be resettled before we yield. Rather, their ruthlessness tells me that as soon as they can bring enough

34

soldiers, they will carry fire and sword from end to end of Taia. Should I not let spokesmen of ours bring them my salted corpse in token of surrender?'

Parasan shook his wise white head. He was shorter and darker than most of his countrymen, with more Negro blood in him, but always they heard his soft words with respect. 'No, Ausar, abandon us not so soon. It would do no good in any case. You are our natural leader – chief of Clan Varanghi, descendant of our kings, thus foremost man of us and known to be a redoubtable one. But if you die, the outrage in the people will not die with you. Another will take your place and fight on. It is for our god, our land, and our blood.'

Ausar laughed bitterly. 'Our blood? What is that? The Hyborians among our ancestors soon mingled theirs with Stygian, Kushite, and Shemite. Keshan is now almost purely black, and we can hardly call ourselves white, can we? As for our land, once it was great, but nearly all that we know about civilization today, we have from our Stygian masters.' He paused. 'And our gods . . . I speak no blasphemy against All-Highest Mitra, but you must agree – it surely distresses you – how bastardized his cult has become, over the centuries, from the paganisms everywhere around.'

'Aye,' Parasan murmured. 'Yet though his flame gutters low, it will never go out.' He straightened in his chair. 'Are your men as discouraged as you?'

'No. They are barbarians who take whatever fate sends them, heedless of everything but the wish to leave an honored name in their clan sagas. I, however . . . You remember that as a boy I was sent here to study Taian chronicles. Afterward I fared for some years through both Stygia and Shem, seeking to learn about civilization. I see things too clearly.'

'But you also see too shallowly, my son. Come.' Parasan rose and limped to the doorway. 'It will not be new to you, and most of it is known to them, but I will declare again the Prophecy of the Ax.'

Ausar obeyed, half unwilling, half eager to have his spirits restored, if the priest could do that for him. They trod out on the portico of the building. The marble, once white, had worn to a deep golden tone. The friezes were nearly gone, and the fluting of the pillars was blurred. Only snags and rubble showed that once there had been two wings behind. Nonetheless this remnant dreamed gracious, in an odor and a whisper of sun-dried grass.

The warriors, males and a few fiercely chaste females, were encamped on the slope below, among fragments of walls and fallen columns. The smoke of their campfires drifted on a warm breeze, into a sky where hawks caught sunlight on wings. Upon seeing their leader and his companion, they hurried to stand below the staircase, rank after rank of lithe brown bodies.

Parasan lifted a hand. Somehow his thin voice carried:

'You who fight for Taia the beloved, hearken. Hear, though you have heard before, the story of your motherland.

'Mighty were your forebears. They came down from afar, from the cold North, Hyboria of the legends, first as wanderers, then as conquerors, then as settlers. Barbarians, they bore a destiny just the same. For they adored Mitra, and the Sun Lord desired them to bring his clean faith to these realms where flourished beast gods, human sacrifice, black magic, and all other manner of abominations.

'Some crossed the highlands and entered Keshan. There they founded cities which became great; but presently they languished in that sultry clime, the jungle reclaimed most of what they built, and nothing is left but a rude black kingdom – which, however, stands yet as a bulwark against cruel outsiders.

'Better did the Hyborians fare in these cooler, drier hills. Varanghi led that branch of them to victory. Even over sorceries, heritage of lost races who were not human, did Varanghi prevail. For he bore into battle an ax given him by Mitra's own hand. As long as the wielder was worthy, this weapon made him invincible.

'It became the treasure and the emblem of the dynasty Varanghi begot. Long did his kingdom of Taia flourish, in achievement, wealth, happiness, and the radiance of Mitra. That light was unendurable to murk Stygia. Again and again through centuries, the worshippers of Set strove to overthrow Taia, and ever were they repulsed.

'At last, though, an unworthy heir mounted the throne. He allowed himself to be seduced by Stygian magic and fell in battle.

36

He fell childless, too; your leader Ausar, here beside me, descends from an upright brother. The Stygians overran and annexed Taia. For centuries has it groaned beneath their yoke.

'The Ax of Varanghi lay not on the stricken field where the last king died. No living person has seen it since. Yet a holy man prophesied up and down the country that it had been hidden away, to await the coming of a deliverer fit to bear it; and he will be of the old Northern blood. The Stygians captured and crucified the prophet; but they could not kill his words, which live to our own day.

'Often in prayer have the priests of Mitra, at this sacred place, asked him for a sign. He has given dreams and visions, which tell us we must never abandon hope.

'They say nothing about the advent of the liberator. But they do not deny that verse in the prophecy which says that this shall come to pass after a hand of centuries.

'A hand of centuries – five fingers, five hundred years? I know not. But that is indeed how long Taia has been enslaved. *Yours* may be the generation that sets her free!'

The warriors brandished weapons and roared forth the savage cries of their clans.

The Stygians bound the few prisoners they had taken but did not otherwise abuse any. At dawn, when mists rolled chill off the river, Shuat came on inspection. For a minute or two he regarded the Taians, and they glared defiance at him. The noises of the torrent and of the regiment moving about seemed remote.

'Is this all?' he growled. 'And we scarcely killed more of them than they of us.' To his adjutant: 'I do not abide by a plan that is a failure. We return at once.' His gaze went back and came to rest on Daris. 'Who is the woman?'

'If it please my lord, I helped capture her,' a sergeant said. 'And a hellcat she was.' He leered. 'I and my friends can soon tame her. We'll forego breakfast.'

Daris snarled. Shame seared her.

'No, you idiot,' the commander rapped. 'See that golden disc on her brow. The natives reserve it for their highest-ranking family. I will not have her hostage or exchange value lessened.' He addressed her. 'Who are you?'

Stygian was not her mother tongue, but like most Taians, Daris had learned it well. She straightened herself, met his eyes, spoke her name, and added, 'I am a daughter of Ausar, rightful king of this country.'

'A-a-ah,' Shuat said. 'Very good. My scheme has paid better than I knew.' Sickened, Daris realized what she had given away.

On his orders, she was separated from her fellows. They bade her a stoic good-bye. They were bound for slavery. Her fate might prove worse.

She was not immediately mistreated. Her guards allowed her to wash – at the end of a leash around her neck. She hated their remarks when she stripped, but cleanliness felt good. She also rinsed her tunic and skirt; they soon dried. Her cuirass and weapons were booty, of course. She shared the men's lentils and walked among them on the march downrive . They tried once or twice to make conversation, but she spoke no word in reply, so they cursed her for a surly she-cur and explained at length what could happen to her later on.

She gave that small heed. The anguish of captivity drowned all else. She moved as in an evil dream.

Hard-driving, Shuat brought his troop back to Seyan in three days. This little town of whitewashed mud buildings, at the confluence of the Helu and the Styx, was yet the largest in today's Taia, and the seat of the governor. His palace stood grand on the outskirts, amidst its gardens, close to the military base. Daris was led there and locked in an offside room while Shuat went to report.

A pair of soldiers soon fetched her forth. 'When you enter the presence, be sure to fall prostrate on the floor,' one warned.

Daris bridled. 'What, has the governor given himself royal honors?'

'No, but he is with a wizard-priest of Set.' Dread freighted the man's voice.

During her journey, Daris had recovered her wits. With them had come resolution. There was no sense in dying for the sake of pride; that would not serve her father's cause. No, let her do whatever was necessary for survival, as long as she could bring

38

herself to it. Let her bide her time, ever alert for a chance to escape or at least to kill a few Stygians. Thus when she was ushered into the great chamber, she made the required abasement, flat on the reed matting.

'Rise,' came sibilant from the far end. 'Draw nigh.'

Meekly, Daris advanced between walls painted with beast-headed human figures. Before her Shuat and corpulent Wenamon sat on stools under the dais of the governor's throne. It was occupied by a shaven-skulled man in a black robe. She was chiefly conscious of his eyes. They smoldered upon her.

'Halt,' he commanded. She obeyed. Silence waxed in the dimness. She felt as if those eyes probed through garb and flesh to her soul.

'Aye,' he said at last, 'there is something dire about the destiny of this maiden. What it is, I cannot see. I must convey her to Khemi for my master to examine closer.'

'When do we suffer the loss of your company, holy Hakketh?' Wenamon asked unctuously

'At once.' The wizard got up. 'Guards, follow me with the girl. You others, have my servants meet me at the wingboat.'

Wenamon and Shuat bowed deeply as he swept past them.

Daris' heart stammered. Sweat broke forth, cold on her skin. To Khemi the Black – for . . . examination?

She mustered courage. By river, the forbidden city was two thousand or more miles distant, she knew. In weeks of travel, surely she could find a way to a clean death.

The path from the palace did not lead to the civilian docks, but to a closely guarded wharf for war craft. None were there at the moment. Instead, Daris beheld a vessel such as she had never heard of before. Almost fifty feet in length, the hull shimmered dull white, metallic. A high prow bore the image of the head and neck of a sword-beaked reptile, whose folded leathery wings seemed to be modeled along the sides. The hull was open except for a smoothly shaped deckhouse, and revealed no sign of mast or oars. In the stern, on an iron-clawed tripod, was a large crystal globe wherein flickered something like fire, red and blue.

A servile, muscular acolyte, one of several in attendance on Hakketh, drew the boat alongside the pier. The party boarded by way of a ladder molded into the bulwark, leaving the soldiers to watch in awe. At a word from the magician, a servitor locked a fetter about Daris' ankle, attached to a light chain that in turn was shackled to a ring in the deck. She had reasonable scope for movement, but saw with horror that she would not be able to leap overboard.

Hakketh gestured. The guardsmen cast off. The boat drifted out on the current. Hakketh turned to one of the acolytes. 'Take the first watch,' he directed.

'Yes, my lord.' The man went to stand before the globe. He lifted his hands. *'Zayen,'* he intoned, a word in no language that Daris recognised. The fires in the globe strengthened. The wings along the hull extended until they stood straight from it. Silently, the vessel gathered speed as the Stygian raised his arms higher.

Perhaps because he wanted to see how she would react, Hakketh told the woman: 'Know that you ride in the sacred wingboat of Set, the last of its kind in the world. The magical formula of its making was lost when Acheron perished, three thousand years ago.'

Faster the craft went and faster. Wind, deflected by the prow, began to whistle.

Hakketh nodded at the deckhouse. 'You will have a compartment in there, and will be unchained when you wish to use it. You will have food and drink. None will harm you, but if you attempt anything untoward, you will be bound.'

The boat no longer threw up a bow wave. It had risen on the wind it raised to skim the dark surface of the river. The acolyte let his arms drop and simply pointed when he wished a change of direction. Sometimes, spying a possible hazard such as a floating log, he reduced speed by raising his arms again skyward, saying the word *'Aaleth,'* and lowering them to a degree commensurate with how fast he wanted to go. Then he would utter *'Memn'* and be free to stand as he chose until time to hasten again.

'Three nights and three days will see us in Khemi,' Hakketh finished.

Daris fought not to cry out or weep. Westward, the sun sank behind the hills that had been her home.

V

THE WORK OF THE WITCH

Near the Crocodile Gate stood the Keep of the Manticore. A huge, nearly cubical pile of dark stone around a central courtyard, it took its name from a figure chiseled above its iron-doored main entrance. Tortures, executions, and vindictive imprisonments had engaged its lower levels for centuries; common dwellers in Khemi shunned its neighborhood as ill-omened. They did not know that on two higher floors were luxurious apartments, an elegant kitchen, secret access for entertainers who were brought there and back blindfolded, but were well paid for performing. Sometimes the hierarchy had reasons to make a detention comfortable. They did not on that account leave it unguarded.

Clad in a silken robe, Jehanan, brother of Bêlit, lounged on a couch. Beside him, a door stood open on a balcony where flowering vines grew across trellises to give shade and fragrance. The chamber was large, lavishly furnished, beautifully decorated with gilt arabesques. Inner doors led to a bathroom that was almost as big, for it included a swimming pool, and a small but sybaritic bedroom.

His days here had fleshed him out, restored his full strength, removed the craziness from his eyes. His face was still scarred and battered; but washed, barbered, smiling, it was a face that some women would have found attractive.

Nehekba perched beside him. A film of gown and a few jewels only accentuated her utter femaleness. She smiled and stroked his cheek. 'What happened then, beloved?' she crooned.

'Why –' Jehanan looked puzzled. 'Why do you care? It is a trivial thing from my childhood. I stopped because of realizing I myself do not remember it well.'

'Oh, but I care about everything that ever concerned you,' she said.

He flushed in joy, reached out to lay a hand on her thigh, and said, 'Well, then, as I was telling you, Bêlit and I came back from our jungle venture safe, though muddy and out of breath. Our father was furious at the risk we had taken and was about to punish us. But our mother told him – now what were her words? – she told him he should not punish venturesomeness, for we got it from him and we would have need of it in later life. Better to put us on our honor to be more careful in future. He agreed. Bêlit and I were glad to be spared a paddling ... at first. Afterward, though, having thought further, we joined in a secret wish that he had simply chastised us. For of course we could never break a promise given him.'

'You were a happy family in truth,' Nehekba observed.

'Aye. You should know that, dear Heterka, as much as you have gotten me to recall those years for you.' Jehanan sat straight. He took her by the slim waist with both hands, looked into her eyes, and said, 'I still cannot believe my fortune – from a slave, in such pain always that only exhaustion let me sleep, to beatific lover of the most wonderful woman that ever lived. *Why?*'

'I have explained. I glimpsed you, your steadfastness in misery, and was enchanted. I could not buy and manumit you, for the law here recognizes no foreign-born freedmen. But I could have you brought to this place, with the idea of making a better arrangement later.'

'Yes, yes, darling, of course. But you are so mysterious that – Oh, no more words for now.' Jehanan gathered her to him and began to kiss her.

Abruptly he winced, let go, dropped his glance, and muttered, 'I fear I need a fresh draught of the potion that frees me of pain. Else I – I will have no manhood in me.'

Nehekba rose. 'I brought some, dear.' She flowed across the room to a purse she had left by the entrance. He stood to watch as she took out a golden vial.

'I will fetch wine to mingle it in, and drink to my love for you, Heterka,' he said.

Her smile turned cruel. 'Trouble yourself not. You have no more need of this.' She unstoppered the vial and emptied it onto the floor. 'I am done with you.'

He howled like a wolf when the jaws of a trap close on it.

'Oh, we will keep you here a while yet,' she taunted. 'We may get a little further use out of you, or amusement.'

'Are you a demon?' he screamed. His big form lurched toward her, fingers held talon-crooked. Those muscles had lost no power in anguish.

Nehekba touched a small mirror at her throat. From it sprang a ray, not of light but of dark. When that struck Jehanan, he crashed down and lay motionless, staring at her in overwhelming horror.

She opened a foot-square hinged panel in the massive outer door and called softly. The turnkey arrived to unlock it for her. 'Farewell, lover who was,' she said to Jehanan, and departed.

The paralysis left him eventually. He crawled to the threshold and tried to suck the spilled potion out of the carpet.

Nehekba went down a stair and through a tunnel that were both secret. She walked fast, the gauzy gown aflutter behind her in cresset-lighted gloom, for Tothapis required her presence and she was belated.

By further devious ways she entered his house. The slaves who had been mutilated into muteness brought her to the centrum. He ignored her at first, continuing his interview with a man who stood respectful before his chair.

Nehekba considered this person closely, for though she had heard of Amnun, they had not met before. He was slender, erect, good-looking in an alien fashion; he favored his mother, who had been a Taian slave in Luxur. In spirit, however, he drew from his Stygian father. Long had he been among the many laymen in the service of the priest-magician.

'The pirate galley is prowling up our coast,' Tothapis said. His vulture countenance jutted forward. Shadows played in the wrinkles of it and in the hollows of his eyes, as they did among the objects of sorcery round about. 'You wondered why I have not raised a gale to sink her. I will tell you; but if you ever reveal it to anyone else, you will soon long for the torments of hell.'

'I am my lord's faithful servant,' Amnun replied boldly.

Tothapis' bald head nodded. 'So you have been. Well, then our sacred duty, lifetime after lifetime, is to strive to increase the power of Set.' He made a reverent sign; Amnun genuflected; Nehekba briefly covered her face as befitted a woman. 'There are other gods than Set,' Tothapis continued. 'They have their own dominions. He has none over the sea – not yet, not yet. Therefore I, his priest, can work only small magics above the deeps out yonder. For the most part we must use our human intelligence.'

He lifted a bony finger. 'Now. The freighter *Meniti* sails out on tomorrow morning's tide. Her captain and crew believe they are conveying cargo south to Umr. That course is such that Bêlit's *Tigress* will soon intercept her – given the minor guidance that I am able to impose on winds of these shores. The matter is so vital that this is but a small sacrifice to make. You go aboard this evening, in the role I explained days ago.' He pointed to a scroll lying wrapped about its rollers on a table. 'There is the documentation you require. Is all clear to you?'

'No, lord,' Amnun admitted. 'I am supposed to pretend familiarity with a person I have never encountered. How?'

Tothapis beckoned to Nehekba. She came forward. Amnun regarded her with the strife between lust and fear that she ever found delectable. 'Know you who I am?' she asked.

He bent his knee. 'You are the lady Nehekba, high priestess of Derketa, and I am humble before you,' he answered.

'I am she who has gathered the knowledge you must have,' she told him, 'and who is about to impart it unto you. Look up.'

He lifted his eyes. She turned the mirror at her throat. A light-ray sprang from the side now exposed. He shivered and froze. His features went blank. She kept the beam in his eyes while her left hand gestured and her tongue whispered words.

After a few minutes, she let the talisman dangle free on its chain. 'Amnun, arouse!' she exclaimed.

He shivered again, blinked, returned to awareness. 'You now know what I have learned from Jehanan,' Nehekba said. 'Use it well, and great shall be your reward.'

Astonishment made the man stagger. 'I – I know, I know!' he cried. 'It is as if I myself heard –'

'Peace,' Tothapis said from beneath the carven cobra hood. 'You will have this evening, and tomorrow, and the night that follows, to consider what our lady of Derketa has imparted to you, and order it

44

in your mind. Thereafter ... for a while, Amnun, you will be the embodiment of fate. Set prosper you, Amnun, who go forth in his cause.'

There was a little more talk, before the agent bowed and was conducted out. Silence lingered after him, while the wizard sat in deep reverie. Nehekba shifted restless from foot to foot. At last she asked, 'Have I your leave to go, lord?'

His attention locked onto her. 'Where?' he demanded. 'The hour draws nigh for us and for Conan. We must not rest idle meanwhile.'

'I will not,' she said. 'Rather, I think I should return to the Keep at once – to Falco.'

Tothapis frowned. 'The Ophirite spy? What more can you do with the ignorant boy?'

'Bind him closer to me. Remember, my lord, we ascertained he too is in some unfathomable way linked with Conan's future. Best he be our tool.'

'Have you not already made him your own, as you did Jehanan?'

The midnight tresses stirred as Nehekba shook her head. 'Not absolutely. He loves me, yes, but he nourishes still an idea of duty above self. Let me keep trying to undermine that. It must needs be done slowly, subtly.' She flashed an impudent grin. 'Not unpleasantly, though. For all his youth, he is an excellent lover.'

'No, let him wait,' Tothapis said in glacial anger. 'You spend too much of your vitality in carnal matters.'

'I serve Derketa, to whom they belong,' she challenged.

'You serve great Set before her – before all else in his universe, Nehekba. Have you dared forget?' Chilled, the witch fell silent. The wizard pursued: 'I have urgent need of your assistance. This day I received a message through the homunculus we sent to Luxur. It was from Hakketh. He is bound here with a prisoner of war, a daughter of the ringleader in the Taian revolt. He has sensed fate in her, danger. He knows not what, but he brings her to me. Surely she too is enwebbed with Conan. I stand aloof from the female mind and soul, Nehekba. You must help me prepare the plans and the spells that may also make of her an instrument for the thwarting of Mitra and the triumph of Set.'

VI

PIRATE, BARBARIAN, RESCUER

'Sail ho-o!'

The shout from the masthead of *Tigress* wakened an answering roar on deck. Her crew bounded about like black panthers, to drag forth chests stowed under rowers' benches, open them, take out battle gear, spring to stations. In the prow, Belit laughed aloud and pointed into the starboard quarter. There was no necessity for that; teeth gleamed ivory-white in the faces of the two helmsmen as they changed course. Conan snatched his mate to him and kissed her briefly and fiercely, before he jumped down to equip himself.

A brisk wind filled the sail and sent the galley soaring across wrinkled, glittery green-and-blue whitecaps. Limber hull and taut rigging creaked, as if to add their voices to the war chant that rose among the buccaneers. The mainland lay below the eastern horizon, but a mile or so to port, surf beat on an islet whose rocks lifted bleached and barren toward the azure emptiness above.

Conan rejoined Belit. His great form now shone in hauberk and horned helmet; sword and dirk were sheathed at his waist and an elliptical Suba shield was on his left arm. For her part she had merely fetched a pair of slender blades, and otherwise wore the same tunic and headband as before. Her hair was braided and coiled for action.

He peered ahead. They were closing in rapidly on their prey, a big-bellied Stygian merchantman. He could see her crew scramble about, trying to coax more speed out of the square sail, then readying themselves for an encounter they realized was inevitable.

'Here continues my revenge,' Belit exulted.

'She ought to have a cargo worth taking,' Conan opined, 'and in frankness, dearest, I've gotten hungry for a good fight.' He scowled. 'Yet I wish you would put on more protection.'

'I told you before, a woman lacks a man's sheer strength,' she explained. 'Armor would but weight me down, without fending off a hard-driven arrow or keeping a solid blow from breaking my neck. But when we come to close quarters, you have seen I am as agile as any and more so than most.'

He put uneasiness from him. Crom, chief god of the Cimmerians, gave might and heart to those he favored, and nothing else, that they may be able to hew their own ways through the world. Had the land of Crom reached down to the Black Coast and touched Belit in her mother's womb? Conan could well believe that.

For a moment he recalled his stark homeland. Far indeed had he wandered from it, and wild had been his adventures. Finally he had come upon love, but he knew that was by the same blind chance that could at any instant reave it away again. He squared his shoulders. It behoved a man – or a woman – to stand up to every onslaught of the fates, unquelled.

Besides, he thought with a quick grin, it did look like a fine scrap ahead. The freighter's crew did not include many full-fledged warriors, to judge by their conduct, but they outnumbered the pirates, and every sailor learned early on how to handle himself in a tussle.

Arrows began to fly from her decks. Archers among the Suba returned the barrage, while their comrades gibed and howled at the foe. Sunlight glittered off spears shaken aloft. A shaft thunked into the figurehead of *Tigress*, an inch from Belit, and Conan snarled. She laughed. Down below, a Negro took one in his right thigh. He wrenched it loose, staunched the wound, and resumed his eager stance at the rail. A man aboard the Stygian vessel lurched, smitten in the throat, crumpled, and toppled over the side. As he splashed, a triangular fin cruised forward.

Belit yelled orders. *Tigress* drew upwind of her quarry. Hauled sharply about and poled out, her sail brought her toward the other hull. A huge ebon warrior amidships whirled a grapnel over his head and let it fly. Trailing a cord, it bit fast in the bulwarks. Immediately he sent another. 'Wa-ho-ah!' roared his fellows, and hauled so the muscles moved like snakes under sweat-shiny hides. Stygian axmen sought to cut the lines. A volley of arrows dropped some and drove the rest back. Planks banged together. *Tigress* shuddered from the impact but lay hard alongside.

'Get aboard before they torch us!' Conan bawled. He had seen what fire could do to a ship. His sword flared free, and he sped along the catwalk.

Crewmen of his had already brought up a boarding plank. Its teeth crunched into a rail several feet higher than that of *Tigress*. Conan shoved through the group and was first in their attack. Behind him stormed those few who had the armor to serve as shock troops. Most bore simply kilts or tunics, with the plumes and weapons of their native country, but they seemed all the more fearsome for that as they gathered to follow. *'Wakonga mutusi!'* Their screams overran the shouts of the merchant sailors.

Three men in Stygian military mail stood shoulder to shoulder at the head of the plank. Conan's blade whirred on high and sang downward. It belled on the metal of a shield. The bearer staggered from the force, but thrust from behind his protection. Conan's clumsy assault had been a ruse. His steel chopped sideways, caught the enemy's wrist, and raised a gout of blood. The man stared unbelieving at his dangling hand and reeled back, to sit down and die.

Conan had already used his own shield to catch that of his opponent on the left by the rim, hook it aside, and leave a leg exposed to a murderous sweep. As he smote, he gave a further twist that threw his foe against the one on the right. While the first wailed and sagged, the barbarian turned on the second. That fellow was more skilled. He kept his shield before him, moving it just enough to counter blows, and worked around its sides. Conan stepped back a pace to gain room. When the shortsword probed after him, his own long blade rang down upon it. Sheer impact tore it loose from the Stygian's grasp. He retreated. Conan sprang forward and onto the freighter's main deck.

He had needed scarcely three minutes to clear the way. Honed metal gathered nigh, in a frantic attempt to slay him and close the gap. He bellowed for glee and laid about him. Most of the defenders, like most of the pirates, had little more than shields to aid them, if that. Their bare brown bodies were terribly vulnerable to his ironclad violence. Crash and clang mingled with the shrieks of those

48

he drove back or brought low. And now Belit's warriors were swarming aboard.

The Stygian captain shouted from the poop. His men heard. They were a well-drilled crew. Such of them as were able formed into a tight squad and retreated aft. They inflicted as well as took losses. The Suba were mainly engaged with those who had not managed to join that band but nevertheless put up a stiff battle. Thus a score or better of the merchant seamen gained the higher deck.

Belit hurried over red-running planks, writhing wounded, contorted dead, to Conan. Arrows from the poop whistled after her. He drew her close to him and held up his shield for whatever safety it afforded. 'They can stand us off, where they are, for a long while,' she said. 'There is ample shipping in these waters, and pirates are the enemy of every seafaring nation. They can hope another vessel will chance by in time to help them. Then I fear we must make off.'

'We can plunder this – No,' Conan decided. It would be impossible to transfer cargo under a barrage. Already the buccaneers had been forced to take shelter behind deckhouse, mast, and bollards. He felt an arrow ram into his shield and urged Belit away.

'Well, we can at least set her afire!' she said viciously.

The wastefulness of that offended Conan's sense of workmanship. 'Hold,' he said. 'I have a notion. They can keep the ladder against us, aye ... *if* they have nobody at their backs.' He was now forward of the deckhouse. 'Help me, will you?' He dropped the shield.

'What –' she began. He told her. For a heartbeat she stood appalled, then understanding flamed in her, and she barked a she-wolf's laughter. 'You are mad, Conan, but you are wonderful! Yes, go!' She kissed him, so hard that her teeth drew blood from his lips, and knelt to unlace his boots.

He sent his encumbering chain mail rattling to the deck and slung his sword across his back. Barefoot, garbed merely in breeches and helmet, he darted forth. At the mast he studied the rigging for a moment, chose a halyard, and drew his dirk to cut it across. Thereafter he sought a rail and the shrouds on that side. His fingers and toes gripped tarry ratlines. Swift as a squirrel, he scampered aloft.

The Stygians did not appear to have noticed him. Belit had gotten her own archers to keep them occupied. A bulwark around the poop protected them fairly well, but they must keep their heads beneath except when rising briefly for a return shot.

Perched on the yardarm above the slatting sail, Conan hauled in the severed line. The backstay offered him a way down, but one that would be fatally slow. Instead, he cut the halyard again at its block and ran out along the pole. Unsteered, the ship wallowed in billows, her mast drawing wild arcs across the sky. Conan balanced himself without thinking. Near the tip of the yard he slashed enough of the sail loose that it would not interfere with him. Having gauged what length he wanted, he made the line fast. Taking the free end in both hands, he sprang.

He fell, shocked to a halt as the cordage drew taut, and swung. Forward over deck, cabin, warriors, *Tigress*, and ever-hungry sea he swept, jubilating like the boy who had once played this game in the treetops of Cimmeria. Back aft he whirled, low above the poop, and let go.

His feet caught the bulwark, a brunt that went through his bones. He rebounded and came to a crouch even as his sword hissed from its sheath. Shieldless, he drew dagger as well. A sailor gaped at him, stupefied. Conan hewed. A skull clove.

'Hoy-ho!' Conan trumpeted, and smote right and left. A pike jabbed at him. He used his sword to deflect it, and slithered inward. His dirk found the pikeman's throat. He hurled the dying body against another, and brought his blade around in bare time to fend off an ax. No single, unarmored man could stand before a massed attack; but he forced himself in among the Stygians, where they could not work together, and sowed havoc.

A shortsword grazed him. He smashed the pommel of his own weapon into the face behind and felt bone crunch. His edge sliced over the man's shoulder before that one could fall, and laid a belly open. Meanwhile he had locked the guard of his knife into that of another sword. He held it immobilized until he was ready to twist about and chop through the arm that wielded it.

Towering over the tumult, he saw Belit's black fighters dash to a ladder now undefended. Abruptly he heard a laugh, long, savage, descending. Belit flew onto the poop, in the same wise as he had done. He gasped. He had not intended that. She bounced about, her steel aflicker. He roared. The fury of his combatting redoubled. He would kill every last Stygian wretch aboard before any of them could harm his beloved!

In the event, he did not, for her men arrived and soon completed the task.

Sails furled, the linked ships rolled easily in the marching seas. More coolly than exuberant Belit, Conan took stock. Their crew had lost three, and five had such bad wounds that they would be out of action for a while, if infection did not take them off. No Stygians appeared to remain. The buccaneers had thrown all overboard, dead or alive; they were not in the slave trade. However, Conan saw that eventually Belit would have to do what she had done before, return to Suba country for fresh recruits. She said there was no dearth of those.

Hatches yawned where men had gone below to find out what cargo they had acquired. He heard happy noises and gathered that it was not only valuable but readily transferable – spices, perhaps. He himself approached the deckhouse, Belit at his side. Both had cast off their bloody, sweaty garb. Her glorious body still shimmered wet from the bucket of seawater she had dashed across them both. They kept swords in hand; predators who have not learned caution reach no great age.

Before them, a cabin door suddenly swung open. The man who came forth wore the iron collar of a slave. Yet his tunic was white and clean, and he bore his slender frame with a certain elegance. Darker-hued and finer-featured than his shipmates, he seemed foreign to them.

'Greeting,' he said calmly, and bowed his head above folded hands. The rest of his words were lost on Conan, who knew almost nothing of the Stygian language.

Belit answered him in her own limited vocabulary. He smiled and broke into Shemitish, which Conan did know fairly well: 'Congratulations upon your victory, my lord and lady. In what may Otanis of Taia serve you?'

'Huh!' grunted Conan. 'You are quick to change masters, you.'

Otanis shrugged. 'What loyalty do I owe him who made property of me?' His gaze intensified. Yearning filled his voice. 'Perhaps you will make a man of me, in your kindness. That would earn you, in truth, the devotion that never dies.'

Belit explained to Conan: 'He is a Taian. His people are not Stygians, though their land has long been a province of the kingdom, and they have often risen against their rulers. It has always been in vain, but you must admire their courage the more for that.' She addressed the other. 'What was your fate?'

Otanis frowned. 'Once more the war arrow goes among the clans, and Taia strives for her ancient freedom,' he said. 'I was captured in an engagement and sent to the slave market.'

Conan studied him and observed shrewdly: 'You do not seem to have suffered too much.'

'No, I was fortunate, if such a thing as good fortune can exist in a cage,' Otanis replied. 'The Stygian who bought me, a merchant of Khemi named Bahotep, has the wit to recognize that one gets more out of an animal if it is properly treated. I happen to be literate – not very common among Taians in these sad years, as my lady doubtless knows – and he put me in his counting house. Lately he appointed me his supercargo for this precious shipment. He had come to trust me, you see; besides, he charged the captain to keep me under guard while in port.' Otanis shrugged again. 'Well, if we balance the fact that he is not unkindly against the fact that he claims me for his slave, I seem to owe him nothing, good or ill. Therefore, my lord and lady, I am at your service.' He repeated his bow. 'May I ask who you are?'

'I am Belit, of the corsair *Tigress*,' the woman said proudly, 'and this is my fellow captain Conan –' She broke off. Otanis stood agape. 'What is the matter?'

'You . . . are Belit . . . of Shem and the Black Coast?' he inquired.

Light rippled along her obsidian-dark tresses as she nodded. 'Yes,' she said, 'I am Belit, who like you has much to avenge upon Stygia.'

'Why, I – I know your brother,' Otanis stammered.

Belit stiffened. 'What?' she said in a shuddering breath.

'Yes, Jehanan, is he not your brother? How often and with what

52

love has he told me of you.'

Belit's sword clattered to the deck. She seized Otanis by the forearm. Her nails dug into his flesh till he winced. He stood fast, though, which Conan liked. The Cimmerian's own broad palm sought the shoulder of his beloved. Beneath the silken skin, he felt how flesh tensed and shivered.

'Tell me!' she commanded. 'Tell me everything!'

'Why ... well, there is a great deal,' Otanis said hesitantly. 'We became close friends, he and I.'

'He is no longer the victim of that Ramwas beast?' she cried.

Otanis shook his head. 'No. He is not.' After a search for words, he proceeded: 'He has told me how Ramwas bought you both, and you apparently got away. He dared hope for no more than that you met a decent death. How overjoyed he would be to see you here, queen of battle! But in any case, Jehanan had made such trouble on his own that Ramwas decided to get rid of him and put him up for sale. My master Bahotep bought him. As I said, Bahotep knows better than to make a field hand of a gifted and educated man. Jehanan responded well to reasonable treatment.' Otanis cast a smirk at Conan. 'We may even visit a certain female he keeps, once a week, if we behave ourselves.' He grew serious anew, met Belit's tearful regard, and went on: 'Yes, Jehanan works beside me, or did until I was sent on this voyage. Of course, his heart ever hungers for freedom. But he is too intelligent to risk what he has, little though that be, unless the gods give him a better chance of escape than has yet appeared.'

'Jehanan –in Khemi? –Jehanan!' Belit wailed. She cast herself into Conan's arms and sobbed. He held her close, stroked her hair and back, murmured what comfort he could. Such of her men as were topside stared white-eyed but did not venture near.

'Where is he, Otanis?' Belit tore loose from her lover and whirled on the other man. 'We will make a raid. Guide us to him, and all the gold in Stygia shall be yours!'

Conan understood, down to his marrow, what she was feeling. Yet becase he was, in some measure, still an outsider, he was able to maintain calm. Beneath it, rage and eagerness seethed in him. To give Belit this gift! But he had the power to stand back and study how the thing might be done.

53

He pinioned her, made her look at him, and said most carefully: 'My dearest, you rave. One ship against a city and a fleet? That is no rescue, that is suicide. Let us use our brains as well as our blades,' his tone strengthened, 'and Jehanan will indeed walk the decks of *Tigress*.'

She hauled herself, almost hand over hand, back toward steadiness. 'Yes, you are right, of coure,' she could finally say. 'We need a plan. But this is going to be what we live for – Jehanan's freedom – until we have won it.'

Conan's ice-blue gaze went above her head and speared Otanis. 'We shall require your help,' the Cimmerian said. 'No doubt the venture will be dangerous. You have fought for your country. Now be true to us, and you shall have not only your liberty, but shiploads of wealth. Would those not buy plenty of mercenaries for your cause?' He pondered a moment, silent amidst the sea wind. 'If you fail us,' he finished bluntly, 'you die.'

Otanis smiled. 'It may not even be so difficult,' he responded. 'Shall we talk further?'

Belit put the first mate in charge of transshipping cargo, and accompanied the two men beside her into the former captain's cabin. She and Conan sat down at its table. Otanis fetched wine and joined them. A sunbeam sickled through a glazed window, back and forth as the vessel rolled. There came sounds of men talking and laughing at work, creak of wheeling gulls, whoosh and smack of waves. Though the room was small and sparsely furnished, air blew past a door secured half open, to fill it with salty breath and hope.

Otanis took a sip from his goblet, leaned back, bridged his fingers, and said: 'Bahotep's mansion and warehouse are not heavily watched. His slaves know they have the best – the least bad – master in Khemi, and are anxious to stay in his good graces. Yes, Jehanan likewise, unless and until a clear chance to run away comes along. My lady Belit must have had incredible luck in her own escape. I would be interested to hear what happened.'

'I stole a boat,' the woman snapped.

'And were not intercepted before then – by a sacred python, for example?' Otanis clicked his tongue. 'Moreover, when a missing slave and a missing craft were reported next morning, certainly three or four ships went out in search. The Stygians always want to make examples of contumacious underlings, and a ship has greater hull speed than a boat. It was sheer fortune that none chanced to sight you, and that nobody thought it worthwhile to ask a magician to scry your exact whereabouts, until too late. Jehanan can not expect similar luck; and a flight overland would be more futile yet. Remember, the punishment for a fugitive slave is not death – not for days.'

He paused. Conan drank deep of the acid Stygian wine and regarded him dourly. Otanis resumed:

'However, as I said, Jehanan would have no special difficulty in leaving Bahotep's place. He, like me, often does, on this or that errand. He could readily invent a reason to be absent for two or three days, a reason that would convince the guard, such as a message to bear to the superintendent of one of Bahotep's plantations. It is unlikely that the guard would query the master about this. I could send him a note instructing him about it – give it into the hand of some mutual, illiterate friend in the household, as soon as that person passes by the spot where I lurk. He and I could then hasten to the boat that brought me ashore, take off well ahead of any pursuit, and seek back to this ship, my lady.'

Wine slopped from the cup that Belit raised to her lips.

'You are very glib, Otanis,' Conan growled. 'Why should we believe we have not seen the last of you, once you are in that boat?'

'A good question, sir,' the dark man replied, unruffled. 'My answer is threefold. First and least, you have offered great reward for my service – reward not only to me but my poor oppressed motherland. Second, I am truly a friend of Jehanan. If you doubt this, let me spend a few hours telling you what he has told me about himself – and about you, my lady – yes, tales reaching far back into childhood. You know your brother; you know he would not relate intimate matters to anyone whom he did not feel was trustworthy. Third, I am a Taian, a mountaineer, no sailor. I will need someone to man the boat that carries me. It is also best I bring a strong sword arm along, in case something goes awry.'

Conan's fist boomed on the tabletop. 'You have one!' he exclaimed.

'No, not you, dearest,' Belit protested. She clutched his wrist. 'I will go.'

He shook his head. 'Impossible. You could never pass yourself off as a noblewoman or a harlot – the only kinds of female who may wander freely about in Khemi, if it is true what I have heard. Besides, though you are a bonny fighter, I shall have a better chance in a heavy set-to – better than any of the crew, in fact. Also, they are none of them used to cities, right? Such a fellow would all too likely blunder and draw attention. Mainly, you call me your co-captain, Belit, but the truth is that you are the one those wild blacks obey. I cannot even speak their language. We must keep *Tigress* yare for ... for Jehanan.'

She gulped, then said with steely realism: 'So be it, Conan. I will scuttle this ship and hold our galley near yonder isle. Akhbet, it is called, and I will teach you how to navigate your way between it and Khemi. It is unpeopled, a handy rendezvous.'

The barbarian stroked his massive chin. 'Hm, you do understand there is no way of foretelling how long this will take? We don't want to be rash, Otanis and I. And sheer misfortune could delay us – maybe force us inland after we have Jehanan.'

Belit nodded. 'Yes, surely I understand.' Her voice broke. 'But, oh, Conan, never will I forsake you, in life or in death! I am torn between my love for you and my love for my brother – unwilling am I to see you go in to danger, even on his account, and yet he *is* the son of my father. No, never will I forsake. Here *Tigress* shall abide, off Akhbet isle. If you are long gone, we may have to steer off in search of supplies; or caution may send us away, if warcraft come by; but always, always we will return and wait.' She entered his embrace. 'Always, Conan!'

Soon, though, she was calm enough that she could ask Otanis about Jehanan, how he fared and what he had had to tell. As she listened, an ardor kindled in her that flared high in Conan, too.

VII

TRAITORS' TAVERN

Night had fallen when a gig taken from the merchantman reached the mainland, but a gibbous moon gave ample light for eyes that had served their possessor in the darkness of Cimmerian forests. The beams glimmered on low, lapping waves and lateen sail. Ahead, Stygia stretched dim beneath the faintly gilded eastern sky. The breeze was still off the sea, and Conan felt the heat thicken as he neared his goal.

That was not Khemi harbor. No craft entered it without permission, nor would Conan have wanted his to be in the view of police; his departure might have to be abrupt and violent. Otanis had suggested a cove south of the estuary, which Bêlit agreed on; she had noticed it on passages between her parents' trading post and their home city in former days. She gave Conan instructions in steering by the heavens, which he quickly mastered, for he had often guided himself overland in similar fashion. Her farewell yet thrilled in his spirit.

The boat lost wind as she entered the little bay, screened by liana-clad mangroves and palms on its miry sides. 'Furl the sail,' Conan told Otanis, and took up a sweep. Water churned to the force of his sculling. Serpents and crocodiles glided off in alarm, shiny-scaled. 'Ho, you are a lubber, aren't you?' the barbarian added after seeing how clumsily his companion labored. 'Let me do it when we make land.'

That happened shortly. He secured the hull fore and aft to trees growing on a bank at the low-water line; it would be unwise to leave himself dependent on the tide. Their drooping branches and the vines growing leafily along these ought to protect the gig from observation by chance wayfarers. Having made things shipshape, he garbed his sweating form in kaftan, cowled mantle, and sandals

57

that had been part of the booty. The cloak hid his illegal sword and dirk, and should enable him to pass casual inspection, at least by night. His size was unusual but not extraordinary among the generally tall Stygians, his skin was tanned to much the same hue as that of their aristocrats, and his blue eyes and foreign cast features were shadowed.

'I envy you in your cool tunic,' he remarked to Otanis. A whine filled the sultry air. He felt a sting, swatted the mosquito, and chuckled. 'Or maybe I don't. Well, from here on, you are in charge, my friend.'

In practice he found he must be the leader through the march, for the older man stumbled and fumbled. It struck Conan odd that one who had been a hunter and herdsman should be as inept as any city dweller. However, the Cimmerian supposed a native of highlands might well fare badly in this wet, entangled gloom. Few people had had as wide an experience of nature in all her aspects as he had.

Otanis did take over after they emerged in cultivated fields. Dust-gray by moonlight, a road ran north beside an irrigation ditch, for them to follow. Twice they came by villages of serfs, miserable clusters of mud hovels. Starveling dogs yelped at them but did not rouse humans who slept the sleep of exhaustion.

'Why do they live like this?' Conan wondered. 'What do they get from their lives but toil – for the good of their overlords, not themselves – and want and an overseer's lash across their backs if they flag?'

'It is the only life they know,' Otanis replied.

'But can they not even imagine something better? The only life I knew as a boy was that of my barbarian homeland. It was paradise set beside this, but nonetheless it grew wearisome to me, and I started out to see the greater world beyond.' Conan reflected. 'Oh, a single man or a single family who tried to run away from here would doubtless come to grief. But if enough of them gathered together, sworn to be free or else dead, they could cast that monstrous load of the state off themselves.'

Otanis was shocked. 'Why, that would bring the end of civilization!'

'So it would,' Conan agreed cheerfully.

'The heritage of the ages – learning, art, refinement – abolished for the sake of – of those beasts of burden?'

'I have been in many civilized realms, and it is true they had much to offer; but always the price was having a state and always that price was too high.' Conan threw a sharp glance at his associate. 'You talk rather strangely for a Taian, from what little I have heard about Taians.'

Otanis pinched his lips together. 'Best we do not discuss politics,' he said, and fell into a silence that Conan could not make him break. The Cimmerian finally shrugged and gave himself to remembering Bêlit.

The distance to cover was just a few miles, and the travelers reached Khemi well before midnight. Walls and towers loomed mountainous above the darkly gleaming River Styx. Here and there a window shone, yellow and lonely, but otherwise the city was sheer murk that seemed to drink down what moonlight fell upon its stones. On a warm night like this most towns would have given forth a few sounds of revelry, but silence lay heavy on the capital of the wizard priests.

Otanis led Conan toward the waterfront, by a paved road under the walls. That brought them in sight of the Great Pyramid, a hulk overtopping the loftiest battlements. This being high ground, Conan also glimpsed the pale jungle of old quarries and tombs below it, descending to the streamside. He curbed a shiver of fear. Mortal foes of any sort he gloried in meeting, but he nursed a primitive dread of the supernatural, and folk whispered that the ghosts of uncounted centuries haunted yonder brae. As for Khemi itself – he had not told Bêlit what courage he must summon to enter such a place.

Yet he was in truth the man best suited by far to accompany Otanis and fetch her brother back for his dearest. In his mind he stamped on his terrors; in his body he paced with tigerish steadiness.

The gates were closed to traffic between sunset and sunrise, unless it was in the service of the hierarchy. But only a pair of flanking walls and watchtowers confronted the docks, which otherwise stood open. Anything else would have hampered the waterborne commerce on which Khemi, like most of Stygia, depended. For defense on that side, the city had the royal fleet, the steep upward approach, and ultimately the powers of its sorcerers. Not for hundreds of years had any hostile force been so foolish as to attack it. Even its landward fortifications were mainly for the purpose of enabling the hierarchy to keep close control over its life.

Thus Conan and Otanis could enter as belated fishermen might, though they did keep to the deeper shadows, and sometimes hunched waiting for the opportunity to advance a few more yards, lest the harbor police notice them and ask their business. In the streets beyond, they had no further need for stealth.

'What a pit,' Conan muttered. 'Is not a single honest inn awake, for a horn of beer against this accursed heat?'

'You can get that where we are bound, but few places else,' Otanis declared softly. 'Now be quiet. We do not want to draw the heed of certain things that go abroad after dark.'

Beneath his cloak, Conan clapped hand on sword hilt. He had heard of the giant pythons sacred to Set, allowed to rove freely in the night when they grew hungry and take what prey they found. Almost, he would have welcomed such a monster, something real to fight. He was no Stygian, to let himself be crushed and devoured unresisting because that was the will of the god!

Though the street was broad, high buildings on either side shut off the moon and most of the stars, making it a canyon of gloom.

He appreciated, grudgingly, the absence of the filth common to thoroughfares elsewhere – until he glimpsed a party of the slaves who cleaned it up each night. They were the emaciated, the diseased, the insane, deemed worthless for any other duty in this last stretch of their lives, and it was as if nothing but their foremen's whips kept them tottering along. Elsewhere a flaring torch would show an occasional laborer of a slightly more fortunate kind, a messenger, a robed and bestially masked priest, or a courtesan naked save for the high, plumed headdress required of her. Those people were few and joyless. Aside from them, Khemi was an abyss wherein went slitherings and hissings.

The blackness deepened as Otanis brought Conan into a meaner section. Here the ways were narrow, twisting, and foul, between crumbling walls of tenements and workshops. Flat roofs were lumpy with sleepers who had fled ovenlike interiors. Once a pair of young men slunk close, spooky in their kaftans, and Conan saw knives glimmer forth. He drew his sword, and they thought better of whatever they had intended and slipped back into their alley.

'Yes,' he said, 'this hyena's den has no right to rule over a country such as yours, Otanis.' His guide made no reply.

Presently they stopped at a certain doorway. A withered palm frond proclaimed the house an inn, and light trickled faintly through cracks in panels and window shutters. Conan's keen ears caught sound from within, and among the stenches of the street he snuffed an odor of cooked meat. 'Have we found the hostel you bespoke?' he asked.

Otanis nodded. 'Yes, Uminankh's.' Aboard the ship he had explained that, while unregistered foreigners were absolutely forbidden to be harbored in Khemi, there were landlords who would ask no questions if a person had payment. The purse at Conan's hip was well filled. He had inquired how Otanis, brought from the highlands to the service of a respectable merchant, knew about such things. The answer had been that the minions of Bahotep occasionally got curious assignments; then, too, gossip was rife in the household.

Otanis knocked. The door, chained, opened an inch, and a surly face peered out. Conan grinned and held up a gold coin. The chain clacked loose, and the newcomers passed through.

They found themselves in a tiny taproom, beneath whose ceiling the Cimmerian must lower his head. Rushes underfoot had not been changed for weeks, and stank of sour beer and uncollected offal. Stone lamps cast dull smoky light over a few wicked-looking men attired in kilts and dagger belts, who sat cross-legged on the floor. A harlot, hideous and pathetic in old age, huddled nearby, ignored. A haunch of pork on a skewer kept somewhat warm above a charcoal brazier that made the air still more stifling than outside.

Otanis exchanged Stygian words with the one-eyed taverner, and passed money across. Glancing at Conan, he pointed to an inner doorway and said in Shemitish, 'You have a doss – to

61

yourself, except for the vermin – in the first chamber on your right as you go through there. I have paid your keep for a week. Do not let Uminankh charge you for food or drink. He will try, of course.'

Conan grimaced. 'A week, locked in this sty?'

'We talked that out before we set sail,' Otanis reminded him. 'Wandering loose, you would much too likely become suspect. Besides, how then could we find each other at need? No, stay hidden. I cannot say how long it will take me to get a message to Jehanan, or when he can safely leave after that. If the gods favor us, it may only be a day or two.'

'And you will seek me here,' Conan agreed. 'Very well. Though if Bêlit could see where I must wait, she would have no doubt that I love her!'

'I go now. Sleep well.'

'Hm, better I sleep lightly. But are you leaving without rest or refreshment?'

'I know where to find those near Bahotep's house, and can begin at once to scout the area.'

Conan gripped Otanis by the shoulders. 'You are a good fellow,' the Cimmerian said gruffly. 'May luck fare beside you.'

The dark man smiled, bowed a little, and departed. Uminankh chained the door behind him. Conan approached the meat. It was not especially appetizing, but he was hungry. As he drew his knife to cut off a slice or two, Uminankh scurried up. Conan did not know the words the landlord spoke, but clearly he was demanding money. Conan told him in Cimmerian, 'You have been paid,' and elbowed him off. Uminankh broke into an arm-waving tirade. He appealed to his patrons, two of whom rose with hands upon daggers. Conan flipped his cloak aside to show his scabbarded sword. One man promptly sat back down. The other held out his palm and whined, 'Baksheesh?' Half amused, Conan gave him a copper, and was immediately surrounded by everybody in the room. 'Baksheesh, baksheesh!' they clamored. He had had less trouble hewing his way through an enemy troop than he did in winning to his bedchamber.

That was scarcely the proper name for a such a dirty, windowless cubicle, but it did have a reed mat hung in the entrance, a moldy straw pallet on the clay floor, and a pot. Conan undressed and spread his clothes to serve as a lower sheet. His weapons he placed on either side; and he would indeed sleep lightly, his fingers never far from their hilts.

He drifted off into a dream of Bêlit.

Noise woke him, harsh voices and metallic clatter. The air had cooled and filled with gray light, seeping in from dawn outside. He heard Uminankh expostulate – a thud that might be a fist as it struck the innkeeper, for it was followed by a whimper – barked commands, tramping feet. He bounded erect, armed.

A shortsword slashed across the curtain. It fell, dryly rustling, and revealed two Stygian soldiers. They were fully accoutered, in helmets, cuirasses, studded kilts, greaves, shields on arms, and blades in hand. Behind them massed the rest of their squad. And behind those stood Otanis.

'Conan, yield!' he cried. 'You have no hope except the mercy of my lord Tothapis.'

Rage whitened the barbarian's visage and thundered in his ears. '*Your* lord, you jackal?' he roared. 'With what piece of carrion did he buy you last night?'

Taller than the rest, the betrayer raised his head haughtily and replied: 'I was never bought. I am no Taian, but a true Stygian – Amnun my name, if you would know – and gladly did I set forth on my mission to entrap you for the priest Tothapis whom I serve. Set himself has ordained this, and potent sorcery has brought it about. Strive not against Him Who Is, Conan. Surrender and keep your life.'

'Not along with yours, cur!' The Cimmerian braced his huge frame in a corner. His steel wove back and forth in menace. 'Come and get me.'

Amnun spoke to the squad leader, who rapped orders to his men. They advanced into the room.

They did so warily, professionally. Amnun must have cautioned them about the person they were to arrest. Shield nestled by shield, the front line made a walking wall to curtain the pikemen behind. Given more space, Conan could have bounded around them, killing two or three on his way. Here he was boxed in.

He smote. A Stygian helmet rang. The wearer's head snapped back. Dazed by the pain in his neck, he faltered. His shield sank. Conan's sword screamed as it swung into the upper spine of the soldier beside the first. Blood spouted. A third man stumbled over the falling corpse, and Conan slew him on the return swing.

But their chief called the remainder toward the door. There they re-formed, and came forward again. This time the pikes of the second and third ranks jutted ahead of the advance. Suddenly Conan was caged among steel-tipped shafts.

'Yield, yield!' Amnun urged from the entrance.

Conan bellowed. Right and left his sword flew, to knock pikes aside. Barely for a moment did he have a clear shot past them, but that was enough. His left hand rose and whipped through an arc. The dirk flew from it. Amnun screamed as that weapon pierced his throat; then he sank to earth, the lifeblood gushing out of him. 'Take your reward!' Conan bawled.

He fully expected to die. He merely hoped to send a few more Stygians down hell-road before him. But the squad's orders were to bring him in alive. The officer called a new command. Several pikemen reversed their weapons and used them as clubs. Though Conan raged forth, striking, slaying two more and wounding nearly everyone else, the rain of blows to his skull became too much at last. He went down, on the floor and into darkness. The soldiers pounded him vindictively until their officer bade them stop.

VIII

CAPTIVES OF
THE BLACK RING

Tothapis' vulture countenance drew into a scowl. His fingers tapped the right arm of his cobra throne. For a moment that tattoo was the solitary sound among the shadows bulking and swaying misshapen in his centrum.

'I like it not,' he said finally. 'It is reckless.'

Nehekba, seated on a stool at his feet, let great bronze-hued eyes go wider still. Catching the candlelight, they seemed to turn the entire loveliness of her face luminous. 'Why, what would you do, my lord?' she murmured.

'The more I think about this thing,' he answered, 'the wiser it appears to me that we have the lot of them killed out of hand: Conan, the Taian princess, Jehanan, yes, and that Ophirite Falco. Abort his deadly destiny, together with the three lesser fates which are somehow linked to it.'

'My lord, forgive me, but I must say that fear speaks through your lips, not reason,' the priestess-witch retorted. 'We *must* probe deeper, learn more, before we take any such drastic action. Else the chain of future events that we sever could recoil upon us in unforeseeable ways. For example, Mitra,' at the name of the hated Sun god, both persons uttered a hiss and drew a serpentine line through the air, 'might find another than Conan able to wield the Ax that was forged in heaven, if that is indeed what he is intended for; and this time we would have no forewarning of who or where. We must gather clues, trace out the possibilities in him, before we can ascertain how the deeds he is to do may safely and permanently be prevented from ever coming to pass.'

'Aye, true,' Tothapis conceded. 'But we have drugs and torture for quick interrogation of him and the rest. Instead, not only have you demanded he be luxuriously maintained in the Keep of the Manticore, you want all of them brought together. No!'

'Potions and pangs will get but little out of that strong, stubborn warrior,' Nehekba argued. 'They should be our last resort, short of his execution, not our first. Whereas if we let the prisoners meet, let them talk and act freely, unaware they are observed, they will reveal everything about themselves – including, I am sure, whatever weaknesses Conan has that we can use against him.'

Tothapis remained uneasy. Nehekba persisted: 'What is to fear? No mortal has ever escaped from the Manticore. Be zealous in the service of Set, and Our Master of Night will aid you. Does he not delight in guile?'

Decision crystallized in the wizard. 'Very well,' he said, 'we will try it.'

He traced the sign and spoke the words that opened a way for vision and hearing between this house and the castle. The scene that appeared was of a room occupied by the officer of the day. He saw nothing in return, and started apprehensively when the voice of Tothapis addressed him. Scrambling to his feet, he saluted and heard his orders, while sweat sprang forth on his skin. 'Yes, great lord, it shall be done at once,' he chattered.

Tothapis and Nehekba followed the progress of the men he summoned. Those carried their assignments through without incident. After they had departed from the common room, the priest kept his view on the four who were now there. Getting her first close look at Conan, Nehekba drew a sharp breath and leaned avidly forward.

When the door of his apartment opened, the Cimmerian snatched up a chair. His wild hope was that he could brain whoever entered and somehow make his way out of prison. He snarled in disappointment and dropped the weapon as he saw an entire squad of fully armed soldiers. If they were here to fetch him for torture or worse, he would attack and die fighting. But the treatment he had received thus far, baffling though it was, made that seem unlikely.

Instead of chains and a dungeon cell, he had been given palatial quarters high in this great building. A physician had poulticed his injuries. A barber came in daily, well guarded, to shave him. The trays that passed through a small hinged panel in the door carried delicious food and drink, in abundance. A closet held a variety of fine garments in his size. There was a pool in which he could swim as well as bathe, with fresh water pumped in from outside each time he had drained it. After three days of such conditions he suffered from no more than rage at being confined, longing for Bêlit, and puzzlement tinged with fear of what this might portend.

'Rejoice,' said the chief of the squad in accented Shemitish. 'In his kindness, lord Tothapis has decided you should not languish alone, but may have company during certain hours. Come with us.'

Bewildered, heart thumping beneath his tunic, Conan obeyed. The men conducted him down a corridor whose doors resembled those of his place and doubtless concealed similar appointments. At the end, it gave on a large chamber, richly carpeted, well furnished, full of light and soft air from open windows. Whitewashed walls bore murals of flowers and wildfowl. A large carafe of wine and four crystal goblets stood on a table. Three people, already present, stared as Conan entered.

'We will bring you back at dinnertime,' the Stygian officer said. He and his men withdrew. Conan heard a heavy bolt slam down. The chamber had but one single exit. Driven by his wish to be free, he went to the nearest window and glanced out. As he had expected, it offered no egress, just a sheer wall going down to the same paved courtyard that his balcony overhung, impossible to climb or jump without smashing himself.

He turned to confront the others. 'My name is Conan, and I hail from the far northern country of the Cimmerians,' he declared in Shemitish. 'Are you captives here, too?'

'I – I believe so,' replied the youth. 'I certainly am. We have none of us met before. I am Falco, a son of the Baron of Kirjahan in Ophir.'

Conan nodded. The fellow's nationality was plain to see, despite Stygian garb. Perhaps eighteen years old, he stood slim, a trifle on the short side, but lithely muscled. Fair-skinned, hazel-eyed, hair ruddy brown, his regular features showed him to be of the westerm Ophirites, civilized, courtly-mannered, often commercial-minded, rather than of the hard-riding plainsmen in the east of that kingdom; but he would surely have been taught to keep a saddle, shoot a bow, and wield a blade as well as to read, write, and make music for ladies. Conan recalled maps he had seen. Ophir lay north of Shem, and Kirjahan was not far from the Aquilonian border.

Falco bowed to the woman in the group. 'And may we ask your name, my lady?' he said.

Conan regarded her with pleasure. She was very tall for her sex, slender but well proportioned and firm-fleshed in a gauzy gown, her hair and eyes dark but her complexion more nearly golden, her countenance molded out of those of several races but finely formed. The look she gave him was bold, in no way coquettish. She started to address them in a language he did not recognize, except that it seemed to belong to the Hyborian family. Seeing that nobody understood, she changed over to Stygian.

'She is Daris of Taia,' Falco interpreted. 'Her father Ausar has taken the lead in the revolt of that province against King Mentuphera.' He hesitated, concern upon his boyish visage. 'If her father yet lives.'

Conan frowned. After his experience he could not help feeling wary of anyone called Taian. 'How came she here?' he asked.

Falco inquired, got a reply, and explained briefly what had happened. Conan's suspicions fell from him. 'Why, good for you, girl!' he said. 'Your heart is sister to Bêlit's.'

The fourth person present uttered a broken cry. The attention of the rest swung to him. A big, sturdily built Shemite, he had stood apart, silent, shoulders stooped, grief etched in every line of his cruelly maltreated face. 'Who are you?' Conan inquired.

'I am no one, nothing,' was the mumbled response. Abruptly the downcast eyes lifted to meet the Cimmerian's. 'But did I hear you speak a name?'

'Yes. Bêlit's, the corsair queen of the Black Coast –'

Conan got no chance to finish. The stranger stumbled forward and seized his arms in a grip that even he found painful. He heard a hoarse scream: 'Lives she, then? How fares she?'

'As well as may be,' Conan said. 'She has a galley and a crew of Suba pirates to harry ships and shores in vengeance –' A terrible thought struck home. 'Who *are* you?'

The Shemite let him go. 'I was Jehanan, her brother.' He slumped onto a chair, his body driven by sobs that came from the depths of his breast.

'Jehanan!' Conan squatted down beside the weeping man, embraced him, and said quickly, 'Hearken. I am Bêlit's lover now, and we were utterly happy together until I was lured ashore by a false promise that I could liberate you, Jehanan, and bring you back to her. By the lance of Crom, I will do that yet!'

'No. No. She would not want to see what I have become.'

'What do some scars matter?'

'In these of mine –' Jehanan touched face, left shoulder, ribs – 'dwells pain unending. I can move about despite it, work, fight, aye. But it unmans me, and sleep comes only with exhaustion.'

Conan gasped. He released the other and rose, to stand white-cheeked, nostrils wide, muscles aquiver and iron-hard throughout his mighty frame. Falco drew Daris clear of him. After a moment, Conan roared. The lion sound echoed and reechoed in the room. He seized a heavy table and battered it to kindling against the floor.

Then he could speak. 'They will pay, they will pay, they will pay such a weregild as the world never knew erenow.' He began to prowl, back and forth. His tone became swordblade-flat. 'Jehanan, do not despair. If nothing else, there is revenge to be had. And later, well, cool sea air and wide sea horizons bring much peace to the soul. What we must do is plan our escape. To that end, first we must all of us exchange all the information we have.'

He bent his glare on Falco. 'We start with you, young sir,' he said. 'How do you come to be here, and what do you know about the place?'

The Ophirite flushed. He was not used to being ordered around like a commoner. But having considered more closely the giant who paced before him, he said respectfully, 'If you wish it – of course. May I suggest we sit down over some wine?'

Conan shook his head. 'Do as you please, but talk,' he grated. His wrath was his own intoxication; it was as if he could hear edged metal whistling and clattering in his skull, and a bitter taste was on his tongue.

Falco filled three glasses. The first he offered to Daris, who took it and perched alertly on a settee. The next was for Jehanan, who snatched and gulped while tears still cataracted from his eyes. The third he brought over to the Taian maiden, joined her, sipped, murmured, 'Excellent,' and leaned back to converse.

'I sorrow at the tragedy I have learned of,' he said, 'but frankly, sir, I cannot believe escape is possible, and I actually wonder if it would be quite desirable. Perhaps I should begin at the beginning.

'I am a younger son of the Baron of Kirjahan, and thus my hope of advancement has lain away from home, in the direct service of my king. A year or more ago, his intelligence officers had assembled facts that, taken together, appeared ominous – things that travelers abroad had seen and heard, reports of troop recruitment here, invoices of exports to Stygia, and the like. Its King Mentuphera is known to be a man vauntingly ambitious for power and glory. Could he be preparing a venture that would threaten Ophir?

'Finally, Lord Zarus of Vendishan was dispatched to Luxur, the Stygian royal seat. Ostensibly he was – is – a special ambassador, sent to discuss such matters as the improvement of trade relations between our countries and cooperation in the suppression of piracy. In fact, he is to gather what intelligence he can. I was in his entourage as an amanuensis.

'Forbidden to go more than a few miles from the city, discouraged from meeting people, incessantly spied upon, our mission nevertheless collected enough clues in the course of several months that Zarus did come to fear something dangerous was in train. Finally, I offered to burgle the Stygian foreign office, where more evidence should be. I had memorized much about the building plan and the routine of workers and guards. Lord Zarus warned me that if I was caught, he would have to disown me and my fate would likely be grim. I went ahead regardless.'

Contemplating the Ophirite, Conan thought, with a hint of wryness in the middle of his fury, that no boy of spirit ever really believes he can die. Still, it was a spirit the Cimmerian admired.

'I wormed my way in one night,' Falco continued. 'By a dark lantern I found and read a file of correspondence meant for very few eyes. Yes, it showed that King Mentuphera has made secret allies of

70

several city-states in Shem, as well as those tributary to him. They plan a joint invasion and conquest of Ophir. If that succeeds, they will be at the frontier of Aquilonia. Weakly and foolishly ruled, racked by civil strife, it will soon fall to them, isolating Argos for later attention. Vast will be the domains of Mentuphera and the cold glee of Set.'

He winced, then shrugged in an effort to appear a self-possessed man of the world. 'Unfortunately, I was caught. Perhaps somebody noticed my lantern beam by sheer ill fortune, or perhaps a magician's familiar scuttled off to bear tidings – I know not. I drew my rapier, killed one guard –' surely his first kill, Conan thought – 'and wounded more, but their numbers overcame me.'

He stared out a window. His voice dropped. 'What followed was eldritch. I was not tortured or beheaded or anything like that. Instead, they soon took me by hidden ways to a dock where a priest-manned boat waited, a boat driven not by oars or sail but by demonic fires, spreading wings to skim the water so fast that we reached Khemi in two nights and a day. I heard it is the sole vessel of its kind, built in ancient Acheron by magical arts since lost. The chief priest aboard spoke little to me but did admit that seldom have prisoners been thus conveyed. He also told me that his government would make no complaint about my action, would not mention me at all, and leave Lord Zarus to wonder what had happened.

'At journey's end I was brought here and put in soft confinement. Here I have been since, a matter of weeks.'

'Have you any idea why you are so carefully handled?' Conan asked.

Falco nodded. A blush reddened his face. 'Yes, sir, I do, and that is the reason I wonder if our escape would necessarily be a good thing. Instead, perhaps we should hope for eventual release.'

Conan halted, folded his great arms, and scowled. 'Say on.'

Falco drank deep and avoided the Cimmerian's whetted gaze. 'Well, I have been having a frequent visitor. The most wondrous lady –'

Jehanan brought his head sharply up. He tensed.

Falco sighed. 'Yes, the lady Senufer is a dream of beauty and, well, love. I have, uh, some knowledge of women, but never had I

71

imagined there could be one like her. She is living proof that not all Stygians are bad and, and, in fact, peace is not a lost cause.'

'Never mind her body,' Conan said with a sardonic grin. 'Tell me about her business.'

'Well,' Falco responded, 'she has explained to me that a strong party in favor of peace does exist among the nobility. They see no gain worth making in foreign adventures. Rather, many of them would like the country opened up, letting new ideas come in from abroad. They are striving to change the king's mind, and they do have considerable influence. One of them learned about my capture immediately afterward and thought I should be preserved as a – oh – a potential liaison. His associates could not get me freed, but they could arrange for my detention here. Senufer is ... remarkable in every way. At first she simply came wanting to make my acquaintance, that she might report on me to her kinsmen, but soon –' Fiery red, he tossed off his wine.

Jehanan could endure no more. He sprang to his feet and croaked, 'Believe her not. She is another fiend, like her who sought me out. You will learn that to your sorrow, boy.'

'What do you mean?' Conan rapped.

Slowly, the shame of it often locking his tongue, Jehanan forced himself to relate his woes, and how a gorgeous wanton who called herself Heterka had restored his joy in life, only to dash it from him again for her sport.

Conan's expression grew stark. He did accomplish going over to Belit's brother, wringing the hand that trembled before him, and murmuring a few words of consolation. Thereafter he cast his glance at Daris. 'Best we hear her entire story,' he said. 'I think we are all in the same spiderweb.'

Falco translating her Stygian, the woman described her own experiences. At mention of the wingboat, the Ophirite was surprised, and surprised her in turn by relating his tale. Conan merely nodded. Jehanan had sunk back into misery.

'Well,' the barbarian said, 'time that I spun you my yarn. I am, you remember, an adventurer from the far North, who has knocked about the world for a number of years. I suppose the part of my life that matters to us here began when I met Belit.'

Jehanan seemed rather heartened by the account of his sister. 'She got herself a fine man, it seems,' he even said. Conan continued. The effort of putting words together, telling the basic story without giving away information that might be useful to possible eavesdroppers, took his mind away from overt anger. Down below, it seethed onward, white-hot. He poured himself a glass of wine to cool it a little.

At the end, the three who were seated looked up his height into his glacier-blue eyes and heard him say:

'Clear is to see, we are in a weird affair. I gather this Tothapis I heard mention of is a leading priest-magician, right?' Falco nodded confirmation. 'Now why should he go to such trouble to snare me, a plain buccaneer? That is the job of the royal navy. Why are the rest of you also so important to somebody – a spy, a slave, and a prisoner of war, albeit she is a princess of sorts? Why are we suddenly brought together and left alone like this? Who has profited from any of it?'

'Senufer's people must have been working on our behalf,' Falco suggested. 'Probably she can tell me more when next we meet.'

'Trust not a Stygian witch!' Jehanan rasped.

Falco bridled. 'You were unlucky,' he said, 'but of Senufer I will hear no evil spoken.'

Though Daris could not follow their Shemitish, she sensed the tension and spoke in Stygian. Falco relaxed and told Conan: 'The lady proposes that if we have no further questions, we spend the rest of the afternoon getting to know each other, swapping memories and tales and songs, over this wine.'

'You have the right idea there, lass,' Conan said – in Cimmerian, which he might as well. He smiled at her, and she smiled back.

When the prisoners had been returned to their separate quarters, Tothapis obliterated the image. He sat pondering while Nehekba rose and stretched her supple form.

'Well, my lord?' she challenged. 'Do you agree this was worthwhile?'

'Perhaps,' he replied. 'We did get a heap of personal information about them. It remains to be seen how much can be used in the necromancy that traces out and cuts the skein of their fate.'

73

'Why, I think already I have learned what may suffice,' she said.

He peered at her through the gloom. 'Eh?'

She laughed, a clear and malicious sound. 'Conan may love his little Belit, but he has been parted from her for days, and he is plainly bull-virile. Did you not see how he ogled Daris? It may take a while, but I judge he is corruptible through this, if by no different means. And once he is corrupted, in the priggish eyes of Mitra ... s-s-s-s ... once he is enslaved to me, ah, *then* we have him, whether he recognizes it or not. His destiny will be lost, his soul rudderless – and yet, while he lives, none else can have the honor of being the god's warrior. For is it not written that "The pledges of Mitra ... s-s-s-s ... are for eternity"? You can keep him alive a very long while, Tothapis.' Sharp fingernails combed flowing tresses. 'And I – I expect to enjoy myself unusually much.'

IX

A WARRIOR'S WELCOME

That evening a full moon rose out of the Styx. It would not be visible from Conan's balcony for some while, but he saw how the sky lightened to a deep purple over the battlemented walls across the courtyard. Stars were coming forth. The weather had turned milder, the night was balmy.

He picked out the North Star, by which he could steer home to his own people if he were free. Not that he would leave Bêlit, but she had said that someday she would like to visit the land that had bred him. He looked upward and found Jupiter, a silvery-golden brilliance. The same planet shone down on her where she waited at sea. Did she watch it at this moment, held wakeful by her yearning and fears for him?

Pain stabbed afresh. He drew a quick breath. It turned into an oath. He spun on his heel and stalked back inside. Hours of vigorous exercise every day had kept him fit, while somewhat assuaging his boredom. Well, he would do an extra round now, in hopes that that would enable him to sleep.

Candles glowed throughout the main room. He ignored its richness, peeled off his tunic, dropped the garment on the floor and, attired in nothing save a loincloth, started a set of deep knee bends.

A click and rattle sounded through the stillness. Conan crouched in immediate readiness for action. His heart galloped. That had been a key in the lock securing the outer door.

Its iron-bound massiveness swung wide. An armored soldier stepped warily back, cocked crossbow aimed at the barbarian. Listening through a slightly opened trap, Conan had already ascertained that the night watch on this floor consisted of a single such turnkey. For an instant, hope flared in him. If he moved fast enough and had rare good luck, he might elude the shaft and get his hands on the Stygian!

Even then he knew how desperate any such attempt would be against a fully alert bowman. He checked the impulse entirely when a second figure came in sight and passed through the entrance – a woman.

She addressed the guard, who genuflected without shifting his aim, then quickly shut, bolted, and relocked the door behind her. Conan stood motionless, though the blood coursed hot in his veins and every sense was heightened. He heard cat-soft footfalls as she crossed the carpet, he caught a musky breath of perfume, his gaze ranged up and down and around her. Never had he seen a woman more beautiful, and few to match this one. Well-nigh transparent, her gown floated and sheened above a form whose slenderness somehow made it all the more voluptuous. Her face was a perfection of the Stygian racial type. Amber skin and ebon hair were lustrous in the candlelight.

She flowed to a halt six or seven feet from him, gave him a slow smile full of promise, and raised her left palm as if to warn him against violence. He no longer kept any such intention. Besides an ingrained reluctance to harm a female, he had a realization that, as things were, it would be worse than useless – whereas if he bided his time, he might get answers to the riddles that encompassed him.

He wet his lips. 'Do – do you speak Shemitish?' he asked, feeling how inane that must sound.

She brought her right hand to a tiny mirror suspended beneath her throat. Conan tautened, suddenly uneasy. Her musical voice spoke, her left fingers gestured.

A beam of light sprang from the mirror to strike him in the eyes. It seemed to burn on into his brain. The whiteness filled him. It chanted in words unknown. His mind went under in a vortex of luminance and sound. Barely did he know that he stood paralyzed, yet did not fall.

After a time that was not truly time, the light blinked out, the singing ended, and he heard, 'Conan, arouse!' Awareness returned in a rush. He stumbled backward from the stranger. 'What witchcraft have you wrought on me?' he groaned.

She smiled again, held her arms wide in a gesture of benediction, and said gently, 'None to harm you, Conan. Only to help. I am your friend.'

He summoned the courage to stand fast. 'Then why did you do that thing?'

She trilled laughter. 'What language are we speaking?'

'Why – it's – ' Thunderstruck, Conan realized. 'Stygian!'

She nodded. 'Yes. I know Shemitish, and many tongues more, but I felt you would find it helpful if you could make yourself understood in that of the people around you. My spell did nothing but teach it to you in a matter of minutes.'

He shook his head, trying to clear out stupefaction. 'Really?' he mumbled, and ran through a number of words for a test. 'Man, woman, sword, ship, horse, battle –'

She sighed. 'Ah, I failed to rid you of a Cimmerian accent. Well, no matter. That burr sounds manly, exciting.' She moved toward him. 'Shall we pour wine, sit down, and talk?'

He mastered astonishment and quelled his dread of things uncanny. He actually felt enjoyment of her presence. Bêlit and, yes, Daris had a more wholesome kind of comeliness, but this exotic creature lured forth dreams he might be wise to dismiss – if he could. 'Who are you?' he demanded.

'Nehekba, high priestess of Derketa here in Khemi,' she answered, 'and, as I said before, your friend.'

If that was true, she would be a powerful ally. He was no worshipper of her deity, but was not repelled either, as he was by Set. The goddess of love and death had devotees throughout these parts, well beyond the borders of Stygia. Bêlit sometimes invoked her.

Nehekba reached him and offered her hand. He took it in his great paw, then, awkwardly, bent to kiss its delicacy. Her skin was like silk. When he straightened, she gave him a smile that was at once languorous and radiant. 'I will fetch the wine,' he said thickly, and sought the carafe set on a table for his use. Several goblets stood by, since he was also offered water, beer, and milk each day. He filled two and brought them to Nehekba, who had taken a seat

77

on his couch and leaned back against a cushion, legs curled trim beneath her. She took a glass and beckoned him to the same resting place. When he had joined her there, she raised the vessel and said – almost sang, 'To your happiness, Conan. May I aid you in regaining it.'

'Thank you,' he said lamely.

'Will you drink to me in turn – no, to us?'

He sipped without uttering any toast and plunged ahead: 'You must know I am completely in the dark about everything. Why am I here? Why are you? What is going on?'

'You must have learned a little from your fellow captives today,' she said. 'It was I who prevailed on Tothapis to give you those hours.'

Indeed he had made certain discoveries, the Cimmerian thought, and was now making more. 'We talked, yes,' he said, choosing each word. 'One among us believes he knows the reason he is confined on this floor, rather than a dungeon or grave. That is young Falco, who has also received a lady visitor.'

Nehekba nodded. Light rippled along her hair. 'Ah, yes, Senufer. She is a noblewoman serving the same cause I do, the cause of peace.'

'And pleasure, I hear,' Conan said bluntly.

Full lips curved again upward. 'Why not? What harm? She is a wealthy widow, thus free to indulge herself if she stays reasonably discreet. Besides, we do wish to maintain contact with Falco. The time may come when his connections in Ophir prove invaluable to us. A man who visited him regularly might fall under suspicion of conspiracy, but a woman obviously having an affair need fear nothing except that a new guardsman may require a fresh bribe.'

'What about Heterka?' Conan snapped.

Nehekba raised her brows. 'Who?'

The wine glass shook a little in Conan's fingers. 'It is a horrible story.'

'I know nothing of it – well, I do know another noblewoman of that name, who dabbles in leechcraft but is said to have certain nasty inclinations. We Stygians are human, dear. Therefore we number among us the good, the bad, and the indifferent, and our affairs are as tangled as any elsewhere in the world.'

Conan decided not to pursue the matter. Instead, he cried low, 'Enough! I pray you, tell me how I come to be here, and what you mean to do.'

'You must understand, I am no confidante of Tothapis,' she said in a tone of sympathy. 'He is a mighty wizard as well as a priest, the present head of that society of sorcerers called the Black Ring. Hence I likewise remain in the dark about much of what happened, though I cherish hopes of finding it out. Meanwhile, let me tell you what I can.

'Tales have been reaching Stygia of a rover from the far North, a peerless warrior, at large in these southlands. Turned pirate, you could become a significant danger to us in a wartime that seems all too likely. Tothapis may well have used his arts to trap you for no other reason than that, though perhaps his plans go deeper. I must agree it would be wrong to let you harry my people. I am not angry at you; piracy is reckoned an honorable trade among you barbarians, no? But I do aim to teach you better, and bring forth a chivalry I am certain is innate in you.

'The factions favoring peace and war are not at sword's point. It is a matter of disputation and politicking, which does not prevent persons of opposed views on that issue from cooperating otherwise. As a member of the hierarchy, I heard about you, and persuaded Tothapis to order you detained here. He himself supports the expansion of Imperial Stygia, but he is not bloodthirsty and it suffices him to have rendered you harmless. In due course, after getting to know you well, Conan, I believe I can convince him that you will honor a parole to wreak no further harm on Stygians. Then he can let you go free.'

'How long might this take?' the Cimmerian asked.

'A year or two, perhaps.' Nehekba gave him a lingering look. 'It depends on how quickly and closely acquainted we become, you and I,' she purred.

He clenched a fist. 'What do *you* want of me?'

'It may be that you can vitally serve the cause of peace,' she said. 'Quite possibly a magical intimation of this was what made Tothapis alarmed enough to act against you. If that is so, then I think I can gradually lull his fears. Not that I would ever employ you or anyone in treason. It is only that I sincerely believe the good of Stygia, too, lies in peace. What might you be willing to do in aid – for generous pay, of course? Well, that remains to be seen; but I can imagine you, for instance, as a swift courier whom no bandit or secret agent can stop. Messages to the governments of such countries as Ophir, Argos, Nemedia, Koth, Corinthia, even bedeviled Aquilonia, may encourage them to unite in exerting diplomatic and trade pressure on King Mentuphera to alter his plans. It helps that his heir, Crown Prince Ctesphon, does not share his ambitions.'

Conan stroked his chin. 'Hm-m, these matters get too entwined for my stiff brain to follow,' he said. 'Nevertheless – Wait. To judge from what Falco told me, war against Ophir will begin soon, well before you could talk me out of my cage.'

Nehekba shook her diademed head. 'No, nothing can be done while Taia is in rebellion,' she reminded him. 'I was instrumental in having the chief's daughter brought here. Perhaps, after she and I have talked, she will agree to serve as a go-between, negotiating an end to both revolt and injustice. An accomplishment like that would vastly strengthen the hand of the peace party.'

'You leave Jehanan's presence unexplained,' he snapped.

'Jehanan?' she responded innocently. 'Who is that?'

Before he could speak, she set down her goblet and leaned close to him. 'We will get chances aplenty to discuss politics,' she breathed. 'Need we carry it on this evening?'

'What do you mean?' he asked hoarsely.

Her lashes fluttered. 'Best I use the same excuse as Senufer to keep seeing you. It will be no play-acting, either. By the gods, Conan, but you are a *man*!'

Desire blazed high in him, unmistakable to her knowing eyes. She half-closed them, half-parted her lips and swayed toward his opened arms. Their mouths came together. Bêlit herself had never given him a more passionate kiss.

Their hands roved.

Conan's reached her neck. Muscles surged as he took hold of the chain that held the mirror and snapped its silver links. He threw the amulet to the far end of the room.

Nehekba screamed. He clapped a palm over her face. She raked nails along his cheek. His left hand caught that wrist. Holding fast, he moved to grab the other arm as well. A shin of his, laid across her thighs, pinned her to the couch. Though she writhed and panted, she was helpless against his bearlike strength.

'Slack off,' he told her. 'Else I'll choke you unconscious. I can do that without any real damage, but would rather not.'

The glorious eyes scorched hatred at him. Perforce, she obeyed. Conan nodded grimly. With the trap in the door closed, her yell had not been heard by the guard. The risk he had taken was that some kind of watch was being kept on him, as he suspected had been the case earlier this day. But he had guessed that she would not want her amours observed, and would have supposed her talisman was ample protection if her wiles failed.

Besides, she would scarcely have expected any such ignominy.

Conan maintained a grip on her wrists while, with his free hand, he ripped the gown from her. 'Have no fears,' he said. 'I have never taken a woman against her will. Anyway, that would hardly have been needful, would it? I just mean to secure you.'

'Are you mad?' she moaned.

He shook his black-mane head. 'No, nor as stupid as you took for given. You civilized people think that because we barbarians have no cities or books we must be a lot of dumb animals. Hell, we need our wits more than you do!'

'But – but I am your friend, Conan,' she pleaded, 'I would be your lover if you let me, yes, even now.'

He stood, made her rise, and forced her to face away from him. Using the torn silks, he tied her arms behind her. 'No, my guess is that you are friend to that Tothapis fellow,' he said. 'I also believe you are sweet Senufer and vile Heterka. It doesn't make sense that this gaol should simply happen to be crawling with lust-crazed brunettes, or that the lord of the Black Ring would not know you were plotting against him and take measures. In any case, I trust no witch.'

'You are wrong – you are wrong.' She wept.

'Crocodile tears, are they called?' he retorted, unmoved. 'Well, supposing you are innocent, which I cannot do for half a heartbeat, you did admit I would be here for a matter of years before I might maybe go free. Never! I am bound back to my own woman, tonight, or else I shall die along the way.' He laid her down on the floor and kept a knee on her thighs, while he fastened her ankles. 'Furthermore,' he added, 'you slipped me fine words about peace, but Bêlit and her brother still have revenge to take on Stygia. Therefore I do myself.'

Having rendered her immobile, he rose, and for a moment regarded her nearly nude body. A sigh gusted from him. 'What a waste,' he said. 'How tempted I was to have my sport with you first. But you are a witch. I dared not risk you somehow binding my spirit here, away from Bêlit.'

He stooped and effortlessly picked her up. 'Call the watchman to let you out,' he instructed. 'After I am done with him, I will leave you here. The change of guard will find you in the morning.'

'No, you blind beast!' she flared.

Conan gave her a terrible stare. 'If you do not obey,' he said, 'I will break you in twain, for what you did to Jehanan.'

She cowered in his arms. 'I will – I will.'

He nodded and stalked to the door. Actually, he had lied, or so he thought. He doubted he could bring himself to such a deed against a woman, no matter how evil she might be; and he lacked absolute proof of Nehekba's iniquity. However, the rage that had not left him gave the threat convincing force.

At the door, he elbowed the panel open and brought Nehekba's head close to it. 'Sound calm,' he whispered in her ear.

She gave a convulsive nod, and cried with a coolness which bespoke her powers of deceit: 'O soldier my business is done. Come unlock, that I may go home.'

Immediately Conan laid her down and used two remaining scraps of cloth to gag her. She found time to hiss vindictively, 'You have made your death certain, barbarian. If you are lucky, it will be swift. If I am lucky, it will take many days.'

He disregarded her, except for the reflection that in her fury she had revealed her true colors. Rising, he snatched from a shelf a brass candlestick in the form of three serpents. Bolt slid, wards clicked, the door swung wide, the turnkey stepped back, bringing crossbow to shoulder.

He was, though, less wary than erstwhile, thanks to Nehekba's tone. Conan sprang from behind the jamb and hurled his metal. It smote before the bow could twang. The shaft skittered harmlessly down the hall. Conan was already upon the Stygian. His hands flew to the man's throat, took hold, contracted. He felt the larynx snap between his fingers. Blood gushed from the soldier's mouth. He fell and flopped. Conan drew his sword and ended his pain.

Ferally quick, the Cimmerian returned to his chambers. A tunic would be less conspicuous than a loincloth if he got as far as the street. He donned the one he had dropped and added a cowled mantle. Having strapped on sandals as well, he went back out. Nehekba gave him so poisonous a glare that he wondered if he should kill her. But no, he could not bring himself to that, nor did he want any part of the talisman he had torn from her. Best would be if he could get rid of the thing, but he was unsure how and dared not experiment.

He took the Stygian's sword belt and put it on. A key was still in the door, attached to a ring from which several more hung. Conan plucked them free and started down the corridor. He would not leave behind him the friends he had made this day.

X

A NIGHT IN KHEMI

Falco sat up in bed with a start. The big man who had shaken his shoulder let go and loomed over him. Light from candles sconced in the hall came dimly through open doors; Conan's eyes, catching it, burned like blue torches. 'On your feet, lad,' the Cimmerian said. 'We're bound out of here.'

'But – but – what –' Falco stuttered.

'I'll tell you later, if we outlive the next few hours. We've got a dead guard on this floor, but we'll need to make more as we go along.'

Falco hunched away. 'No,' he protested. 'This is lunacy. Have you forgotten what the lady Senufer promised?'

Conan spat. 'I will explain what her promises are worth, when I get the chance. Now come, for Crom's uncaring sake! We don't have time to jabber.'

Resolution congealed in the Ophirite. He sat straight amidst the sheets and said, 'No. Do what you like, and I will wish you well though I doubt if anything can save you. But I am not leaving Senufer whom I love and trust.'

Conan glowered. 'Why, you white-livered pup! What is *your* oath worth, that you gave to your king? You are the one who can bring him warning of what Mentuphera plots against him. The rest of us would scarcely be let into his court, let alone believed. Stay, then, and be a lapdog.'

Falco doubled his fists and bit his lip till blood ran. In a convulsive motion, he swung feet to floor and rose. 'I am sorry,' he said in a voice that wavered. 'You are right about my duty to – to try.'

'Much better. Get dressed. Quickly!'

Falco drew on tunic and footgear. 'Do you actually imagine we can break free? How in the world?'

'By what I have used thus far, surprise and speed. I paid attention while they brought me here. Did you not?'

Falco made no answer. Staring beyond his companion, he whispered, 'I will return to you, Senufer, if I live – return to you bringing peace between our nations, O my darling.'

Conan snorted and led the way forth, to unlock Jehanan's door. The Shemite slept restlessly, tossing and muttering in nightmare. When Conan shook him awake, he gasped and flailed about.

'Easy, fellow,' the Cimmerian said. 'Save that for the Stygians.'

Jehanan sat up. 'You are loose, you two?' he marveled without gladness. 'What will you do?'

'Get you and me back to Bêlit, for a start. I told you earlier I have a boat tucked away, and the traitor who knew where she lies is dog meat. We shall have to fight clear of this kennel first, but –'

Jehanan slumped. He shook his head. 'What is the use?' he mumbled.

'Name of Ymir!' Conan exploded. 'What gutless wonders I am among, that I must talk them into seizing their freedom? If nothing else, man, don't you want to kill Stygians?'

Jehanan's back stiffened. 'There is that left in life,' he said slowly. 'Very well.'

'Dress, then.' It wrung Conan's heart to see how the other must fight agony with every movement as he got out of bed. 'Come over here, Falco,' the barbarian directed, turning his back and taking the youth's elbow. 'We should decide what equipment we can improvise.'

Remembering Bêlit, he took a glass decanter, smashed the bottom against a table, and gave the Ophirite the jagged remnant to hold by the neck. Muscles stood forth in his limbs, cable-thick, when he wrenched a leg from the same heavy piece of furniture. He tucked that club under an arm, loosened his sword belt, and handed the metal weapon to a now-clad Jehanan. 'You Shemites favor sword blades,' he remarked. 'You ought to do right well.'

Somber anticipation touched the ruined countenance, and the scarred frame moved more smoothly after having been used a little. 'Let us be off,' said Bêlit's brother.

'We have the girl left,' Conan reminded. 'If nothing else, she deserves a chance to dare this, too.'

Daris of Taia must have roused when the key turned in the lock on her door. As the Cimmerian entered, she came bounding into the main room from her bedchamber. Her naked form was leopard-lithe; the dark hair rippled behind at her speed. She saw him, stopped in midcareer, and reached out. Eyes blazed, teeth flashed. 'Have you broken loose?' she cried. 'O Mitra, oh, wonder!'

'We are on our way.' Even now, Conan found himself admiring the sight before him. She seemed quite unaware of her nudity. 'If you wish to come along, get dressed fast.'

'Not in a gown meant for a rich man's plaything,' she scoffed. 'Let me go to – yes, to your place, Falco, and find a proper tunic. I won't be a minute.'

She was as good as her word. Returning, she still revealed shapeliness of leg, for the garment was a trifle short on her, and the hard-soled feet were still bare. She had also found a leather belt with a heavy bronze buckle. 'I shall have a use for this,' she said almost merrily.

Conan grinned back at her. 'A soldier and three tavern brawlers, eh? I thought you might use yonder crossbow, though.' They had emerged in the hall, and he pointed toward the corpse.

'For a single shot, if you like. But thereafter we shall be in a melee, true?' Daris did pause to retrieve and make ready the bow, while she observed: 'Suddenly you speak Stygian. Much that is strange has happened this night, and I think much more will yet.'

'Silence,' Conan warned, and led the way to a stairwell.

Progress down the murky stone flights was slow, for caution. At each landing the barbarian stopped, listened, finally peered down, before he waved his followers on. The first two floors below appeared empty, perhaps because nobody else was currently detained under the conditions granted him. Farther down, however, was considerable activity, both penitential and military. Night watches would not consist of a single man. Twice Conan gestured his party to a halt and let feet go by. Given such care, the escapers at last reached ground level undetected.

The stairway debouched on a hall. No person was in sight, but a few sounds drifted through its hollowness. On the right, Conan remembered, it led to a large anteroom where guards stood at the main door. He could not be sure how many they numbered at this hour, but he had counted ten when he came by earlier, and doubtless plenty more were in earshot. What was to his left, he had no idea. He might find a safer exit, or he might get lost in a labyrinth or otherwise come to grief.

He needed but a second to abide by the provisional decision he had already made. Crom favored, if he did not actually help, the bold. Conan turned right. He broke into a noiseless run.

At the ends of the passage, he did not pause to look everywhere around, nor did he waste breath in a shout. He continued his charge, on across bare stones to the squad, whose helmets, cuirasses, and pike heads glimmered. The vaulted ceiling outranged the light of scattered lamps, but bats darted in and out of the shadows up there. From the muraled walls, beast-headed gods and the Great Serpent himself cast menacing looks. Acrid incense burned below them.

The sentries were indeed ten, Conan saw, At glimpse of him, they called out and moved into tight formation, swords and shields in front of pikemen. From behind Conan, the crossbow went *snap*. Daris's aim was true; a Stygian clanged to the pavement, the bolt standing deep in his face. Daris whooped.

Conan reached the nine foemen who were left. Pikes thrust at him. He swung his club through a whirring arc that battered one aside, knocked the point of the other down against the floor and splintered its shaft. Then he was too close to be speared, hard against the shortsword wielders. A man stabbed from around a shield – and screamed as the club broke his arm. Conan struck the helmet beside it so that metal rang. The user staggered back. That exposed a leg for Conan to break.

The formation dissolved in chaos. Jehanan's blade rattled on another. Armored, the Stygian forced the Shemite to give ground. Daris' belt flew, the buckle took the soldier across the eyes, he let his defense slip aside and Jehanan pierced his throat. Falco bounded about, too swift to hit, darted in whenever he saw a chance, and used his glass to frightful effect. Conan raged everywhere, cracked the neck of the pikeman, snatched the weapon

87

for himself, employed butt and point alike. Blood made slippery the floor.

More guards came into view from the archways at either end of the anteroom. Conan had hoped they would not arrive so soon, in such numbers. 'Get that door open, you!' he roared.

Side by side, he and Jehanan held off the survivors of the squad while Falco, his glass now shattered, and Daris struggled with a ponderous, chain-secured latch. The newly arrived Stygians milled about in the background. Most were unarmored and all were astounded. Their confusion would not endure past a minute or two. Conan smote, Bêlit's brother thrust, forgetful of pain in his battle ardor.

The portal creaked. A breath of night screamed through to the fetor inside. 'Out!' Conan bawled. He stood fast while his comrades left. An officer cried, 'Kill him!' and led a band in attack. The Cimmerian hurled his pike and skewered the man. A lamp flickered on a stand nearby. The barbarian flung that and its burning oil on the next Stygian who headed a party. Both charges faltered. Conan slipped through the door and caught up to his own folk.

The moon had risen high enough to drench the street in cold brilliance. Conan thought that nonetheless he could outrun pursuit until he was lost to sight. He might have done that, and Daris beside him, but they soon realized that Falco and Jehanan could not match them. By unspoken agreement, they slowed. A glance rearward showed a swarm of guardsmen following.

Conan thought of ducking into some black, tortuous lane such as met the avenue here and there, and shaking off the enemy in the warren beyond. But no. Neither he nor any of his band knew this accursed town to speak of. They would blunder about lost while the Stygians spread out a human net that must inevitably close on them.

The waterfront offered a slight chance, maybe. He had seen a little of it when he entered. 'This way,' he rasped.

Stone sphinxes and inscribed stelae glimmered on either hand, unreal in the moonlight. A few times a belated passerby saw the chase and fled.

Stateliness yielded to bulky warehouses, deserted at sundown, between which rats scuttered. Ahead, Conan glimpsed masts raking aloft from wharfs and moonglimmers deceptively lovely on the stream. Lanterns bobbed, carried by a squad of harbor police. Conan eased his pace. Now it might be possible to elude the enemy by darkened ways.

Behind him, a trumpet clamored. The notes were not music, they were long and short blasts of varied pitch. 'Stygian army code,' Daris panted. 'Surely they warn all warders hereabouts against us.'

'We shall be surrounded,' Falco groaned.

'At least we can find a spot to make a stand that will cost them,' Conan said.

'No,' Jehanan replied, through his heavy breath and the thud of his trotting feet. 'If we can get by them at this end before they cordon us off, I know where we can shake them.'

'Huh?' Conan grunted. Hope crackled anew in his breast.

'The old tombs and quarries below the Grand Pyramid,' Jehanan said. 'They are a jumble, and feared. None go there save slaves like me, by day, who dig what limestone is left to take. I have come to know them a bit, trudging across them to my toil.'

The hope froze in Conan. A prickling went along his spine, and the sweat of his efforts felt suddenly chill. 'Are they not haunted, those?' he muttered.

Falco showed cheer. 'Better the risk of a ghoul than the certainty of being caught,' he said. Action had roused his natural boyish exuberance, and for the time being set aside obsession with his love. She was doubtless denied to him anyway, after what had happened, unless and until he returned in some official capacity. Moreover, as a literate aristocrat of a civilized, practical-minded region, he bore scant awe of the supernatural.

Daris, half-barbarian, had herself been taken aback. She rallied and said dauntlessly, 'If that is the road home, so be it.'

Yes, Conan thought, if he must fight through graveyard horrors to regain Bêlit, he would. The lanterns of the harbor police were drawing nearer and their bearers heeded the trumpet. Arms and armor sheened visible. Dark under moonlight, the soldiers from the keep likewise approached at a flagging but dogged run.

'Lead on,' Conan ordered, around a tightness in his gullet. Jehanan nodded and spurted ahead.

At an alley, which two buildings walled in blackness, he turned. The party linked hands to follow. He brought them, surely more by sense of direction than knowledge, through several tangled passages and out by a watchtower at the edge of the flanking wall. Moonlight flooded them again. Stones clattered, sand gritted under their feet. They were beyond the city. It sheered sable above them. Jehanan ran slantwise over ground which sloped sharply from those ramparts toward the broad, gliding, moon-polished River Styx. The Grand Pyramid's mass hove in view, ghostly in that luminance, seeming almost to float under a sky where a few stars gleamed.

A brazen tone clove the night silence. Conan looked over his shoulder. Lanterns gleamed fireflylike. Had his group been seen from the tower maybe? More lanterns came from behind the half-wall.

The terrain across which he sped grew rough, treacherous, pocked and skeleton-white. Pits yawned on every hand. Shadows cast by huge, tumbled blocks made them hard to identify before one fell over an edge. Jehanan skipped like a mountain goat; somehow he had mastered the ceaseless torment that would have crippled most men altogether. Daris fared still more nimbly. Conan saw Falco trip again and again, often nearly going into a hole. He joined the Ophirite and lent a guiding clasp. A remote part of him felt glad that this added trouble kept him too busy to dread demons.

Halloos lifted. Stygians had reached the rugged stretch. They ventured forward slowly and clumsily, but their officers screamed commands that did send them onward.

Jehanan beckoned. An excavation was at his feet, wide enough for moonbeams to reach its depth. He went on all fours and groped his way down a rough slope. His friends came along. Stones tumbled free, a sound like dry bones. Conan fought not to shudder. At the bottom, Jehanan scouted among boulders and sharp ridges until he found what he sought and vanished. His followers crawled over the same barrier as he had done, and saw before them a low, oblong structure of chiseled blocks. Its entrance gaped open on murk. Conan clenched his teeth and crept into the ancient tomb with the rest.

After his pupils had dilated, he found that barely sufficient light was reflected that he was not altogether blind. 'To me,' echoed Jehanan's hoarse whisper. The Shemite stood, a blot of darkness, in the center of some object. When he got there, touch more than sight told Conan what it must be – a lidless sarcophagus, plundered ages since.

The four crawled into it and lay huddled close. The barbarian felt something hard against his ribs. His fingers traced a curve, holes, teeth: a human skull. The olden owner's? Scarcely, after millennia. Besides, he brushed shreds of flesh. Some creature had brought the head here to devour, belike from a recent grave elsewhere. What kind of beast or being?

Voices called back and forth, feet scrambled, metal clanked. The Stygians had attained to this area and were casting about in search. Conan thrust aside his qualms and made a warrior's calculation. Jehanan's sword and Daris' belt were the last weapons left to his band, but the tomb was highly defensible and plenty of rocks lay around to throw or to weight a fist.

The noise faded away. The enemy had not made as thorough a search as they might have. No doubt dazzling moonlight and inky shadows, in this ripped-up, barren patch of wilderness, confused their vision. But no doubt, also, they were not eager to stay.

When they were gone, Jehanan said, 'We move again. If we go carefully, mostly creeping, they won't see us. They will come hunting in force at sunrise, I suppose, but by then we can be in a place I know where they cannot find us in less than a month.'

'A month, waterless?' Conan muttered.

'If we can endure till tomorrow night, I will lead you out toward the hinterland,' Jehanan promised. 'Then you can guide us to your boat.'

XI

THE VESSEL OF
THE SERPENT

The refuge was a niche or shallow cave near the top of a bluff, screened from sight below by a ledge. Sand had blown in to soften the floor a trifle. As night wore on, air grew chill; sleepers huddled together for warmth. None were free of frequent dreams that made them struggle, moan, and waken aghast. Dawn was infinitely welcome.

Conan was first to grow quite conscious. He gently disengaged the arms Daris had cast about him in slumber, and slipped outside. Prone on the ledge, he squinted over its rim. The sun, clearing the river, turned stream and eastern sky silver. Black Khemi and dull-hued Grand Pyramid loomed athwart western blueness. Underneath him, the limestone wreckage was pale yellowish and purple-shadowed. He saw troopers clamber about down there in quest of him. Though light winked off their metal, at their distance they resembled ants, and he heard no breach of the stillness around.

He drew a deep breath and felt memory of nightmares slipping away. Whatever had brewed them must have slunk back into the tombs. He and his people could get well rested during the day, recover strength in spite of thirst and hunger, and after dark depart. No doubt the Stygians would try to ring this area in, but no doubt there would be gaps in their lines ample for an athletic, determined, knowledgeably guided party to get through unobserved. If need be, the escapers could crawl for two or three miles over the farmlands beyond, until distance veiled them. Thereafter it would be no long walk to the gig, nor an extremely long sail to Akhbet isle, *Tigress*, Belit. Conan stretched cramped muscles and smiled.

Suddenly he tensed. An oath cracked from his lips.

Out of the harbor, spidery-oared, slipped a war galley. Another followed, and another, and another ... In midstream they raised sail, caught a westerly breeze but continued rowing against the tide, and moved off between the headlands enclosing the bay, seaward bound.

Conan counted them. 'Why, that must be nearly the whole flaming fleet!' he exclaimed.

His companions, roused by the noise, crowded about him. 'Where are they going?' Falco cried. 'Has the war on Ophir started?'

'I much doubt that,' said Conan grimly. 'No, likeliest it is us they are after.'

'Four runaways, causing that small armada to go forth?' Daris sounded incredulous.

'I know not why, but plain it is to see that we matter greatly to some powerful persons,' Conan answered. 'I seem to be right in my guess that the wretch who trapped me never thought to tell his masters where we had hidden the boat. Why should he? Nor did I tell you yesterday, in case we were being spied on. Else they need but plant an ambush there. They know, however, that the craft cannot be far off. Thus they have no great stretch to blockade, and are certain of intercepting us if we sail.' He shrugged. 'They cannot expect to be out for more than a few days. Meanwhile the sailors get exercised.'

'I told you we might lie hidden for a month,' said Jehanan in a dead voice. 'Of course, we would wither well before then. Let us plan how to sally forth so that we are sure to die fighting.'

Daris shook her dark head violently. 'No! If we can reach the hinterland as you claimed, we can seek a way to – to Taia.'

'Scant hope in that,' Falco replied. 'We would be better off trying for Kush, due south, though the odds against us will still be overwhelming.'

'Why not north, across the river and into Shem?' Conan inquired. 'Even in the parts tributary to Stygia, we should find hiding places and helpers.'

The rest regarded him in surprise. 'Did you not know?' Daris said. 'West of the Taian highlands, the Styx is death to swimmers. Those who try fall mortally ill within a day or two. Even wading across at one of the few fords is dangerous; you must wash tainted water off your skin with fresh, immediately afterward.'

'Well, can we not steal a boat to ferry us over?' Conan snapped.

'The harbor police, both ashore and afloat, will doubtless stand doubly alert against any such attempt,' Jehanan warned.

Daris leapt to her feet. *'The wingboat!'* she shouted.

Conan seized her and hauled her down. 'Keep low,' he growled. 'You might be seen from afar, standing on this brink.'

Her suppleness shivered in his arms, her eyes looked straight into his, and she said in a rush of sweet breath: 'The magical boat that carried me here, I remember where it lies docked – it is lightly guarded and – and kept supplied, and can outrun everything else –'

Conan gripped her till she winced. He eased his hold, but not the excitement that soared aloft in him. 'Can you handle that thing?'

She nodded. 'I paid heed on the way, just to keep my mind from breaking apart in despair.'

'I too!' Falco shrilled. 'The spell is very simple, and you need not be a magician. Ordinary acolytes did the piloting.'

Conan released Daris. A while he crouched, chin in fist, and stared into heaven. A hawk soared there. Finally he nodded, 'Aye, this seems our best hope by far,' he rumbled. 'Unless we can head straight to sea – failing that, we fare to Taia and seek the rebels. We three outlanders get help from them to start us on our treks. Overland to Ophir, thence Jehanan and I onward to Argos, where we will take a boat for a rendezvous with Belit.'

'I have a better thought still,' Falco urged. 'Outpacing any word from Khemi, we can stop at Luxur and take refuge in Lord Zarus' embassy. Warned of what I have discovered, he will go home on the first excuse he can contrive. We board his ship in disguise, and he lets you two off at the isle. Daris, of course, can take the wingboat east. Maybe her people will find it useful in their cause.'

'We shall think that over once we have our transportation,' Conan declared. 'For now, we should rest, yes, get some decent sleep.'

Admiration filled the gaze Daris laid upon him. 'As you will,' she murmured. 'You are he who brought us thus far. How?'

Never reluctant to shine before an attractive woman, Conan took his party back into the cave and settled down to relate past events. They heard him breathlessly, though Jehanan showed renewed pain and Falco flushed.

At the end the Shemite nodded. 'Yes,' he said in a sick man's voice, 'everyone in Khemi has heard of Nehekba and how she is hand

94

in glove with Tothapis, the wizard priest of Set. I did not imagine it at the time, but, yes, she must have been my cruel Heterka – and your Senufer, Falco.'

'No!' the youth cried. 'Impossible! If – if you but met her for a single time, you would understand.'

'What have these women looked like?' Daris asked shrewdly.

Her idea failed, because none of her companions had much ability to describe a person in unmistakable words. From their attempts emerged little more than a vague picture of a Stygian female aristocrat, typical except for her beauty. The mirror talisman was a revealing detail.

'But she never wore any such thing, did my Senufer,' Falco said triumphantly. 'There, are you satisfied?'

The Cimmerian gave up. He could not see that it made any difference at present; and the Ophirite would presumably gain a minim of wisdom before time gave him a chance to seek his paramour again. What mattered immediately was to keep this band united. While the plan did hold promise, Conan hardly expected that theft of the black magicians' sacred craft would prove safe or easy.

They left before moonrise. A dry and foodless day had not unduly diminished either strength or alertness in them. All had keen senses and had often stalked game in wild country. The early part of their passage went fast. Later they inched along. By the time the moon cleared the hazes that at first reddened it, the last Stygian picket was behind them and they stood in shadow under a rampart.

'The wingboat has a roofed dock of its own on a short canal that must have been dug for it, west of the city,' Daris had explained. 'A double row of monoliths guards the path to a sally port; I read upon them terrible curses against trespassers when I was marched away. Otherwise I saw only four sentinels.'

Conan had dismissed unease about those curses. Anybody could write a threat on a stone, and the Stygians were utterly subservient to the hierarchy. Were the necromancers really worried about their vessel they would have fenced that path with flames or adders or something else deadly. This he must believe, and otherwise put his trust in ... in Mitra?

Now he led the way south, since he dared not cross through the harbor area. Locked gates, a ban on land traffic, ought to keep them unnoticed if they hugged the base as they rounded three fortified sides. The moon was too bright for his liking, but the western ground would be shaded from it.

Halfway along the first wall, a portcullis stood lowered. Conan did not expect sentries at the foot of it after dark. Too valuable to endanger needlessly, they would be aloft in the towers flanking the gate and, if they actually paid much attention to anything, would keep eyes on the horizon. Yet he signaled for redoubled caution as he started past.

A hiss brought him leaping about. Moonlight glistened on the scales of an enormous snake, which undulated forth between the bars. It moved toward him, mouth agape, tongue aflicker. Lidless eyes gleamed in a head raised man-high.

Jehanan drew blade. Daris whispered shakenly, 'A python of Set, after prey. We can run faster than it can crawl.'

'No, both of you,' Conan murmured back. 'Either way, we would make too much noise. Hold off – against the wall – keep silent!'

He poised motionless, as if he were a Stygian who would meekly accept being choked and engulfed. The serpent hissed again and drew nigh. Thunderbolt swift, it struck to seize him in its fangs and throw coils about his body.

Conan's fist met the snout in midair. The thud was soft but the pain to that sensitive spot great. The snake went backward in waves. Hope that it would flee broke asunder, for in twisting about it spied Daris. The manthick length surged toward her.

Conan sprang. He cast himself on the cold neck, just behind the head, the one place where no rib-crushing loop could reach him. His legs clamped tight. His arms came around the head, his hands gripped the lower jaw and heaved downward. The reptile thrashed in maelstrom violence, but otherwise the struggle was silent, an icy flowing beneath the moon.

A crack resounded. Conan had ripped the forward part of the mandible free. He clung the tighter to the wildly lashing body, while he brought the bleeding piece above the skull. With all the might that was in him, he smashed its teeth downward. The blow drove them through the scales and bone into the brain.

Barely did he cast himself free of loops that still churned about. He struck the ground, rolled over, and bounced to his feet, gasping. Let the dead monster flop until sunrise quieted it, if that saying about reptiles was true. The guards above would not come down to see why.

Conan's wind returned, and he sought the others. They pressed close. Fingers and eyes asked mutely, pleadingly, how he fared. He gave a curt nod for reply and set forth afresh.

Southeast corner, south wall, southwest corner, and northward.

Shadow cloaked the west side of Khemi, out to where farmland stretched gray-white in the moonbeams. The boat canal was closer than that. Conan kept his glance well away from the illuminated ground and let his night vision sharpen. Crouched above the deeply cut channel, by starlight he saw water like a ribbon of tarnished silver. At its end stood a dock and a roof built out on slanting poles, all in silhouette. Likewise featureless were the menhirs whose double line marked a path from the bank to a gate in the city wall.

He drew his companions into a huddle. 'We must either be quiet about this, or quick, or both if we can,' he muttered, 'for any racket will surely draw men from yon towers. Follow me, but do not act unless I tell you to.'

'Oh . . . you, alone?' Anguish pulsed in Daris' voice. Her fingers clutched his wrist.

'No, us together,' he answered, 'but being sensible about it. Heed me! Come!'

He avoided the stairway down the bank and, like a prowling tiger, slipped over the earth toward the pier. Soon he made out the vessel berthed there, long, metallic, figureheaded by some beaked reptile. Bent nearly double, he glided close. Four sentinels were on duty. Two stood, spears grounded against the planks; two rested on a bench close by. While young and burly, they were not soldiers, but shaven-pated, garbed in black tunics – acolytes.

Conan padded up behind the seated pair. He rose. His great hands seized both heads and dashed them together. There was a cracking sound, and the bodies went limp.

The guards afoot whirled about. Conan leapt over the bench. A

Stygian tried to bring spear against him. Conan was too quick. The edge of his right hand chopped past the shaft, into the neck behind. The guard lurched and crumpled. The Cimmerian caught him before he could splash into the water and lowered him with care.

That took a brief time, though. Yet the fourth warder had not yelled for help. Conan looked and saw why. Daris had laid a knee in the small of his back, slipped her belt around his throat, and hauled it tight. She lacked the power to strangle him, but she kept him dumb, and his sandals made scant noise as he struggled. Jehanan arrived, sword in hand, to finish him.

Conan decided he could not well reprimand such a pair for disregarding his orders. Anyway, speed remained vital. He beckoned his company to gather the strewn weapons and come aboard.

Had his course of late not been headlong, he might have had trouble forcing himself to do likewise. Fires in a crystal globe the size of three human skulls glowed and wavered astern. The metal of deck and hull felt chill to his touch, nothing like warm, life-remembering wood. Forward of a deckhouse, whose unlighted ports resembled empty eye sockets, rose the terrifying figurehead.

However, if this was his roundabout way to Belit, he would not hesitate. He had proposed going straight to sea, but Falco and Daris did not think that would be wise. Naval vessels were bound to spy both this craft and the fact that she was not manned as she ought to be. She was not so fast that she could evade stones or flaming missiles from well-aimed catapults. It was not even sure that the magic which ran her would prevail far from Stygia; Set's power appeared to be slight out on the clean ocean.

Inland, then!

'Take over, Daris,' Conan said low. 'Stand by her, Falco. Jehanan, help me cast off.'

The woman's eyes gleamed wide, but she nerved herself to go before the globe, speak the word, and make the gestures. The youth kept close watch on her. Well-nigh soundless, the boat slipped from shore, backed out the narrow channel, entered the river, and turned her prow toward the moon. Wings spread wide. Speed increased. The hull lifted to slide on the very surface. Cleft air whistled. Khemi receded into night.

Conan wrestled down his fears and took charge. He sent Jehanan forward as a lookout. Himself, by the glow of moon and brightened demon-fires, he explored. In the deckhouse he found small separate cabins, lanterns, flint and steel for kindling them, no galley but ample stores of food and drink that did not require cooking, assorted clothes and weapons and the like, and instruments he neither recognized nor desired to know about.

He considered casting those overboard, but decided to leave well enough alone. Minute by minute he felt calmer, happier. A night and a day and a night to Luxur – an arrow or a galloping horse could perhaps outstrip that, but who could shoot an arrow or ride a horse untiring through almost a thousand miles?

Exultant, he loaded hardtack, cheese, raisins, wine, and water on a tray. First he served Jehanan in the bow, then he went aft. When Daris and Falco had theirs, he allowed himself an enormous draught and a bite. Presently he inquired how this witch-vessel was controlled. They demonstrated the simple art. He paid as much heed to Daris as to it. How like Belit she was, how fair to see in moonlight and freedom.

Tothapis, who had been ageless as a mummy, all at once looked old. He sat well back in his throne, as if its cobra hood might shield him, and rustled: 'They have escaped us, then. They have done the impossible, and now they are off in Set's own boat . . . to Taia.'

'How can you be sure?' Nehekba asked.

She knew it was not by scrying. After his god revealed the location of the corsair ship to him, the sorcerer had been able to track her continuously from afar. But once Amnun was aboard, he had let this surveillance lapse, for it was a demanding thing to maintain. Indeed, in his haste to organize the seizure of Conan, he had neglected to ask Amnun what Belit's plans were; and an agent on whom he had laid spells protective against hostile magic in life, could not be summoned back from death. If he sent his remote vision scanning widely about, the chance of its lighting upon his enemies was very slight, and meanwhile time slipped away between his fingers.

'Who but Conan, were-lion Conan, could thus have killed three strong men, bare-handed, in silence, after having slain a python sacred to the lord of the universe?' Tothapis shuddered. 'And I sense fate at work. Powers from the heavens themselves. O Set, be with your servants, make us strong against the unmerciful Sun!'

'Is he indeed bound for Taia? Has he not likelier put to sea?'

Tothapis' bald head wove back and forth in negation. 'Would he had tried that. The boat would soon wallow helpless on waves that annul its fires. No, he must have headed oppositely, toward his destiny.'

Nehekba gave him a look not entirely reverent. 'Then why have you not scryed upstream till your view overtook him?'

'Were you not aware? They were puissant magicians who built that craft. As long as it remains on the river whose soul it embodies, no spell can prevail against or reveal it.'

Standing in the gloom, still disheveled from her experience, Nehekba said, venom in each word, 'Yet since it is visible to mortal eyes, tangible to mortal hands – and, yes, stealable by mortals – it must be vulnerable to ordinary force.'

Tothapis gave her a lengthy stare. Will flowed slowly back into him, to lift his head and make his shoulders less stooped. 'What do you mean?' he inquired.

'We know, within a few hours, when those criminals left Khemi,' the witch replied. 'We know how fast they can travel. Thus we may easily calculate the farthest distance they can have gone. My lord, use your skills, your command over certain beasts. Your spirit can wing at the speed of thought, to lay under command a herd of behemoths upstream. Let the great river horses swim out to meet the boat when they see it, rise from below, crush it with bulk and tushes, bear Conan's bones down into the silt of the Styx!'

Tothapis considered. 'We would lose a most valuable instrumentality,' he said.

'If Set spoke truly, and every necromantic indication we have since forgotten, then the fulfillment of that ruffian's destiny would cost us far more.'

Tothapis meditated, his gaze lost in shadows. Finally he said: 'No. Huge though behemoths be, harpooners in reed boats have often slain them. Consider what those four have already wrought, and what they now have at their disposal, and the fact that their fate is again in motion, more powerfully by far than erstwhile. They would win through. I would have spilt priceless time and energy for nothing.'

'Will you then simply wait for yon ape to prevail?' Nehekba screeched.

Tothapis studied her. 'You hate him, do you not?' the sorcerer asked.

'After what he did to me, aye, revenge will be more precious than rubies.' The witch checked her passion. 'Brute I called him. I was right about that, my lord, and wrong in what I just proposed. Raw strength and reckless courage, those make his dominion. We must fight him on a different ground.'

Her laugh shivered forth. 'Why, my lord, he has stunned us till we were bumbling along as brainless as him. Let us use our wits. You did earlier, when you dispatched Ramwas and a homunculus to Luxur. Never has investment shown higher profit than yours will.'

'What mean you?' Tothapis demanded.

'Our enemies will make halt there,' Nehekba said eagerly. 'Falco will insist on it. See, was I not wise in getting to know him well? He will argue that Zarus must be warned, and furthermore can smuggle them directly out of Stygia. Conan ought to agree. He has no reason to suppose they are not well ahead of even the fastest carrier pigeon. But you can send an instant message to Ramwas, ordering he keep clandestine watch on the Ophirite embassy, and stand prepared to take the gang when they approach.'

Tothapis came as near showing enthusiasm as he ever did. 'By the Underworld, yes! We will do it so.' A shade of fearfulness crept back over him. 'Yet if somehow, through some damnable quirk of chance, the barbarian does elude our trap –'

'Forget not my featherskin,' Nehekba said. 'In bird guise, I will depart east within this hour. I can go faster thus than the wingboat itself, and have spells to keep me untiring aflight. It should not be long after the vessel gets to Luxur that I do, to hover aloft and observe.'

'You lack the means of communicating mind to mind,' he objected.

'What of that?' she replied. 'Do I lack intelligence to do whatever proves needful,' her fingers crooked talon-like, 'for bringing Conan the brute to destruction?'

XII

THE CITY OF KINGS

Luxur lay about a hundred miles south of the Styx. Once it had been the oasis lair of wild nomads. After their chieftains had conquered widely around and established the First Dynasty, its central location made it a good choice for a royal seat. With the growth of civilization, the city had engulfed the oasis. However, irrigation made agriculture possible nearby, and a ship canal was dug to connect it with the river. Trade flourished, for while the comings and goings of foreigners were regulated, they were not virtually forbidden as at Khemi. Besides visitors from every part of vast Stygia, Luxur saw Shemites, Kushites, Keshanites, and more exotic folk. Occasional vessels brought goods from far Argos or Zingara, rowing the long way upstream for the sake of prices that even made the dismal inns endurable to their crews.

The wingboat slipped up the canal by night, not to attract notice. As if to aid her wayfarers, a wind off the desert blew dust, which stung their eyes and gritted in their nostrils but obscured the moon. It died down toward morning. By then they were not far from the capital, in an area Falco remembered from excursions of limited range that the embassy staff had had permission to make. Here a gradual slope of ground to the water and below created a marsh full of reeds and wildfowl. The boat nudged into that whispery thickness until she lay well hidden against a bank.

'Let us get going,' said Conan impatiently. 'Remember, lad, if you have not heard from us after three days, do not try to be a hero on the spot. Hasten on to Taia, find Daris' father Ausar, tell him what you know, give and take what help from him you may.'

'Y – yes,' the Ophirite said unsteadily. 'But oh, do return! Mitra and Varuna guard you!'

On the journey, he had not only rested and recuperated like his

102

comrades, he had acquired worshipfulness for the mighty Cimmerian. Daris likewise often found her gaze drifting toward the leader, and herself unwontedly shy when he spoke to her. Jehanan was mostly sunk in silence, though he did his share of work and tried hard not to inflict his suffering on the rest. It had been a strange trip, through landscape sometimes barren, sometimes intensely green. No pilot of ship, barge, felucca, or canoe but sheered well off from the eldritch craft and dared not hail her. Serfs abandoned flocks, hoes, shadoofs to pelt inland at the sight. Yet those aboard were peaceful, and three of them were sometimes merry, with wine and song and tales and hopes for the future.

Now, though, action was again upon them. Falco had best stay behind, as caretaker and because he might be recognized on his way to the embassy. If all went well, his countrymen could fetch him after sundown, bringing a forged pass to get him by the nighttime pickets at every city gate; darkness ought to obscure his features. For this first contact, Conan wanted Daris and Jehanan along. Despite cowl and kaftan, he would be fairly conspicuous in the streets. It should lull suspicion if he was accompanied by an obvious Shemite and Taian; then people could assume they were three of mixed race in the service of a caravaneer, as was common. Not all Taians were in revolt. Some, descendants of slaves or hirelings, had never seen their ancestral hills. In garb like his and Jehanan's, Daris might be a beardless youth.

They had scrubbed their faces, and Conan had shaved. Otherwise they depended on clothes to hide grime, since they dared not draw washwater from the Styx and felt it best to conserve what they had that was potable. They were not unduly gamy, having been outdoors nearly the whole time, in dry air.

Conan took Falco by the hand. 'Thank you,' he said. 'Fare you also well. But do not fret more than you can help. That which will be, will be. Our pride is to meet it boldly.'

He swung himself onto the rail and sprang ashore. His two waymates followed. On firm ground, they struck across a paddock to a dirt road. Running parallel to the canal, it pointed at towers which bulked on the southern horizon. False dawn became sunrise.

A flock of ducks beat clamorous up from the marsh. Mud hamlets dotted a terrain of croplands, date groves, and ditches. Southwest and southeast, the desert that stretched beyond it thrust ruddy wedges into its green. Air was still cool, but rapidly warming.

After a while, Conan reminded: 'Falco described well how to find Zarus' place. But we should not seem too eager or purposeful. Best we loaf through the streets like newcomers off duty, sightseeing, keeping an eye out for a pleasant way to spend some of our pay. A town like this must know many such drifters each year.'

'Be not so sure how the Stygians will take to us,' Jehanan said harshly. 'Those grovelers before snakes are unlike any people anywhere else. Are they even human?'

'Oh, yes,' Daris replied. She touched his cheek in compassion. 'Some of them have misused you and yours, as some of them have misused my folk. But I have met a number of ordinary ones, and heard tell of many more – decent persons little different from you or me, simply concerned to make a living for their families after paying their extortionate taxes – and what harm have these poor toilers we see coming forth ever done to anybody? The common Stygians are the first victims of their own overbearing nobles and fanatical priests.'

Conan grunted. He cared nothing for such fine distinctions. In his world view, apart from fierce immediate loyalties, the hand of every man was against every other man. At best there was truce, for practical reasons and always fragile. That did not mean that individuals could not share work, trade, enjoyment, liking, respect. He had been sorry to kill certain men in the past, though he lost no sleep afterward. Strife was the natural order of things.

Luxur grew in sight. The outer defenses were yellow sandstone, formidable but not forbidding in the way that Khemi's were. Banners on cross-poles hung arrogant above battlements. Gates stood wide, and while sentinels were present, they did not check the traffic, which by now had become dense – foot, cart, litter, chariot, horse, ox, donkey, camel. Laborers in loincloths, drovers in ragged tunics, desert nomads in white and black robes, merchants in garb more colorful, courtesans in gossamer, soldiers, hawkers, strolling performers, housewives, children, foreigners, a bewildering variety of individuals surged to and fro. They crowded, jostled, chattered, quarreled, screamed curses, yelped laughter, importuned, haggled, intrigued, shouted, wailed, crooned, made a maelstrom of sound between high, drab walls whose balconies were festooned with garments hung out to dry. The streets, mostly cobbled, littered and dirty as was usual in cities, were redolent of smoke, grease, dung, roast meat, oils, perfumes, drugs, humankind, beastkind.

Conan's party entered and pushed a slow way through. A monument – on a pillar the statue of an ancient king trampled a Shemite and a Kushite underfoot – marked their turn into the Street of Weavers. Here, cross-legged in booths, sellers held out fabrics and chanted their virtues to every passerby. It was less jammed than the main artery, and the newcomers could walk somewhat faster. According to plan, they pretended to marvel at the spectacle as they sauntered.

'Allo, allo!' cried a voice. Conan glanced behind him and saw a man in a shabby kaftan running to catch up. He carried a load of trinkets: crudely whittled toy camels in his hands, strings of bone beads hung on his arms. Drawing close, he said in Argossean, 'Welcome to Luxur. You are from Argos?'

'No,' Conan replied, annoyed.

'Ah, Zingara!' The man slipped into an accented version of the tongue of that country. 'Beautiful Zingara. You take home souvenir.'

'No,' Conan said in Stygian, 'I do not want to buy anything.'

'You speak this language!' exclaimed the vendor likewise. He smiled across his entire weathered face. The effect was somewhat diminished by his few snags of teeth. 'You are a world traveler, then. You know fine wares when you see them. Here, look at this camel. Beautiful workmanship.' He thrust one of the little models into the Cimmerian's palm. 'Only five lunars.' His reference was to a small copper coin of the realm.

'I don't want it.' Conan sought to give it back. The hawker's fingers were not there to receive.

'Four lunars,' the Stygian offered.

'No, by Crom!' Conan suppressed a desire to bring out the ax concealed beneath his robe. That would be madness.

'For four lunars, I will give you two camels,' the man said. 'Take them home to your children.'

'I tell you, no!'

'Three camels.'

'*No!*'

'Three camels and a necklace.'

Conan strode on. The vendor kept pace. 'You must not steal a poor man's stock in trade, sir,' he scolded in a loud singsong designed to draw attention. 'Think of my babies at home.'

'Take the damned thing,' Conan snarled, tried again to return it, and failed again.

Suddenly he noticed Jehanan and Daris were not beside him. He stopped and looked behind. The owner of a real, if rather motheaten camel had cornered the maiden and was insisting that she wanted a ride on it, and he would take her to all the interesting parts of town. 'Here,' he said, and made the animal kneel. He pushed her toward the saddle. 'It is easy. It is fun. You pay me only what you wish.'

Jehanan sought to deny a fellow who proffered grubby confections off a tray. 'Ah,' that Stygian leered. 'I know. You want *numi.*' From a flowing sleeve, he produced a packet. 'Finest *numi.* Burn it, breathe the smoke, get lovely dreams and feel wonderful. Just two silver stellars.' Jehanan whitened.

'Three lunars,' proposed Conan's pest. The barbarian was about to cast the gimcrack he had onto the street, when he realized what a scene that would bring on. Already, curious denizens had paused to watch. They included a mounted guardsman a few yards off.

Somehow Daris had been eased onto the live camel. It lurched to its feet. The owner grabbed the bridle and trotted off, tongue clacking.

'For three lunars, three camels and two necklaces,' Conan heard.

The seller of sweetmeats and drugs beamed and suggested, 'You would like to meet my sister. Young, beautiful, very, very good. Take *numi,* feel fine, make love to her, be happy. Come.' He plucked at the Shemite's robe. Jenanan's breath rasped, his fists doubled.

106

'*Hold!*' Conan roared. 'We must go on. No time. Here, I will take your toy for three lunars. Daris, Jehanan, for everything's sake, give those scoundrels a ransom and let us get out of here!'

'You are buying three camels and two necklaces,' the vendor told him. 'One more necklace for one more lunar will bring you luck.'

Conan opened his purse and shuffled forth money. The wingboat was well supplied with Stygian coinage. Daris terminated her ride by paying over what she guessed the cameldriver would have expected for an entire day. Jehanan's hand shook as he bought himself free; even that Stygian was subdued by the look he got and bowed before he slipped off.

More of the kind converged on the travelers. 'See, behold what I offer! . . . You are my father and my mother! . . . Alms, baksheesh, for the love of the gods!'

'I have heard about this, but never quite believed it,' Daris said, breathless.

'And I have met something of the sort before, but naught to match,' Conan answered.

'We were mistaken,' Jehanan said. 'We must stride straight forward, fast, scowling, fists closed and at our sides, looking neither to right nor to left.'

Conan gripped his shoulder. 'You can speak so well, now?' the Cimmerian murmured. 'O brother of Bêlit, you are unwounded in your heart!'

The peddlers and beggars presently quit and disappeared into the ruck. Conan wondered how to get rid of the gewgaws that had been thrust upon him. If he gave them to any of the naked children who scampered and scrambled around, that would bring a fresh horde. In the Street of Jars, he managed surreptitiously to drop them into a large specimen.

Soon afterward, his party entered quite a different sort of thoroughfare. At the middle of Luxur, royal generations had built a grandiose complex reserved for the great and their attendants. The palace, the fane of Set, the barracks and parade grounds of the king's household troops, the archives, the office buildings for his counsellors and their staffs, surrounded a broad plaza. Across the way from the latter stood a row of aristocratic mansions, some of

107

which held foreign embassies. Toward this row, as Conan's band approached from the north, led the Avenue of Kings. Broad and smoothly paved, it displayed a double line of olden monarchs in stone; inscriptions on bases reiterated the haughtiness on images. Behind them reared buildings whose walls were of granite, not clay, and painted in symbols of the gods. Here traffic was scant and dignified – a lord or lady borne in her litter, a couple of wellborn boys off to school under ward of their pedagogue, a scribe bearing the apparatus of his trade, an occasional priest, official, wealthy merchant, military officer, liveried servant, veiled wife, delivery-man bringing wares that had been ordered. These cast sidelong glances at three plebeian strangers, but raised no inquiry. Falco had said, 'Behave as if you have a proper errand there, and everybody will take for granted you do. Who would dare carry defiance into the citadel of Stygia?'

Conan's pulse knocked. He was almost at his goal.

The avenue ended at a cross street, less imposing though also clean, quiet, flagged. This was flanked by town houses on whose flat roofs blossomed gardens. Narrow lanes went between them. Beyond, above, Conan saw higher structures, those that surrounded the royal plaza, rise massive. Here there were just a few people. Stillness hung heavy as the gathering warmth. Shadows lay blue.

He turned right. Several entrances down, one façade displayed a lion in gold, rampant, blinding bright. That was the Ophirite embassy, he knew. He hastened his stride.

A Stygian who had been slowly pacing by suddenly halted and stared. He snatched a whistle hung at his neck and blew. The noise whined loud.

Doors to either side of the lion's flew open. Armed soldiers stormed out. 'Halt!' boomed a voice. 'Conan and your companions, halt or be slain!'

'Mitra aid us,' Daris gasped. 'We are betrayed.'

'By witchcraft – Nehekba's, Tothapis' –' Jehanan lifted the hem of his kaftan and drew his shortsword. 'Ishtar,' he prayed in his mother tongue, 'let me go bravely, guide me home to you, make me well again that I may abide in your love.'

108

Conan unslung the ax he had chosen off the boat. It was a Taian weapon, straight-shafted, beaked as well as edged, lively in his hands for all its weight. He spent but an instant feeling sick at the knowledge that he had lost, that he would never again embrace Bêlit – and gallant Daris must die beside him, slain by him if that was needful to forestall her capture – Then he was warrior and naught else. His glance flickered. The Stygians had his party boxed between two long housefronts. They were thirty, half of them closing in from either side, four bearing cocked crossbows, the rest blade and shield. Behind the eastern rank, their commander shouted orders: a burly, grizzled man, equipped with sword but otherwise wearing simply a tunic.

'We will charge toward their officer and try to cut through,' the Cimmerian told his friends. 'Back to back after we have closed.'

In Daris' right hand gleamed a dirk, in her left hung the belt she had borne from Khemi. 'If only my father could know whom I fight beside,' she said low. 'He would be almost as honored as I am.'

XIII

DEATH AND HONOR

The wanderers attacked. They did not rush together in a straight line. Separately, crouched down, they bounded in zigzags. Bolts whirred at them but missed targets so swift and unpredictable. Before the archers could reload, Conan had gotted to the infantry.

Skilled in the use of a battle ax, he held his with left hand near the end of the haft, right near the middle. The Stygian whom he confronted stabbed at him from around a shield-rim. Conan's helve struck the blade downward. Immediately his own weapon swung slantwise above his right shoulder. As it swept back to smite, he shifted his grip at the middle, which had given him close control, down to join the other hand at the end for fullest leverage and driving force. The Stygian brought shield higher to meet that blow. The Cimmerian's whole huge mass and strength were behind it. Metal rang, framework buckled, the swordsman tottered backward. His shield dangled by the straps from a broken arm.

Conan whipped the ax right and struck its pointed beak into the exposed thigh of the foe on that side. The wound was not mortal, but surprise and shock momentarily disabled the man. In that time, Conan turned on the one to his left. Again he parried a sword thrust with his haft. Then, twisting it about in midair, he brought it under this man's shield. Weight and his might forced the shield aside. He hewed into a now unprotected knee. The Stygian screamed and sank down to the pavement. Conan whirled his ax aloft and down to ring on the helmet of the other leg-injured man. Half-stunned, that Stygian also stumbled and fell.

Daris and Jehanan were beside their captain. She snapped her belt at a soldier's hand. The buckle struck so painfully that he dropped his weapon. Jehanan let the Cimmerian ward him for the moment he needed to kill that foeman and take his shield for himself. Rising, the Shemite in turn blocked an assault on Conan.

Though their line had been broken, the Stygians were trained and courageous fighters. Those on the wings dashed to the melee at the center. Their quarry was surrounded before getting a chance to run onward. The second rank of troopers reached the battle and joined in.

Back to back the three stood. Conan's ax roared, Jehanan's sword stabbed and sliced, Daris' belt flailed and her knife darted. Blood flew, dripped off metal, spread in a scarlet lake over the street. Men yelled, iron clanged. Householders looked out in terror. Among them, above the heads of his enemies, Conan glimpsed a graybeard in flowing Ophirite blouse and trousers, beneath the sign of the golden lion. Lord Zarus, no doubt – mere yards away, but the ambassador might as well have been on the moon.

The Cimmerian thought he was at the end of his own career. Well, he had lived more in his two dozen years on earth than most men could in a century. Let him only first slay so many Stygians that afterward the survivors would never sleep soundly. Then let him be sure that he and his comrades were not dragged back to the vile attentions of sorcerers, but died a clean death here.

The officer drew closer, to exhort his platoon. Conan saw him clearly, and smote still harder in the hope of bursting through the pack around him and cleaving that head. The hope was vain. The Stygians pressed too thickly and savagely for even his power.

Jehanan howled. *'Ramwas!'* It was like the baying of a maddened wolf. 'Ramwas! Ramwas!'

And the Shemite went berserk. Where he had fought with care, ever mindful of his friends and how best he could aid them, he shed all heed for anything. His shield became a weapon of offense, edge chopping, boss crunching. His sword flew about, meteor-swift. He did not seem to feel the wounds he took, and they bled little though many were deep. His face was a gorgon mask from which men shrank back appalled. Striking, trampling, become troll-strong, he broke through their crowd. Dead and wounded strewed his path, hideously mangled in those few seconds.

'Ramwas, remember!' he bayed, and was upon the officer. That

111

man drew sword. Jehanan's shield knocked it loose, to spin and twinkle through yards of air. Jehanan's blade pierced the belly of the Stygian. Keening, the Shemite lifted the transfixed noble straight up over his head and threw him at a wall. The skull shattered, the brains exploded forth.

Conan himself had with a chill recalled who Ramwas was. But he remained a lion that saw a way out of the trap. Most soldiers had recoiled in fright and confusion. He charged, Daris beside him. The two who tried to oppose them, he struck down in as many blows.

They reached Jehanan. A human soul had come back into his eyes. His wounds were beginning to open and copiously bleed. A loop of entrail dangled from his ripped, red-soaked kaftan.

'Go,' he croaked. His gesture was at the nearest lane between houses. 'I can hold them for a span ... yet.'

'No, Bêlit's brother, we stand together,' Conan protested.

The Shemite met his gaze. 'I am sped. Let me die in ... her service. If you should win back ... tell her ... I loved her.'

Conan clasped the hand of his which clutched the dripping sword. 'I will tell her more,' the Cimmerian vowed, 'that you died a free man.'

'Aye. Freed of this body, let loose to soar. Fare you well, my brother.'

The words had passed in a single minute, while the Stygians milled or stood shaken, leaderless, more than half of their number dead or disabled. Otherwise only the moans of the maimed had voice. But a member of the troop, perhaps a noncommissioned officer, soon raised a shout. He urged them to attack, he slapped their faces and hustled them into formation.

Conan led Daris, on whose cheeks tears ran down through sweat, into the lane. Jehanan took stance at its mouth. 'Come,' he gibed, 'come, dogs, and we will make rat food of you. What, do you reckon three against you to be heavy odds? Why, then, we will meet you one at a time, dear mongrels.' Even then, he sought to give their dazed minds the idea that his comrades stayed with him, lest the soldiers go roundabout in pursuit. He sought to remind them that they were supposed to take the fugitives alive if at all possible, lest a crossbow make short work of him.

Conan and Daris departed. The last words they heard from Jehanan were in his native speech. 'Ishtar of the lovers, who descended into hell for her man, receive me home to you . . .'

The passageway opened on a street as broad as the Avenue of Kings. Opposite were stately, lotus-columned buildings which fronted on the plaza beyond. Few people were in sight, and those all appeared to wear the collars of slaves, who dared not break off whatever errands were theirs. The racket of combat must have drawn freemen to go watch – none from this particular alley, as had been clear to see from the start, but surely elsewhere – unless certain individuals prudently took refuge in a government office.

'We cannot linger,' Conan panted. 'The hue and cry will be out for us very soon, well before we can get to a city gate. We had best hide somewhere till dawn, I suppose, when the laden caravans enter and the warehousemen bring their goods down to the cargo vessels at dock. In that tumult, we will have a chance of slipping out unnoticed.'

Daris regarded his bloodiness and her own. 'Not as we are.'

'No, curse it, we must tend our cuts, wash our garb and ourselves – better yet, get fresh clothes of a different sort – but where? How? And where can we find refuge in a town we know not, when criers will be telling everybody about us, and doubtless about a reward for information?'

Daris squeezed Conan's arm. 'Think,' she urged. 'Let us hark back to everything Falco has told us – no, wait, let *me* try remembering. I have never been here before, but it is, after all, the royal seat of Stygia, and I was taught about it in my girlhood.' She snapped her fingers. 'Aye! On the left side of the plaza as we stand is a large and famous temple of Set. Behind it lies a walled garden said to be laid out as a maze, where surely is at least one pool. Beneath it are crypts for secret rites. Who would ever think to look for us there?'

Conan stiffened. For a moment he was daunted. Then he cast his maned head back and formed a silent laugh. 'Wonderful! If we have borrowed Set's boat, he should not begrudge us a night's lodging. Come, lead me.'

113

They took care to walk as if they were on legitimate business, weapons again concealed beneath dress, and no slaves were sufficiently close to pay them any heed. From the street they had left drifted shouts and clamor still, as Jehanan fought his last battle. Rounding the corner of the archival building, they came on a nine-foot wall whose colored bricks formed the image of a mighty python and which was topped by iron pickets in the form of cobras. At its rightward end loomed a huge structure in diminishing tiers. Daris had no need to explain that that was the temple, for a cupola on top was in the coils of a gilt snake figure. Beyond its edge, across a plaza inlaid with the crown and scepter of Stygia's kings, Conan glimpsed the palace colonnade.

Nobody else was in sight, but that would not last long. 'Up you go, girl,' he said, and boosted her on a stirrup of his hands. He himself jumped, caught a picket, and hauled his body aloft. The cobras were meant to repel intruders simply by arousing fear. It was no trick to wriggle by them and spring down to the grounds below.

Conan was prepared to kill anyone who might be there, but none were visible. That was not surprising, for in truth the garden was a maze. Though it was formal and trimmed, the word that came to his mind was *rank*. In the gathering breathless heat, palms stood skeletal above man-tall hedges whose dense leaves and thorns confined a person to the paths between. Those paths were decked in moss to muffle every footfall, even as the brooding green masses swallowed spoken sound. Vines trained into serpentine patterns crawled along trees. Their crimson flowers were somehow less vivid than sullen, as were beds of the black and the purple lotus from which subtle poisons were obtained. No bird sang here, but winged beetles toiled through the air, spiders squatted in webs that formed part of the whole pattern, killer ants went in files down the labyrinth.

After walking a while, Daris shuddered and drew close to Conan. 'I am sorry,' she confessed in a thin whisper. 'I did wrong to bring us to this evil place. Fear flows through me like slime, for we are lost.'

He hugged her waist. 'You have never been in a jungle, have

114

you?' he answered. 'I have, and this is not very much worse than some. At least it is free of parrots. There must be water to keep the turf moist. First we look for that. I'm thirsty enough to drain the Vilayet Sea.'

He took off his sandals, to let footsoles feel how textures changed. He snuffed, he listened, he called on woodsman's instinct, and always he read his direction by the sun that was Mitra's. Before long he had found their way to a fountain.

It splashed through a series of onyx basins, into a pool where water lilies grew thick and carp swam. Conan surmised that porous pipes ran everywhere from here, underground, to wet the soil. No matter. He held Daris back when she would drink. 'Could be from the Styx,' he warned, and cautiously tasted it himself. It was cold, pure, artesian. Conan chuckled. 'What did the architect mean by this – or did he simply blunder?'

They drank and drank and drank. They stripped, washed their bodies, rinsed out their tattered clothes. As they did, a flush deepened the gold of Daris' face and bosom. Conan, watching her with honest appreciation, recollected that her nudity had not embarrassed her earlier.

'Best we let our garments dry, so we don't leave tracks later,' he said. They hung the clothes on an over-arching bough. Thereafter they squatted by the poolside, snatched fish out, and ate these raw. There was no telling when they would again get food. By the time they were done, the air had sucked all damp from the linen. 'We're lucky that no gardener has come on us yet,' Conan remarked. 'Or, rather, he is. However, we would be wise to seek a spot where interruptions are less likely.'

Having cut bandages for their wounds, which were superficial, they proceeded. Above the highest trees, the fane gave them a mark to steer by. Now and then they circled bewildered among giant fungi or bestial topiaries, but soon regained lost ground and won closer. Finally the maze ended. Across a flagged strip rose the lowest wall of the temple. The front was ornate, but this rear was plain, in blocks of dark granite, save for a frieze of hieroglyphs. Slit windows and several doors confronted Conan when he peered from the shelter of a clump of deadly nightshade. Silence weighed down emptiness. He wondered at his luck, and if it was really luck, until he recalled that a temple of Set was busiest at night. Priests, acolytes, even most slaves were asleep at this hour.

Entrances were shut and generally barred. Testing them, he found one whose direly inscribed door swung aside for him. It did not have a latch. From the gloom beyond, a breath of cold and dankness blew up a staircase. He nodded. 'The way to the crypts,' he said. 'No need to lock that off. Who but a sorcerer would willingly go in?'

Daris smiled. 'We,' she said, and trod springily forward.

Conan shut the door behind them. Hewn from the living rock, the stairs went down farther than he could see by the bracketed lamps that flickered at intervals. The walls bore scenes of procession, ritual, human sacrifice. The ceiling was low, and bulged outward above each riser in a full-relief image of a serpent. Thus at every step Conan and Daris must bow to Set. Rage flamed white in the Cimmerian. He clenched his teeth till his jaws ached.

'Jehanan, brother of Bêlit,' he vowed under his breath, 'you shall be avenged. In your name will I yet tread the Snake beneath my heel.'

After a passage which seemed endless, the stairs gave on a corridor, also wanly lit, full of shadows and echoes. Occasional doorways broke the parade of sinister murals. The first two that Conan found belonged to chambers for enormous sarcophagi; he wondered if the mummies within were of human beings. The third spilled forth some light of its own. Entering, the pair discovered a room furnished as a shrine. At its far end was an altar whereon a great bronze lamp burned before a full-sized golden eidolon of a cobra, coiled, neck raised, wise wicked eyes staring at any who might enter to do homage. Below the altar stood a crystal bowl of milk. On the side walls, rich hangings framed pictures of men whose heads were ophidian.

Daris considered the hieroglyphs at the rear. They were not the writing of Taia, which had an alphabet of Hyborian origin; but she had studied the Stygian symbols as part of her education. 'The Sanctuary of Set the Hooded, the Venom-fanged,' she translated, adding: 'Dedicated to him in this of his many aspects. That milk is for a sacred cobra which lives somewhere near.' She paused. 'We may not be alone.'

Conan inspected the artifacts. 'This lamp was filled with oil and its wick trimmed a few hours ago,' he declared, 'and it is too big to need further attention until tomorrow. Likewise, the milk is fresh. I daresay an attendant takes care of such things each morning before he retires. We will be gone earlier than that. I do not think any rite will take place hereabouts during the night; the crypts are for special, sorcerous use, are they not? As for the cobra, if he comes by, the worse for him.'

He unslung the ax beneath his kaftan. Stretching, he seized first one velvet hanging, then the other, ripped them loose, and spread them on the stone floor. 'It is chilly here,' he laughed, 'but we have drunk and dined, and now we have light, blankets, good company –' He broke off. 'Why, Daris, you weep.'

'I may, may I not, if we are safe?' she sobbed between the fingers that hid her face. 'For Jehanan, dead in an alien land.'

He went to embrace her. She laid her head against his breast, held him tight in her turn, and cried onward, but quietly, almost stoically. He stroked her hair and back as once he had done to console Bêlit, and murmured into the fragrance of her tresses:

'Do you wonder how I can jest when the brother of my love lies slain? Daris, dear, you are born of a warrior folk. Surely you understand. Death comes to us all when fate wills it, whether we spoil our lives by skulking in fear of the end or enjoy the world while it is ours and depart it uncowed. Jehanan died in glory, in joy. He had had his revenge and he was giving his comrades back their own lives. If his belief was true, at this moment he, made hale again, rides a unicorn through the queendom of Ishtar, toward a tower where a beautiful woman waits to become the mother of his children. If his belief was wrong, well, then he has forgotten, he is at peace. He wanted us to remember him, Daris, but I do not think he ever wanted us to mourn for him.'

She lifted her eyes to his and breathed, 'Conan, here at the gates of hell you give me heart.'

Passionately, defiantly, before the altar of Set, they kissed. But when at last she said in her ardor, 'Oh, beloved, I am yours, take me –' he drew back.

She stared at him. 'I mean it,' she avowed shakenly. 'I love you, Conan.'

'And I am more than fond of you,' he answered. 'Too fond to make you my mate when I shall leave you as soon as may be for Bêlit.'

'She would understand!'

Conan smiled sadly, wryly. 'All too well would she understand, and upbraid me for such treachery to a battle comrade. Be my sister, Daris, and I will be honored.'

She wept again for a while, and he gave her what chaste comfort he was able. Seldom had he required a greater effort of himself.

The wingboat slipped free of the marsh and turned down the canal toward the Styx. Though noonday blazed, there was no further reason for stealth; she could outrun anything on water or land.

Daris stood lookout in the bow. Wind sent her midnight locks flying and pressed a tunic around each graceful curve of her body, but the face was saddened that should have been triumphant. Astern, Falco steered and Conan finished an account in his laconic fashion:

'– So a little before sunrise, as well as I could gauge by the oil in the lamp, we went hunting. First we came on an acolyte. I killed him, tucked the body into a closet, and donned his garb. It was small on me, and of course my scalp is unshaven, but a cowled cloak hid that. Next we met a slave. That poor devil I only stunned and hid away bound and gagged with pieces of Daris' kaftan, while she put on his livery. It disguised the absence of an iron collar on her. We walked right out the main door – few were yet astir – and on to the gate. I doubt anybody would have challenged a pair of temple servants, even without the usual dawntide chaos. And we walked overland to you, and now the three of us are bound for Taia.'

Adoration filled the glance which the youth gave him. 'Never did such a warrior bestride this earth,' Falco said. 'Someday,

Conan, you will win a kingdom of your own; but first you will redeem mine and hers.'

'Maybe,' the Cimmerian replied curtly. 'We shall have a deal of fighting before any of that can happen.'

The Ophirite gave him a closer regard. 'Yes, our plan failed and we lost Jehanan. Yet he got what must have been nearly his dearest wish; you two mocked Set once more, in his very house; we here are free again.' Falco's tone grew worried. 'You and Daris are more subdued than I would have looked for. Did something happen that you have not told me about?'

'We talked about some private matters that are not of the happiest,' Conan said gruffly. 'Listen, we have a couple of days and nights ahead of us with nothing much to do but travel. You are young and lusty, and she is fair to behold and may be just a bit distraught. Take no advantage of any moods she may fall into, do you hear? We will bring her home in honor.'

'Oh, certainly, certainly.' Falco's expression changed from surprised to dreamy. He stared aloft and sighed, 'I have my Senufer. Her day and mine will come.'

Conan looked grim but said naught.

High above the boat, on wings that shone golden in the sun, an eagle kept pace.

XIV

WAYFARERS IN TAIA

Heaven was moonless but crowded with stars when the wanderers reached the mouth of the Helu. That river flowed swifter, louder, and brighter than the Styx into which it emptied. Eastward of the latter, which here ran north, mountains walled off countries still more arid, where nomads roamed. West of it, Taia rose steeply on either side of the Helu Valley, silver-gray in starlight, toward rugged highlands – Taia, which the Stygians called a rebellious province but which the dwellers therein called a nation at war for its liberty. Where the two streams met, on the left bank of the lesser, the white walls of little Seyan town stood amidst slumber and shadow.

'We will go up this tributary,' Daris said, pointing, 'past the cultivated sections, to a grotto I know where we can safely hide the boat. Thence it should be no long stretch afoot to Thuran. If my father is not there now, he will return there in due course, and meanwhile the priests of Mitra will give us hospitality.'

Eagerness tinged her voice, which pleased Conan. She had not done or said anything foolish on the way, as he had feared she might. Far from sulking or crying, she was quietly friendly to both her companions. But the good cheer while bound for Luxur had vanished. He hoped very much that she would get it back.

Having gauged they could pass under a bridge across the Helu, he gave the vessel his command. He had overcome his repugnance for this craft. While he still reckoned such a means of travel unmanly, he must admit its usefulness in a situation like this. The boat swung about. From the bows, Falco signaled everything clear. The force of the mountain river, eddying out into the sullen Styx, vibrated through the hull.

Abruptly the demon-fires sank low. The boat lost speed, her wings began to retract, she drifted back helpless. When well away

120

from the confluence, she regained force.

'What the devil!' Conan exclaimed. Bleak as the upland night, alarm struck through him. What sorcery was at work? He set his teeth and made a second try. Again he failed.

Falco came aft. 'I fear our launch refuses to leave her native waters,' the Ophirite said. 'Rather, I suppose the enchantment rises somehow from the Styx itself. If we want to take her up any other river, we must tow her.'

Conan nodded. A glance upward, at the clean blaze of stars and silvery cataract of Milky Way, drove out his fears. 'Aye, that makes sense,' he replied. 'A good thing we did not try heading out to sea, eh? Well, what shall we do?'

'Let us go on south for a few miles,' Daris proposed. 'I recall a place where we can also conceal the boat fairly well – in these troublous times, when nobody wanders freely about. We will have more of an overland journey than we hoped, but nothing beyond our power.'

Her companions agreed. Seyan disappeared behind. The spot Daris meant proved to be a cleft in a stone bluff, so narrow that they could barely manoeuver through, so deep that the anchored hull would not be visible from the river. They decided they might as well get a night's rest aboard before setting off.

At dawn they scrambled to the heights. From stores in the boat they had equipped themselves well. Their garb was a tunic and rolled-up blanket for each; in addition, the men bore footgear, and kaftans and burnooses against the midday sun. They had dried rations for several days and a waterskin that would see them through to springs and streams which Daris could find. Besides their knives, Conan had his ax, the best weapon for him that had been available; Falco had found a saber and small round shield made in Iranistan; Daris carried bow, full quiver, and the belt that had served her before.

Throughout that day they strode westward. The country rose fast, hills shouldering toward blue-hazed mountains, cliffs, hollows, ravines, ruddy crags, strewn boulders. It was a stern country, dry, treeless save for tamarisk or acacia growing far apart, mostly decked with waist-high tawny grass which whispered and rustled in the wind, often snatching at legs with the cruel hooks of thornbushes. That wind boomed warm across distances which stood sharp to vision in the utterly clear air. It smelled like hay and thunder. Sometimes the travelers passed a stone shelter or saw traces of kine, but herders had fled. Wild animals remained, or had drifted back after man departed – antelope of various kinds, giraffe, zebra, quagga, baboon, lion, seen afar. Butterflies danced gaudy, finches and cranes and francolins flew by, vultures wheeled aloft. Beyond them soared a lone golden eagle.

As she fared, Daris grew ever more happy. 'This is my land,' she exulted. 'I was born to these steep reaches, this huge sky, I am of those who range yonder heights, I have come home!'

Conan made no response. He was a child of Cimmeria in the North, snowy peaks, gloomy forests, chill rains, fugitive sun. Though he might never return there, and though the austere domain around him spoke to something in his spirit, he knew he could not long stay content in this parched brilliance.

Unless he left his bones here, he thought sardonically.

Toward evening of the second day, trouble sprang once again at their throats.

It happened suddenly. With a tor for landmark, Daris had been guiding her party toward a watercourse they could follow for much of the way. Long yellow light-rays in their faces, long shadows at their backs, they climbed a root of the hill and started down its other side. That slope was sharp, into a winding gulch. At the bottom the brook ran fast, noisy, bright in the shade, over smooth-worn rocks. Grass, herbs, rushes, dwarf trees along its banks were startlingly green after mile upon mile of the veldt above. Coolness welled upward.

'Hold!' Conan barked.

His gaze flew ahead. Beside the stream, some two score men had been pitching camp for the night. Large burdens lay stacked beside several pack mules. Cut thornbush did not actually make a defensive zareba in the manner of the Black Coast, but a low ring of it would discourage intruders and give warning of them. Animal chips burned in small flames; chopped deadwood ought to provide

122

a larger fire after dark. The men were variously clad in hides or tattered cloth garments or grass skirts, but they were all of the same breed, and it was not Taian. They were purely Negro.

'Travelers from Keshan?' wondered Daris in a tautened voice. She shaded her eyes against glare from the west and squinted into the early dusk below. 'No, they have not quite that appearance.'

'They look like dwellers along the seacoast of southern Kush,' said Conan. 'What might have brought them this far?'

The strangers had likewise seen his group. Yelps rose from them. They grabbed weapons and elliptical shields. Leaping over the thorn-ring, a few bounded uphill, well to right and left of the newcomers. The intent of these was clearly to see if there was anyone else. The majority drew into combat formation and advanced directly, at a slow walk.

'I like this not,' Conan growled.

'You cannot blame them for being suspicious,' Falco said.

'Well, no. We will try for peace, but keep ready to fight.' Conan lifted both hands, widespread. 'We are friends,' he called in Stygian.

A man who must be the leader stepped a little forth from the line of shields. Unlike the rest, who were young and lean, he was grizzled on his woolly pate and had a substantial paunch above his leopardskin kilt. His frame was big enough to carry it easily. Brass bracelets sheened on his thick arms; a golden torque coiled under his double chin and the wide-nosed, full-mouthed visage above. 'Who you?' he demanded. The almost unintelligible accent made clear that his knowledge of the language was slight. 'You from where? Why for?'

'We will go,' Conan offered. 'Now.'

Above him, the scouts waved and called. The leader paused for a moment, then his laugh rolled. 'Ho, ho, ho!' He bawled orders in his own tongue.

The blacks deployed, carnivore-swift. Half sprinted right and left, to reinforce the scouts or to move directly inward at Conan's band. The rest came straight on. 'You drop weapons,' the leader cried in Stygian. 'You be nice, we no kill.'

'No,' Conan sneered, 'you will only take us for the slave market.

And first Daris –' He unslung his ax. His tone became a roar. 'Better men than you have tried!'

Within, he thought that belike this was the end, for his comrades and himself. It was bitter to be destroyed by nothing more than blind chance; but what else did a soldier of fortune have any right to await? He brought his lips close to the woman's ear and said, 'Whatever happens, they will not get you alive. I swear.'

Her bowstring twanged. Immediately she snatched a fresh arrow. 'Thank you, dearest man,' she said, never looking from her targets. 'If my last kiss is of your ax, I will still know it is given in – in love, and bless you. May we meet again in the halls of Mitra.'

He had no such faith, but her calm eased the anguish in him, and he grinned as he took stance for battle.

'Yaah!' screamed Falco, and started to dash ahead. Conan clapped hold of his shoulder and jerked him to a halt. 'No, you fool,' the Cimmerian snapped. 'We stand back to back. Thus we will slay more of them.'

Daris' arrows caused two or three flesh wounds, but otherwise stuck in shields or missed. As the foe closed in, she dropped the bow, unbuckled her belt, and drew her dirk. Falco's saber glittered through arcs of challenge. Conan stood ominously poised.

The first man came against him, knobkerrie raised. Conan's ax leaped, smashed through a wood-and-leather shield, clove the neck behind. Blood fountained, a head fell and rolled, a body collapsed. 'Bêlit, Bêlit!' Conan shouted. He battered a shortsword from the owner's grasp. At the corners of his eyes he saw Daris drive her knife into an arm, Falco slice open a leg. A Suba war cry he had heard on the pirate galley ripped out of him. '*Wakonga mutusi!* Bêlit, Bêlit!'

The leader jumped backward. He ululated. At that signal, his followers withdrew. Headless corpse at his feet and weapon red in his grip, Conan thought wildly that a faint hope of his might have been realized. His group was still surrounded by armed men who glowered, but at a distance of two or three yards. Maybe the chief had decided three slaves were not worth casualties which might prove high, and would let his intended victims go.

The big-bellied Negro trod closer to confront the Cimmerian.

He uttered something. 'I do not know that language,' Conan told him in Stygian, though it sounded familiar.

'Do you know this?' the stranger asked in the lingua franca of the seaboard.

Conan's pulse fluttered. 'Yes, I do,' he responded likewise. 'See here, we are willing to let bygones be bygones if you are, and betake ourselves hence.'

'You cried a name,' said the black slowly. 'And words of the Suba. Do you know what those words mean?'

'Not really.'

The other's chuckle and grin were engaging, in a rascally fashion. 'I would render them as, "Death be damned; charge!"' He sobered. 'You cried a name. Say it anew, and tell me who bears it.'

For a moment, Conan bristled. However, he knew of no harm his obedience could do; and maybe it would help, if he had indeed stumbled upon members of that one tribe.

Pride rang in his answer. 'I called on Bêlit, because I am her man. She is daughter to Hoiakim of Shem, he whom the Suba entitled Bangulu.'

Awe and delight made the gross countenance almost comely. 'And I am Sakumbe, who knew Bangulu of old and dandled infant Bêlit on my knee,' the Negro said. 'Welcome, welcome!' He dropped his assegai and lumbered forward to enfold Conan in a smelly embrace.

The uncountable stars of Taia wheeled in majesty above its loneliness. Down where a brook chimed, a fire snapped high. Red and yellow light glowed in its pungent smoke and on the men who sat cross-legged around.

As had been the case at sea, the Suba held no grudge for a fellow slain or for injuries, none very serious, that others had sustained. In riotous cordiality, they offered shelter, food, what sour wine was left to them after their trek. They crowded close to listen, albeit none but their chief had a proper command of the lingua franca. From time to time he summarized for them, evidently in phrases more flamboyant than those he had heard.

125

'Aye,' Sakumbe related of himself, 'these have been bad years, since the Stygians found us. Weakened, we have been prey, over and over, to raiders from rival folk. Bêlit and her seafarers have made things better; the loot they bring home hires warriors from farther south for protection. Nevertheless we are but a wraith of what we were in the days of Bangulu. I, who had many cattle and yams and wives, am but a poor tramp who must seek his fortune wherever he can.

'I thought of joining Bêlit, but remembered how seasick I get. So I collected these lads and we fared off as traders. From the coast we bore mainly salt, for little else was left. Inland, we swapped this for ivory, feathers, rare woods, and the like. In Keshan we bartered to get ironwork, jewellery, unguents, spices ... and mules, to be sure, to be sure.' He picked up a wineskin, squirted his mouth full, belched, and passed the drink on. 'Rather than retrace our steps, I took us over the mountains, for word had come that southeastern Stygia was having woes, which might mean poor honest men could glean a trifle extra.'

'Including slaves,' Conan said.

'Why, yes, if that chance came along,' Sakumbe replied, unabashed. 'In fact, often on our trip have we bought a slave or three, to sell farther on at a bit of a profit. But in the case of this realm, well, says I to myself, the Stygians won't be keeping the tight control on trade they usually do; and there might even be a minikin of loot lying about in need of a caretaker.' He gusted a sigh. 'Thus far, though, we have only marched through desolation. You can't blame me for wanting to take three handsome, juicy people like you to market. How glad I am for my mistake! Too bad about Dengeda, of course, but, ah, well –' He slapped the Cimmerian's back. 'Any friend of Bêlit's is a friend of mine. And you are her husband, you say? Ho, ho, were I not a kind of uncle to the dear girl, I could envy you that!'

Conan grew somber. 'Best you turn back at dawn, over the pass to Keshan,' he advised. 'This land is in a sore plight. Not only tyranny and war are loose, but the worst kind of sorcery.'

'What?' Sakumbe registered uneasiness.

'You heard my tale. I do not think the magicians have stopped their malignant striving.'

126

Sakumbe frowned, hiccoughed, and said, 'Let me take counsel.' He indicated one who sat opposite him. Though younger than the chief, this person was older than the rest of his company, gaunt, hard-visaged, bleak-eyed. Cicatrices drew curious patterns over face and torso. 'Gonga is a witch doctor,' Sakumbe explained. 'Not as powerful as Kemoku, his master at home, no, not anywhere near as powerful. As yet, he has learned but a part of the lore. However, neither is he aged and infirm. I figured I would be wise to bring somebody along who knows something about magic. Let me question him.'

While the Suba words went back and forth, Conan related what he had heard to Daris at his side and Falco beyond her, in low-voiced Stygian. 'Honor demanded I warn our host to go back,' he finished. 'Yet I have an idea these bully boys might be useful allies, if we can recruit them. Shall I try?'

The woman nodded. 'Why not? My father needs every spear he can get. My country does.'

'Besides,' Falco added as his grin flashed forth, 'would it not be something if we, three fugitives, arrived at his headquarters with a platoon at our heels?'

After a while, Sakumbe told Conan: 'Against the mighty wizards of the Black Ring, Gonga says he can do nothing. Not even Kemoku could. Gonga does caution against lesser magics, such as are common among the Kushites and have drifted north into Stygia. Above all, body magic.'

'What is that?' the Cimmerian asked.

'Always be careful about anything that is from your body – nail clippings, hair, spittle, blood, sweat, anything – lest it falls into the hands of an enemy. If that enemy knows the spells, he will use the stuff to bring harm or death upon you. Reclaim it if you can, that Gonga may annul the charm. If you cannot, then at least give him a sample of the same, and he will try to use it defensively.'

Conan shrugged. When Falco, curious, inquired what had been communicated, the Cimmerian repeated the information, but added, 'Care about something like that is like care about poison. A measure of forethought is sensible, but too much will soon make a man into a sniveling coward.' He laughed. 'Whatever we do, we walk among snares and pitfalls, and death will take us in the end. I would rather give him a good fight then, than slink about through all the years before.'

He turned to Sakumbe. 'I bespoke hostile sorcery beneath whose feet yonder body magic can but grovel and whimper,' he said. 'Yet thus far we three have outwitted it, yes, tweaked its nose and left it howling. You did not seem unduly scared by my yarn. Well, what do you think about leaguing with us? One way or another, I am going to hew me a path to the sea and Bêlit. There should be plenty of Stygian plunder for you as we fare.'

Half drunk though he was, the Suba retained a trader's wiliness. 'I swear no brotherhood now,' he replied after a minute's pondering. 'But ... yes, why not go take a look? That is why we puffed and groaned over those nastily steep mountains, right? Right. Very well. Ho, ho, ho!' he guffawed. 'A guided tour of Stygia! See the ancient monuments! Visit the quaint shops! Bargains galore! Ho, ho, ho!'

Two days later, Conan and his enlarged band reached Thuran-on-the-Heights.

Warriors sprang from banked fires to challenge them. When some recognized Daris, jubilation winged on high and echoed back. Lissom brown forms leaped, steel flashed, plumes and banners gamboled on the wind. Above grassy slopes, camps, carven fragments, the temple of Mitra glowed in sundown light.

'My father is here,' Daris told Conan. Glory was over her like an aurora. 'So is the army he has gathered. You see but a part of it, because most are scattered across the hills, to have water and fuel. Horn-blasts can summon them within an hour. They have lately fought a pitched battle, when the Stygians moved in the direction of this holy place and were sent back licking their wounds. Oh, Conan!' In innocent exuberance, she seized him to her. Then, as she remembered herself, pain crossed her features.

Side by side, they advanced up the mountain. A tall, gray-haired man with a whetted countenance trod out on the temple portico. Conan knew this must be Ausar. Daris sped into her father's arms.

XV

THE AX AND THE EAGLE

In a big tent near the gracious remnants of the building, a lamp burned, for the two who sat there had talked at length. Light glimmered on racked weapons, a pile of sheepskins for sleeping, a few simple articles of furniture, a wine jug on a small table, the horns from which the men drank. The flap was drawn back on a view of heights and heavens; campfires strewn across the land gave ruddy reply to the stars. Cooling breezes carried odors of smoke and distance-muted snatches of song. Farther off, like a remote landslide, a lion roared.

Ausar rose and, after an instant's hesitation, Conan followed his example, as a third person entered. This was a man short, old, very dark-skinned for a Taian. His blue robe was threadbare. He had donned a pectoral of antique workmanship, lapis lazuli around a golden sunburst, which caused the clan chieftain to bow and sign himself. Yet somehow it was evident that that was not what gave him his air of power great and gentle.

'Parasan, high priest of Mitra, be welcome,' said Ausar. 'We hoped you could come earlier.'

The newcomer smiled as he limped to a seat. Conan took his staff and stowed it while Ausar poured wine for him, not into the horn that was good enough for a fighting man, but into a crystal goblet of the few that survived from ancient times. 'I supposed you would have much to discuss,' Parasan said.

'Yes, sir, but should you not have heard it, too?' the Cimmerian asked. He had been only briefly introduced to the prelate earlier this day, and had been amazed at the look of sheer wonder he got before solemnity masked it.

'I believe the details can wait,' the old man said. 'You twain – well, Ausar, I also have raised girls in my time. It seemed best that

129

you first calm your souls about Daris and about any other worldly business, for we have concerns before us which are not entirely of this world. Have you done so?'

The war lord settled himself, frowning. 'I am in Conan's blood debt,' he said slowly. 'He freed her and conveyed her back in more honorable wise than – Well, what she has confided to me is no fault of his, I suppose. Mainly we two have been telling each other about his journey and my war-waging.'

The Cimmerian flushed in embarrassment. Parasan raised a palm. 'No need to speak out what I can guess,' the priest murmured. 'Let Daris find consolation in pride. Without her, Conan would never have come to us. She has borne destiny, Ausar.'

A chill tingled through the Northerner. He did not understand this at all, and did not think he would like it when he did. Hunched forward on his chair, he strove to be courteous, but his tone roughened: 'What do you mean ... sir? I have told my host how chance brought me, nothing else. I wish you people well, and maybe I can do you some further service in exchange for some things I expect I shall need, but nailed to the masthead is my aim of winning back to my true lady as soon as may be.'

Wise and luminous, the eyes of Parasan caught his and would not let go. 'Do you indeed believe everything has been accident, Conan?' the priest responded as softly as before. 'I know better, and I have not even heard just what happened. Two gods are in struggle. We mortals are not mere instruments – no, it is we who must win or lose by our own efforts, lest the universe be torn asunder as they wrestle – but their wills are manifest. Shall an outpost of Mitra again flourish in freedom, for a light unto this part of the world, or shall the Serpent crush and poison it and the dominion of his sorcerers spread unrestrained abroad? That is what we make trial of.'

The young man sought to protest. Parasan would not let him: 'Of late I have prayed much, and offered Mitra such clean sacrifices as are acceptable to him, and pleaded for a sign. This has been granted me, in dreams and visions. Their meaning was enigmatic until today, but after you had come, I fell into a trance

130

before the altar, and more was revealed to me. I have no further doubt. You are he who shall bear the Ax of Varanghi.'

In grave words, he told the legend and the creed.

'No,' Conan whispered at the end. 'No, I am only a – a rover, a barbarian adventurer. I have been thief, bandit, pirate –'

'And the year will come, if you live, when you are a king,' Parasan said. 'What mortal has never done wrong? The Prophecy declares that the Wielder of the Ax will be of the Northern race which founded Taia, and worthy – not that he will be a saint.'

Excitement drove away Ausar's last reservations. 'The wizards in Khemi must have had reason to believe Conan is a threat to them!' he exclaimed. 'Did Set himself give warning, as Mitra has granted signs to you? Why else would those devils have gone to such trouble over a mere corsair?'

Parasan nodded his winter-crowned head. 'Aye; and indeed, though I am no magician, I dimly sense monstrous forces of evil nigh to us.' He straightened. 'But we can prevail over them. We must. Conan, accept your destiny. It is your way to freedom.'

The Cimmerian gnawed his lip. Having brought Daris home, he had thought he and Falco might return to the wingboat, proceed down the Styx, and at sea, rig a sail to bear them onward.

And yet – he could not but feel he still owed Daris a return for love and loyalty. Far more than that, he had beforehand taken up Bêlit's cause of vengeance upon Stygia; and lately he had promised Jehanan, who had saved his life, that he would tread the Snake underfoot in Jehanan's name. How much could he wreak with a single buccaneer crew?

'I speak no threat against you, who deserve well of us,' Parasan said quietly. 'But I swear by most high Mitra – may he forsake me if I lie – that a man who refuses a sacred duty laid on him is ... not accursed ... but abandoned; never again will he know honor or joy or love. Yes, Conan, our enterprise may fail, you may die in a strange land, but then you will die fulfilled; and if not, then for a time afterward – what little time the gods may allot, yet for a time – you shall have your dearest wish.'

The words struck into the wanderer like a knife. Dry-throated, he whispered, 'Where is this weapon?'

131

Ausar listened, shivering in tension.

'Will you wield it?' Parasan asked, unrelenting.

Conan had never been one to dither. All the storms in him came together and spoke: 'I will! By Crom, I will!'

And what a glorious fight would follow, thought a part of him.

Breath hissed between Ausar's teeth. Parasan nodded again, serene, and told them: 'Now hear what we few priests in Mitra's Taian temple have bequeathed from lifetime to lifetime for a hand of centuries. When the last king fell, he who afterward became the Prophet was at his side. This holy man took the holy implement beneath his cloak and bore it off the field. Well did he know that the Stygians would ransack Taia from end to end in search of a thing so foreboding to them. It must be hidden where no one would ever search.'

Conan's prosaic practicality made him interrupt: 'Why has no magician tracked it down in all this time? If it is from heaven, it ought to show plain against common earth, to any questing spell.'

'The virtue of the Ax wards every kind of magic off itself,' Parasan explained. 'If somehow a wizard did find and seek to recover it, his own powers would recoil and blast him. Even a mortal in a wizard's service would be so tainted by those forces that the Ax would destroy him. An ordinary man, whether a chance adventurer or someone hired for this task only, should be able to take up the weapon without coming to harm. But nobody would go to its hiding place at a mere venture, and belike there is not gold enough in Stygia to pay an expedition.

'For the Ax lies in Pteion.'

Ausar gasped.

'The holy man's sanctity repelled demons and ghouls when he entered and buried it,' Parasan went on. 'Know, Conan, that Pteion is a ruined city of immemorial antiquity, in eastern Stygia just across the Taian border. Chronicles declare it was founded by the Acheronians, thousands of years ago; but legend, which may well be true, says that they were only inheritors, and the true builders were the serpent men of prehistoric Valusia. For untold centuries it was the seat of black magicians and thus of terror; but during the Seventh Dynasty of Stygia, the desert encroached until

132

Pteion was abandoned and the wizards moved their center to Khemi. Uncontrolled, the foul beings they raised or created have haunted the ruins ever since, and no man goes near.'

Conan shuddered. Sweat broke forth upon him. His spirit groaned.

'I repeat, no devil has power over the Ax, which came to Varanghi from Mitra himself,' Parasan said. Each word seemed to peal more dread out of his listeners. 'Bold men, in a noble cause, entering by day, may dare hope to carry out their mission. If they be no saints, as the Prophet was, still they can fare under what benediction is mine to give, and keep their hearts sufficiently pure that evil finds no entry for stinging them from within. Yes, I think you will bear forth the Ax, Conan.'

'And then?' the Cimmerian heard himself mumble.

'Why, then you will lead the warriors of Taia as they win freedom for their land,' Parasan replied. Abruptly, astoundingly, he laughed. 'I leave the details of that to the professionals.'

More than an hour followed, in which Conan and Ausar talked while, for the most part, the priest sat mute. He heard the story of what had happened, he asked questions and made a few suggestions, he saw courage flame up in the others.

They went on to tactics. Further discussion would be necessary in the morning, but the outline of a plan grew rapidly. In the saddle, with ample remounts, at the fastest prudent pace, it was about a week's travel from Thuran to Pteion. That was because much of the route was through the valley of a river that had long since dwindled to a brook, easier going for horses than most of this country was. Let Conan and his guide bring a troop of about a hundred men; such a number ought to suffice against any foreseeable contingency. Meanwhile let Ausar organize his host and move west, recruiting as he went.

After losing the latest engagement, General Shuat had left half his Stygians to garrison Seyan and the lower Helu. He was marching the remainder northwest, on a military road that ran from the governor's seat toward Luxur. Ausar guessed he planned a pincers movement, quite likely in conjunction with re-inforcements sent from the royal capital. Let Conan's band rejoin their kinsmen after the Ax had been retrieved, and they could all seek to reduce the Stygians in detail.

Of course, King Mentuphera and his immense reserves would be left, and he would scarcely let the loss of a detachment or two check his ambitions. However, that worry was best deferred to the unknowable future. If Conan had learned anything about war, it was that the first casualty of a battle is always one's battle plan.

Exalted, he finally rose to say good night. 'May I accompany you back to the temple, sir?' he asked Parasan.

'No, thank you,' said the priest. 'Though you be chosen of Mitra, you are not initiated into his mysteries as Ausar and I are. I think best we two pray together for a while.'

The younger warrior felt no offense, nor for that matter any particular desire to be initiated. Crom was in many ways a much less demanding god. With a wave, Conan stepped forth into darkness.

Brilliant though the stars were, his eyes needed a moment to adapt. He saw his breath smoke white beneath them, and –

And what was the shape rising yonder, as if it had lately been on the ground near Ausar's pavilion? An eagle? No, that could scarcely be; eagles were not nightfowl, nor would one descend this close to humans. It must be some other kind of large bird.

After all, he was in a strange country. He should not let a chance-met wild creature disturb him. Yet he wished he had not been so stubbornly honorable. The human warmth of Daris would have been very welcome just now. Conan hastened toward his lonely tent.

Made tireless by her magic, Nehekba flew across hundreds of miles, faster than aquiline flesh and blood would ever be able. A second false dawn turned the east cold, when she discerned Luxur beneath her and slanted earthward.

At the snake-encircled cupola atop the temple of Set, she glided through an arch to its deck and resumed her human form. Feather-clad, she descended to a suite reserved for members of the Black Ring. There she rested and planned until midmorning. At that time she dispatched a messenger to the king, bearing a token which would get him immediately received and a written request for a confidential audience. It was a request in form only; she required it. The monarch knew that and sent back a prompt invitation.

At the appointed hour, duly stately in crown and robes, she crossed the plaza to the palace. In order to emphasize the gravity of the occasion, she did not go afoot, but in a brazen chariot without wheels or tongue, that bore her along three feet off the ground. Awed guardsmen bowed low, stood well away from her vehicle after it had settled to earth and she stepped out, provided a man to escort her inside.

She was ushered into a room small but well appointed. Scenes of the chase ornamented its walls, and the furniture was lavishly carven and gilt. Mentuphera bade her be seated. He himself filled a silver wine cup for her.

'I hope that my lady, high priestess of Derketa, will accept the presence of my first son,' he said. 'I want him to learn how such things are also a part of statecraft.'

Nehekba shrugged. 'If you desire, Your Majesty,' she replied, careful to observe the niceties. While Mentuphera was apprehensive of her and her colleagues, he was no weakling. On the contrary, Stygia had not had so formidable a secular lord for generations. He was a tall man, heavily muscled in his plain tunic, scarred from many a combat. His face was square, weatherbeaten, broken-nosed, his eyes like metal. Ever at his hip, even when he wore dress of state, hung a sword. Despite his deference to the witch, he did not try to conceal the lechery that flickered in his glance across her beauty; they had often shared a bed.

'In truth,' she continued, 'you are wise to let the crown prince hear. O King, live forever. Yet the gods alone see what lurks behind tomorrow's sunrise, and I bear tidings of peril.'

Ctesphon, heir apparent, a slender man no longer quite young, stirred uneasily on his seat. 'My lord father,' he ventured, 'should we not have your counsellors here as well? The words of a sorcerer are often darkling – no disrespect to my lady – and no single mind can think of every issue that should be raised.'

'I desired private discussion,' Nehekba reminded sharply. 'Much of what I am about to tell Your Majesty should not be noised abroad, lest fear breaks its chains and run loose in Stygian hearts.'

Mentuphera gave his son a doubtful glance, but decided not to dismiss him. Ctesphon had frequently argued that the plan of conquering an empire was unwise. However, since he could not dissuade his father, he worked loyally and ably in the cause; he hunted lions in his chariot; searching for arcane knowledge from which Mentuphera's hard soul shrank, he dared correspond with Tothapis' exiled rival, Thoth-Amon the terrible.

'Say on,' the king rumbled.

'Your Majesty knows the legend the Taians tell, of the Ax of Varanghi,' Nehekba began.

'Wistful folklore,' Mentuphera snorted. Ctesphon grew tense.

'Would that it were,' Nehekba responded. She went on to describe – in a version preserving the dignity of herself and Tothapis – what had happened and what she had lately spied on. 'I fear we cannot get men to Pteion ahead of Conan by any earthly means,' she finished, 'and to transport them magically would be but to send a quite inadequate number against his troop, given the limited time and means available to us. Besides, such an experience would wreck their morale and leave them easy prey to him.'

'By the fangs of Set!' The king's fist crashed on an arm of his chair. 'A lout like that, the chosen instrument of – of Mitra? Why, if the Sun Master can do no better than Conan, what is to fret about?'

'Much, my lord father,' Ctesphon murmured. 'Only think what the barbarian has done thus far, with no supernatural weapon.'

'Yes,' Nehekba agreed. 'Your majesty, hesitation on our part will mean loss of that entire province, which will thereafter stand armed and hostile at your back. What then of your dreams of foreign conquest?

'No, mobilize the strongest force you possibly can on short notice. Command it yourself, leaving the crown prince here as viceroy, for your presence will instill valor no matter what your soldiers meet. March southeast at once, within days, to bring Taia to submission. Meanwhile, we who serve Set will strive by every art we possess to keep the Ax that Mitra forged in the grave where it

136

belongs. Should we fail in that, do not despair, for we shall have further resources. One way or another, given your help in this world, O King, we shall succeed against your enemy in the heavens.'

'Aye!' Mentuphera shouted.

In a crypt below the temple of Set, candle flames flickered blue. There on a table, among the shadows, stood a glass vessel in the form of a womb. Within this floated the pale, curled, half-formed figure of a babe unborn.

Nehekba entered. An acolyte in attendance prostrated himself before her. 'Go,' she said, and he crawled out backward.

Leaning over the womb, staring into the blind face beneath her, she drew signs and muttered words. The homunculus stirred. Agony twisted the blob that was its countenance. Words came out of its throat in little plopping globules: 'Who calls me? What would you?'

'It is I, Nehekba,' the witch hissed. 'Heed well, Tothapis, and set all else aside. I do not say that the Wreck of the Gods draws nigh, though that may be; but surely an hour is upon us when, once more, the Bull and the Serpent make war.'

Across as many miles as she had flown, the wizard spoke through the small monstrosity: 'Tell me what you have learned.'

She did. At the end, she said urgently, 'Fate hangs yet in the balance, and will while Conan lives.' Her nails scratched the air. 'That need not be for long. But it will take mighty magic to halt him; his destiny is in spate. My lord, do not crouch in your house any more. Come forth yourself, on dragon wings, with your spells prepared. Meanwhile I will return to spy on Conan and work what spells I can on whatever weaknesses I sense in him and his companions. By such means did my predecessor, five hundred years ago, finally make vulnerable the last man who wielded the Ax.

'Let us meet at Pteion of the ghouls, my Lord – and you and I destroy him!'

XVI

JOURNEY TO THE DAMNED

Stones rattled beneath hooves. Glowering from the west, a sun tinged bloody by dust made eyes ache that already stung from sweat and were weary after days of squinting at naught but desolation. Light and unmerciful heat rebounded from the walls of the gorge through which the Taians rode. Those red slopes grew lower, less steep and cragged, for every mile; but that was merely because the travelers were approaching open desert. Patches of sand ahead shimmered in an illusion of water that redoubled thirst.

Mostly the warriors fared in silence, nursing their steeds along. Kaftans and burnooses they had donned against this clime fluttered around their lean bodies. Spears swayed to the rhythm of riding, points ablaze with the radiance, as if wind passed over a grainfield on fire. Though the men had no love for the wasteland around them, they suffered less than did their Northern leader. At the head of his hundred, Conan endured.

Some yards behind him, Daris brought her horse next to Falco's. 'How goes it for you, friend?' the woman asked. 'You have said almost nothing on this trip.'

The Ophirite shrugged and did not turn his face to look at her. More than parchedness roughened his voice. 'What has there been to talk about?'

'Why, everything,' she answered softly. 'Hopes, dreams, memories – even fears, if naming those would help give power over them. You were a cheerful soul before, Falco. What gnaws at you of late? That tomorrow we reach dread Pteion?'

'I am not afraid!' he flared. 'I didn't have to come along.'

'Nor did I. But then, Conan is my lord for ... as long as he and Mitra will have it so. You, though, would be no coward, would rather be of service equal to this, if you had accompanied my father instead, as Sakumbe and his men agreed to do.'

'For plunder! Do you liken me to those savages?'

'I think much more than greed is in their hearts, Falco. I think there is love for Bêlit and the shades of her parents, there is a wish to avenge the rape of their motherland.' Daris paused. 'As for you, you chose to follow Conan because in your heart also he has become your lord for whom you would gladly die. Is that not true?'

Falco's knuckles whitened where he held his reins, but he made no reply.

'Yet this journey has oppressed you more for each day that has passed,' Daris murmured. 'Why? If you would tell your friends, maybe they could help.'

'Oh, Conan has burdens enough,' the youth blurted, 'and I scarcely know any Taians.'

'You know me,' Daris said, and reached forth to touch his hand. 'Our comradeship has been short in time, aye, but must go deeper than most, after everything we have done together. Would you like to call on me? I see no more shame in crying for help from a sworn waymate when the soul is beset by devils, than when the flesh is ringed in by enemy swords.'

Goaded, he turned on her and rasped, 'But you are the cause!'

Her dark eyes widened, though the gold-skinned countenance showed compassion rather than surprise. 'In what way?' she responded low. 'Never wittingly or willingly, I swear.'

'Oh, I – you –' Pride and need struggled inside him. His sunburnt cheeks grew redder still. 'Very well,' broke from him at last, in ragged words, while his own gaze roved everywhere except toward her. 'You came along, the only woman among us, and only for Conan's sake. I have not failed to see how your look is ever straying to him and lingering, how often you find excuses to speak with him, short-tempered though he has grown in this hell-country. Oh, I am not jealous, but you are a goodly sight, Daris, and ... you bring back Senufer, who grieves for me in Khemi as I do here for her –' Fist pounded saddlebow. 'She comes back to me too much, too fully. At night I cannot sleep, by day I go about in a dream of her, always her dear voice whispers her name till it sings through me like wind through a harp, Senufer, Senufer, Senufer –'

He gulped air and shuddered his way back toward a degree of calm. 'I'm sorry,' he gulped. 'I spoke wrongly. You are not to blame. But I long for her, Daris, I long for her beyond your understanding.'

He did not see how uneasiness went through his companion. She smoothed off outward signs of it, rode closer until their knees touched, laid a hand on his arm, and said very softly, 'Thank you, Falco. You do bring me to understand, a little – at least about what is troubling you. Keep it not dammed in your breast, till it overflows and bears your spirit off on its torrent. Talk to me, if no one else. Tell me whatever you need to tell. Let me help you look beyond this span of waiting and yearning, to that dawn when you can begin your life anew. Let me invoke hope in you.'

Conan, glancing behind, saw them thus. Unreasonable anger brawled suddenly up in him.

The gorge debouched on a seemingly endless wilderness of ocherous sand dunes. They gritted underfoot. Dust streamed on a droning breeze, to clog nostrils and irritate eyes.

As the sun neared the horizon and shadows grew gigantic, Tyris the guide approached his commander. He had come through these parts in former years when he worked as a caravan guard. 'Best we camp now,' he advised. Pointing to an eroded outcrop in the distance: 'If they spoke aright when I passed by here, we are within a few hours of Pteion. Not that anybody ever went there, but the traders keep their lore from of old.'

Conan scowled. 'We can push on for another of those hours this evening, in cooler air,' he said.

Tyris fingered an amulet on his breast. 'Chieftain, is not our plan that we enter by day, when fiends and phantoms are underground? Well, I do not think we would be wise to sleep any closer than where we are.'

'As you will,' the Cimmerian said contemptuously.

Hurt, Tyris rode from him to convey that order. Mounts, remounts, and pack beasts stopped the instant their masters gave signal; grateful snorts and whickerings resounded. Men cared for them with what scanty water, fodder, and grooming were available, hobbled them, and bivouacked. Soon bedrolls lay spread, chips burned blue, and around each small fire squatted several warriors. Taians were generally not a dour folk; beneath their dignity bubbled considerable joy in life. Now, however, a somberness was upon them and they spoke in few words and hushed voices. Many drew aside to pray, pour out libations, attempt minor magics.

Conan stalked about inspecting the pickets. Often he spoke gruff reprimands for carelessness. They were not really deserved, and were therefore resented, and he knew as much. It was as if he must slap out at someone.

Beyond camp, silhouetted black against a green sunset sky, Daris and Falco stood face to face, hands linked, deep in converse. After a while they walked down the far side of the dune and were lost to sight.

For a moment Conan wondered if the sullenness that had been gathering in him throughout the past few days had any good cause. What son of the North would not grow snappish in these ghastly barrens? He had known countless hardships, but this was the worst, this sucked vampirelike at his very spirit. Yet did it not behoove him to refrain from complaint, even in his own mind? Why did he let mere discomfort prey on him?

Well, there was worse than that. He had gone without a woman for longer stretches in the past than thus far since leaving Bêlit. But lately the time had begun feeling like years. And then that empty-headed Daris had insisted on being in the expedition and kept throwing her presence at him. Could the jill-flirt not see what fires she stoked? Were it not for her countrymen and their disapproval, he might well have kicked his scruples aside and taken her. By Derketa, he might lead her beyond view of the clansmen and do it anyway! Except that now she had begun to play her tricks on that Ophirite brat. What had *he* done to deserve the enjoyment?

Ha, if that was what she wanted, let her eat alone when she got back. Conan was hungry.

He slouched to the place that was his, hers, and Falco's. They had been eating together and spreading their sleeping bags not far apart. The man who had laid out their gear and started a fire for them rose, salaamed, and left. Conan hunkered down. He spitted and toasted slices of dried meat, onions, and peppers; he drank warm, ill-tasting water from a skin; he drew a cloak about his shoulders against the gathering chill. Not sleepy, in no mood for company, he sat alone and considered his wrongs. Bêlit felt unreachably far away. Twilight swiftly became night, and stars crowded forth.

Daris returned, in a scrunch of sand beneath bare feet. He glanced up. Her form was tall and shadowy above him. 'Hunh,' he grunted. 'At last. Where's Falco?'

'He decided he would stay off by himself for a while and think over what we talked about,' she replied.

'Talked? I hope you had a good romp.'

'What?' She settled down opposite him. Dim firelight glimmered in eyeballs. 'What do you mean?'

'What do you suppose?' he retorted. 'Oh, I know, I have no claim on you. Do as you please.'

'Conan!' He had never heard such shock in her before, nor seen it on her. She sat upright, both hands lifted as if to ward off a blow. 'You don't imagine – How could you?'

'Do you suppose I am blind? He's a pretty boy, whereas I have been dull company of late. I tell you, I don't mind. Eat. I am going to my rest.'

'But I love you!' Daris nearly sobbed. She caught hold of herself. After a few heartbeats she said quietly but steadily, looking straight at him. 'Hear me. By Mitra I swear, nothing untoward has happened, unless you count a single brief kiss at the end. Falco and I talked, simply talked. He was sick for that Senufer woman in Khemi.'

'For Nehekba, you mean,' Conan sneered. 'The more fool he.'

'I did not repeat our idea to him, that the two are the same. That would have driven him from me. No, I got him to talk about himself, no hard task for me. After he had spilled out his sorrow, it weighted him much less, and I could lead him back to such fancies of the future as belong to a healthy lad. He is not free of her by any means, but his spirit has returned to him. I think he will sleep well tonight and be able to fight tomorrow if need be. That is all, Conan, all that went on ... though my own thoughts did not end there.'

142

'I must take your word, of course,' he said with studied indifference.

She regarded him in a kind of horror. 'Conan, what has been happening? What sorcery has been at work? It is not like you to be this surly, yes, nasty. Nor was it like Falco to wallow in self-pity till he was almost useless. Have demons of the desert possessed you?'

Her mind racing ahead, she did not see his resentment increase. 'No,' she mused, while her gaze sought the stars, 'not that, when you both kept plodding loyally onward. But a black spell could have played on weaknesses – his infatuation; your vexation by a country never meant for your race, and ... yes ... even more, no doubt, your yearning for Bêlit. Re-echoing such moods, the spell could worsen them beyond what nature would have allowed.' Her look returned to him. Eagerness entered her tone. 'If I am right, it cannot be an actual binding laid on you. Falco has cast if off him, with my help. Let me next help you, my beloved!'

'Why should you trouble?' Conan snapped. 'I am surly, nasty, and weak, remember?'

He saw in the gloom how she flinched, and all at once wanted to take her in his arms and tell her he was sorry. Before he could speak, pride responded to him. The daughter of Ausar rose to her feet under the stars and said, 'We will talk more of this whenever you feel ready. First seek the rest that you desire. Good night.' She took her sleeping bag and walked off into the dark.

Conan lay long awake, trying to puzzle out what he should have done. They could have argued rights and wrongs till dawn, when he needed his sleep against the morrow. Women!

The noonday sun made heaven a furnace, the land beneath a bed of coals. Air wavered until dunes at a distance looked uneasy as flames; but there went no ghost of a breeze. Sounds of hoofbeats, creaking harness, jingling metal vanished into an infinity of silence, like raindrops vanishing into an eternal drought.

Conan slitted his eyes and strove to observe what lay ahead. Glare, mirage, and distance turned the sight unreal, a bad dream. Drifts of sand were piled nearly to the top of what remained of outer walls. Where these had crumbled, he descried buildings within, black stone masses, equally ruinous; yet somehow the shapes kept a hint of the inhuman, too low and narrow for their length, sides slanting at curious angles up to roofs grotesquely decorated. Legend said that most of the city had been underground; it whispered that those vaults and passages were to this day inhabited. A number of monoliths and twisted columns were standing, whether isolated or in groups. At the middle of the city loomed the form of a dolmen, a prehistoric tomb, but built of polished ebon slabs so huge that no man could tell how they had been raised into place.

There, Conan recalled from Parasan's words, was where the Ax of Varanghi awaited him. Despite his ill humor, despite the primitive fears that surged beneath a hard-held determination, his pulse leaped. He drew sword and swung it on high for an oriflamme. 'Onward!' he trumpeted, and spurred his horse to a canter.

His men lifted a ragged cheer and followed. They too felt qualms, but they were all volunteers; if nothing else, the honour of their clans forbade them to be daunted.

As the troop advanced, a wind sprang up. It whined across illimitable wastes, it plucked at garments and sucked at throats and lungs. Dust devils whirled. Grit scudded; Conan crunched it between his teeth.

Faster than he thought should be possible, haze boiled over the horizon and across the sky. The sun reddened, dimmed, vanished. Driving darkness hid his goal. The storm lacerated his skin and well-nigh choked off his breath, before he drew a flap of his burnoose around for a veil. His horse stumbled, whinnying in pain. He roweled the animal savagely and pushed on. If nothing else, he thought amidst the shrill howling, the hiss of dust and sand in flight, his party must find shelter till the weather died down: and where was that but in Pteion?

Blurred vastness appeared to right and left, pieces of the city wall. He flogged his horse to go in between. Though he got some relief beyond, with those ancient defenses for a windbreak, the air was still acrid and murky, and the red-black gloom was thicker still. Ahead, he vaguely made out one or two of the buildings he had seen

144

from afar. A look over his shoulder revealed the nearest of his followers. Those farther back were lost to sight, but doubtless each man kept in view the ones immediately before him. Wind yelled.

No – that screech was something different! Conan twisted round in his saddle and saw what came out of the night suddenly laid on this ground, move toward him in attack.

XVII

QUEST OF THE AX

At first it seemed a troop of human soldiers advanced in a strangely stiff formation from the inner city. The question flashed through him how they could have arrived this fast, when the closest well-populated region in Stygia was remoter than Thuran. He reined in and signaled his men to draw nigh, dismount, secure their animals, prepare for combat. The highlanders had no cavalry tradition. He kept his own stirrups, and gestured Falco to do the same. Theirs were trained war-horses captured from the enemy. A couple of skilled horseback fighters ought to count for much, when yonder force had nobody riding.

Again a horn screamed, like none that Conan had ever heard before. Overtones ripped at his nerves. The noise did not come from the foe, but from above. The barbarian glanced up. Though scudding dust choked off vision within yards, he thought he glimpsed a deeper darkness in motion there, as if great wings wheeled and soared.

The strangers came onward. Now Conan saw their front ranks more clearly. He stiffened. Terror stabbed him. Daris, also still in the saddle, stifled a scream. Falco called on his gods. The Taians wailed.

Those were not living men, they were dried corpses. Some bore archaic helmets and cuirasses over blackened skin, most wore only cerements gone ragged during millennia. In many, bones jutted through desiccated flesh. The sunken faces were unstirring, empty of expression; what eyes remained were dull, tearless, unwinking; breasts drew no breath, hearts did not beat behind ribs. Legs moved puppetlike. The company was armed with shortswords of antique shape or spears whose heads flared in the same fashion. The metal was corroded green bronze. The bodies numbered two hundred or more. The shuffle of their feet was the single sound they made.

'Ghosts, ghosts,' Daris moaned. 'The tombs of Pteion have yielded their dead to go against us.'

Aye, thought Conan fleetingly, in this unnatural gloom all sun-shunning horrors could come forth. But who had raised it before raising them? How could anyone in Stygia have known the Taian plan? A second shock pierced him as he remembered what he had earlier chosen to forget, the eagle outside Ausar's tent.

Tyris the guide screamed. 'Mitra, forgive me that I entered this unholy place!' Conan heard an answering babble among the warriors. He glanced back, saw them assembled but in an array that wavered. At any instant, somebody would bolt. Then blind panic would seize the rest and stampede them forth to perish in the desert.

The horn above the storm laughed.

Conan never knew whether sheer desperation drove out his own fear, or the smouldering anger of his journey burst into flame. Battle fury took hold of him. He spurred forward. 'Hai, Crom!' he roared. 'Varuna of the Lightning! *Wakonga mutusi!* Bêlit, Bêlit!'

A cadaver in the front line jerkily raised its spear and thrust at him. The point glanced off the chain mail beneath his slit kaftan, which he had donned this morning. He struck it aside. His mount pushed on at his behest, into the throng. He leaned over. The sword blazed in his hand. He felt steel hit, meet less resistance than from living muscle, and shear on through. A head flew free, struck the sand, rolled to a halt. Hideously, the body did not bleed or fall – but it tottered about, spear flailing, as might a decapitated insect.

Conan reared his charger. Hooves came down, crushed bone, smashed a form to shapelessness that writhed. He smote at a helmet. The impact clanged dully, split age-eaten metal, did not reach the skull but broke a fragile neck. That head lolled as the owner continued striking. Conan hewed off the sword arm.

Falco had plucked up heart and ridden into the fray. His saber whirred. Daris, inexperienced in this sort of fighting, nonetheless kept her steed a-dance on the fringes and wielded a spear.

Yet the dead were not feeble. Slow, awkward, they felt no pain,

147

lost no blood, could only be disabled by the shrewdest of blows. Gashes reddened the horses, surrounded by thrusters and stabbers. The riders began to take flesh wounds, and might at any moment receive worse. Meanwhile most of the deathling troop had rustled past them and fallen on the Taians.

'Break through!' Conan cried to Falco. In a right-and-left hail of sword-cuts, thunder of kicks and stampings, they did. The corpses they had fought did not pursue, but went on to join battle against the clansmen. Dismembered pieces jerked and squirmed at their rear.

Conan drew deep, shaken breaths through a fold of his burnoose. Shielding eyes with hands, he looked toward the combat. It raged loud and frightful, men sustained slashes and stabs, men fell dead and *they* moved no more. But the Taians held fast. War cries and panted clan chants defied hooting wind and sibilant red dust. He had shown them that a strong arm and an undaunted heart could meet even such as these.

'Shall we attack from behind?' Falco asked. Ardor burned in his eyes.

'No,' Conan decided. 'We would only be two more, and the outcome of that fight is odds-on at best. Also, we know not what further devilments the enemy has at his beck. Best we take this chance to seek the Ax. If Parasan spoke sooth, that is a weapon to use against hell itself.'

Daris drew nigh. 'It is fitting that the three of us go,' she said. Her look upon Conan pleaded, *May I again be your comrade?*

The Cimmerian shook his head. 'No, best you stay here and encourage the men. Some will see Falco and me leave, and wonder, and their will could break yet. If you abide, though, their princess, descendant of Varanghi – do you understand?'

Pain tightened her lips, but she nodded. 'Yes. Mitra ward you.' Unable to say more, she trotted off.

Conan stared after her for a second before he clipped, 'Let's begone,' and led the way on into the city. Sight and sound of the battle were soon lost.

Black walls lined a buried street. Though low and sloping, they gave added protection from the storm. One could see somewhat farther and breathe somewhat easier. But the rusty light was no more than on a moonlit night when demons may wander abroad. Swords unsheathed, Conan and Falco made for the giant dolmen by memory, observation, and sense of direction rather than vision.

'I have heard,' said the Ophirite, 'that after Pteion was abandoned by the living, it was used for several generations as a burial ground.'

Conan wondered momentarily what they had been like in life, those men whose dead bodies he had hacked asunder. Had they also laughed, loved, drunk deep, fared afar, begotten, sorrowed, wished for immortality? Were their liches mere machinery used by a sorcerer – Tothapis, surely Tothapis! – or were their souls still trapped within?

Ahead on his left, he saw a portal yawn wide. Carved in the stone above it, time-blurred by recognizable, was an outsized human skull. Abruptly he halted and cursed. Figures were issuing thence.

They pullulated forth like maggots from rotting flesh till they formed a line three or four deep across the way. Conan's throat constricted, and a cold crawling passed over him. The naked, gray-skinned forms were manlike, in a skeletal fashion, but inhumanly long arms ended in great claws, and many squatted on all fours as jackals might while digging up a grave. Bestial too were the hairless heads, point-eared, muzzled, fanged, with eyes aglow like the eyes of owls. They leered, gibbered, let black tongues hang out, pawed the sand, crouched waiting.

'Ghouls,' Falco groaned. 'What mummies laid away through ages keep them fed?' The hand that drew a Sunsign trembled, the mouth that mumbled a prayer was dry. Thereafter he was able to ask, 'Sh – shall we retreat, try to find a different approach?'

Conan mastered his own dismay, squeezed it down into a solid lump of loathing. 'No,' he grated. 'this dump must be acrawl with different things just as bad. And we could easily get lost. There's no time to waste. We'll go on through.'

'I am afraid that a single bite or scratch from those carrion eaters – deadly infection –'

'Then see to it that they don't get at you.' Conan raked spurs. His steel flashed on high. 'Crom, Varuna, Bêlit!'

Falco swallowed hard and galloped beside him. Hooves thudded, horses neighed, men shouted. The ghouls yowled back.

The riders hit them. Conan's sword flamed downward. He struck a misshapen cranium, felt the force jar back through his shoulders, saw inky blood spout. He must have missed a tiny brain, for the creature did not die; but it fell, yammering, and prattled obscenely.

Another ghoul sprang from the left, to grab him and drag him from the saddle. His left fist smashed into the flat nose. Checked in midleap, the attacker fell under the horse, which trampled it. Hooves lashed and kicked. More beings seethed around. Their howls and cackles drowned out the weather. Conan struck from side to side as fast as they came in reach. His horse screamed when claws raked flanks, but fought the more furiously. Nearby, Falco's saber whined, sliced, stabbed; his shield guarded him on the left against creatures that pounced at him; his own beast reared, smashed, bit, whinnied terrifyingly loud.

Then the riders had broken those disordered ranks and were beyond. They went several yards, slammed to a stop, and looked back. The ghouls milled witless. Some were already tearing at the slain. Conan charged. His lion roar echoed from wall to wall. Panic-smitten, the ghouls fled, streamed back into the house of the skull, left none but their dead and mewling wounded.

Conan returned. 'I thought best to scatter those vermin before they forget the lesson we taught them,' he said. 'Are you all right?'

'They never touched me, praise the kind gods,' Falco replied, breathless. 'You?'

'The same.'

'But I fear for our poor animals.'

'They will bear us a while more. If their wounds get inflamed beyond healing, we will give them the last mercy. Now, onward.'

Deeper into the necropolis the pair rode. From lightless doorways and murky porticos, eyes glistened, they heard voices chitter and feet scuttle, but nothing emerged. 'Keep alert,' Conan warned. 'I doubt Master Tothapis has emptied his whole bag of tricks.'

The streets twisted and intertwined in maddening chaos. He must ever note landmarks – a cockscomb roof, a stump of pillar, a statue eroded to shapelessness – lest he lose direction in the drifting dust. It helped that he could shortcut across buildings which had collapsed to rubble heaps. He swore when a deepening of the gloom ahead proved to be a wall squarely across his path. Which way around would be shorter? It was impossible to see. Well, most folk reckoned right luckier than left. Conan chose it.

The wall ended after about a hundred yards. He and Falco confronted a broad, bare space. Low dunes hid pavement, but this must in its time have been a plaza like that in Luxur, for two enormous ruins stood on either side. Their ebon masses gave less protection from the whistling, scudding storm than had the narrower streets, though they did give some. The far end of the square seemed to be open; Conan got an impression of a broad avenue and of shapes which stood along it, but the murk obscured too much for him to be sure.

Still, as nearly as he could tell, that way pointed straight at the dolmen. He clucked to his weary steed, stroked a mane that sweat had plastered to the neck, and started across. He and Falco were halfway over when the boy yelled.

'Crom!' exploded from Conan. He fought to control a destrier that suddenly plunged, bucked, and whinnied in terror. Falco's had gone just as unruly. What they saw coming woke primordial instincts. How many eons had yonder monsters been locked in enchanted sleep before they were wakened to walk the earth again, ravenous?

From the right-hand edifice bounded an animal akin to a hyena but the size of a bull. Stiff pelt bristled, mouth grinned and slavered around yellow fangs, a howl like a maniac's laughter shuddered through the wind. It paused at the doorway, studied the scene with snuffing nose, cocked ears, intelligent eyes, and loped ahead.

From the left-hand structure stalked a beast on two long, taloned legs. Though the body stooped forward, counterbalanced by a great cudgel of a tail, the blunt reptile head lifted twice a man's height. Small forelimbs were bent, claws laid together in a parody of prayer. Scales on back and sides sheened steel-gray through dimness; the belly sagged white. When it saw prey, the saurian hissed and hastened.

'Stay by me,' Conan snapped. 'We'll see if we can outspeed them.' He nearly broke his horse's neck, but got the hysterical brute pointed toward the avenue opposite and slacked its reins. It shot off. Blind instinct made Falco's follow.

They were nearly across the plaza when Conan heard a scream of agony and a triumphant whoop. He cast a look over his shoulder. The giant hyena had overhauled the Ophirite's mount. A slash had laid open the hindquarters. As the horse stumbled, the hyena snapped onto its throat. Gullet torn out, the charger went down in a red fountain, rider beneath. The saurian lumbered close behind.

Conan forgot his errand. A Cimmerian did not abandon a way-brother while the least hope flickered. He sheathed his sword and sprang from the saddle. In a ball of rubbery muscle, he hit the sand, rolled a few times, and bounced to his feet. The hyena worried the dead horse, snarling and slobbering. Falco, leg pinned under that weight, lay still.

Conan sidled off at an angle. His intention was to keep the saurian's attention locked to his own steed, overlooking him. It worked. The colossus marched on by. Its pace was deliberate, earthshaking, but each step was so long that the speed matched any gallop. Mammal and reptile vanished in the streaming dust.

Conan drew blade and pounded toward the hyena. That beast saw him, raised its grisly head, coughed a warning. 'Aye,' the warrior taunted, 'I am about to rob you of your food.' The hyena left its prey and stood in front, mane erect. Blood dripped from jaws that could halve a man in a bite.

Behind it, Conan saw Falco sit up and strive to work himself free. The barbarian rejoiced. His companion must have been feigning, not to attract a casual snap. Maybe the two of them could retreat after all, leaving the carnivore to its meat.

No! Conan had come too near. The creature howled and charged.

Conan braced himself. The hyena's head gaped nearly level with his own. Through sleeting dust, he stared down a huge maw, he caught a rankness of breath, he felt each thud of paws in his footsoles. His sword went over his shoulder. As the foe came in reach, he smote.

The edge bit through nose and muzzle. The hyena bayed, ear-piercingly, and withdrew. Buried deep in bone, the sword was torn from Conan's grasp. The hyena dashed to and fro, crying its pain, while blood rivered from its snout. But the injury was not mortal. It remembered who had smitten it, halted, growled utter hatred, and advanced stiff-legged. Conan drew his dirk and prepared to die.

Falco limped from the rear, saber in hand. Again the Cimmerian saw a chance. He must hold the monster's entire notice on himself. 'Nice doggie,' he crooned. 'Come here, I have something for you, doggie.'

The titan bunched muscles for a leap. Falco lurched alongside. His saber went in between ribs. The hyena yowled, louder than the gale, and bore off the Ophirite's weapon, too.

Out of hasty red gloom trod an enormous shape. Conan's horse must have escaped in a maze of streets. The saurian had come back in search of easier game.

As the hyena turned on its newest tormentor, Conan attacked. His left hand grabbed wiry hair, yanked it aside. His right drove home the dirk. With every last spark of strength that was in him, he slashed. Blood jetted. He had found a major vein. He did not retrieve this weapon either, for the jaws clashed after him and he sprang back barely in time. The hyena crumpled to the sand and threshed, ululating, geysering. The reptile beheld and approached.

Conan sought Falco. 'Lean on me,' the older human directed, for the younger moved haltingly. 'We don't want to go too fast, lest we draw yon dragon's heed. But if we are careful – he has a good deal more food there, waiting for him, than is on us.'

They made their way onward. Behind them, impervious to every bite, the saurian crouched down and began to devour the hyena.

That sight and its gruesome noises were soon lost in the tempest. Conan stopped. 'How are you, lad?' he asked.

Falco grimaced. 'I don't think anything is broken,' he said. 'The sand cushioned me a little.' Sweat studded his skin.

Conan knelt and made a quick examination. 'No,' he agreed, 'but you seem to have a twisted ankle, and from there to halfway along the thigh, your right leg is one solid bruise. Also, I see your dirk is what we have left for armament.' He rose and sighed. 'Never have I felt more unwelcome than here. Well, I can help you hobble

153

along. It shouldn't be far now.'

Fine, drifting sand had already buried tracks. In the night it made, Conan saw that this avenue had once been stately. The rubble of mansions that formerly stood well back sloped in windows to the feet of a double row of tall monoliths still lining the way. Millennia had scoured off most of the hieroglyphs chiseled into their darkling sides. What blurred traces they glimpsed made Conan and Falco grateful for that.

They slogged on. Wind screamed, grit assailed eyes and nostrils, murk walled off the world, exhaustion dragged. From time to time Falco drew a sharp breath, but else he kept manfully silent.

Something rumbled. The ground shivered. Sand upon it went sliding in little waves.

Only his leonine instincts and speed saved Conan. He saw a menhir topple, snatched Falco so that a shriek broke from the youth, and bounded clear. The stone smashed into the sand where they had been.

The one opposite fell. Conan barely escaped it likewise. The stark knowledge came – Behind him, the saurian feasted. If he tried some roundabout way, he would likeliest soon be lost in this labyrinthine graveyard full of abominations, and he with a crippled companion and no weapon save a knife. He had no choice but to run the gauntlet ahead of him.

From some unknown wellspring deep in his being, new strength flowed. He lifted Falco, placed the Ophirite across his shoulders, and said, 'Hang on.' Then he ran.

Another monolith boomed down, and another, and another. He dodged, he darted, he zigzagged, feinted, and sprinted. Whoever hovered beyond sight had a cyclopean mass to magic loose from its ground each time. The wizard sought to lead his quarry, as an archer leads the animal he would shoot. But Conan was no fowl or deer; he had been a hunter himself.

Nonetheless it was touch and go. A stone crashed before him as he swerved. He started to overleap it, and its mate across the avenue descended. He got past, but chips battered his back. A detached part of him considered going behind either row, where the other could not reach him. But no. The rubble would make slow going, with too much chance of tripping. Here the surface was

154

level. He could manoeuver. He bounded on down the middle of the street.

The menhirs quieted. He had sped between them for yards, when suddenly they fall at once, fore, aft, and to the sides. He had guessed this would happen and made ready. As the nearest pair swept earthward, he gauged exactly where they would land and sprang to a spot within inches. They missed. Conan jeered at the invisible sky and bounded from stone to stone.

And he was out from among them, on another broad square; and in the middle of this rose the dolmen.

'Name of Mitra,' quavered Falco. 'How did you do it?'

'I had to,' Conan said.

The wind fell rapidly. 'I doubt that is because the enemy is giving up,' he added. 'Let's proceed before the next grief gets here.' He trotted on to his goal.

Vertical slabs of black stone sheered too high for him to see the horizontal one that roofed them, through the ruddy night that hung on while dust slowly settled. Before him gaped a cavernous entrance. After his headlong course, he fretted no more about what might lair beyond. Nor did he believe the wizard could bring this tomb down on him. The structure was too massive, it was built to reinforce itself, and besides, within it slept the Ax of Varanghi.

'Against the things we have met,' Falco breathed, 'the good Lord has protected us.'

Conan thought their own actions had had something to do with that but refrained from saying it. He lowered Falco. 'Stand watch here,' he directed. 'I am going in.' The youth regarded him in mute veneration.

The far end of the tomb was shut. Silence closed on Conan as he entered. He heard his footfalls on the undrifted, stone-paved floor echo hollowly back from walls and ceiling lost in darkness. Wings whispered, scales slithered. What light seeped from outside became a distant blur. Yet he did not go on altogether blind: for ahead of him glimmered a blueness.

It waxed as, panther-cautious, he padded forward. Presently he made out what the source was, a crystal globe nested on a great block inscribed with symbols that somehow took the eye down impossible paths and evoked nightmarish visions. Conan wrenched his glance from them. Behind the altar loomed an idol – not of SEt, but of something winged and many-tentacled – a god older still? Conan gave the image a snarl and bent his gaze elsewhere.

Yes, at the fringe of illumination, a loop rose from the floor. He went there. The loop, he saw, was actually an ankh, chiseled from the same stone that formed a man-proportioned element of the paving. A thrill coursed through him. This was what Parasan had described, the lid of an immemorial grave wherein the Prophet hid the Ax.

Where had a priest gotten the might to raise anything that heavy? Conan knew not. He straddled the oblong, gripped the ankh, and strained.

His whole power surged. Muscles stood like iron under his byrnie, in arms and legs; tendons drew taut in hands and neck; sweat washed blood and grime downward in runnels. Just the same, he was careful. It would not do to throw out his back; how the devils in hell would laugh! He lifted straight, letting legs and hips take much of the stress, slowly, slowly.

The slab grated free. Pivoting it on end, Conan hauled it vertical, gave it a final tug, jumped aside and saw it fall and break asunder. The noise reverberated through blackness. At once he knelt to stare into the space below.

A few bones and traces of grave goods lay covered by dust. Conan ignored them. His whole being seized on the thing against which time had not prevailed.

It was a battle ax such as the Taians used to this day, haft long and straight, edge slightly curved, hammer sharpened to a point. It was larger, though, needing a strong man for its wielding. The helve, of some unknown red-brown wood, had not decayed in the least. Etched into the blade – on either side, Conan soon found – was the emblem of the Sun. That steel shimmered like no metal he had ever seen before, blue-white, silken, as if light of its own streamed thence.

With unwonted reverence, Conan reached down, lifted the Ax from its burial, and rose to his feet. He gave it a tentative swing. It came alive in his hands, became a part of him, or he a part of it, himself a war god, a sky god. He checked his exaltation and ran a thumb along the edge. In spite of his caution, blood oozed from a

156

cut. The weapon was razor keen. Parasan had said it never needed honing. He laughed aloud and sent it whistling in front of the eidolon.

A demonic screech resounded. Conan whirled about. He remembered the horn that had summoned the dead against his men. Falco was alone out there. Conan ran.

An asp struck at him, missed, and was crushed underfoot.

He burst from the dolmen. Falco crouched against a slab, dirk free, spitting defiance. From red-veiled sky, through dust and murk, descended a new monster. Now Conan understood why the wind had lowered, so that this thing might descend without risk of being blown against some wall.

He recognized that pointed beak, those naked thirty-foot wings. They were molded into the boat of Set. A tail ending in rudderlike flukes streamed after the reptile. Its talons were small, but they could scoop an eye out, and the bill held fishhook fangs.

A man bestrode it, in front of the racketing wings. The wind of his passage fluttered a black robe around his gaunt body. His head was shaven, his face aged and like a scimitar. Once more he blew the horn slung at his waist, let it go, and shrieked his own shriek of malice turned into madness.

Conan took stance. Flight-gusts buffeted him. The magician grasped a talisman hung on his breast, the articulated skull of a viper. He made a sign and aimed the open jaws.

Lightning struck from between them, blinding. Conan staggered. But the bolt had not smitten him, it had hit the head of the Ax – and rebounded. Thunder bawled. A lurid blaze wrapped the Stygian. He was lost in flames.

His steed was almost upon the man. Conan recovered his footing and swung. The Ax sheared through the long neck. The severed head snapped jaws shut on his left forearm, lacerated it, let go, and dropped at his feet. The body crashed against the tomb. For a while, beak clacked and wings threshed, before the creature lay altogether dead. A little distance from it, unrecognizable, huddled a charred corpse.

The wind sank to nothing. Dust drifted earthward. The sun came back in heaven, radiant.

XVIII

A SNARE IN PTEION

Through a great and blazing silence, the fighters returned.

They meant to skirt the plaza, but a look from behind a heap of shards showed it empty save for remnants of horse and hyena. No reptile could endure desert noonday. Teeth had crumpled Conan's blades, but Falco retrieved his saber and shield. Aided by his comrade's arm, he limped stubbornly on.

They were about halfway back when a wild metallic sound broke the hush. A thrill in them responded. That was no ugly bray of a wizard's horn, it was a bugle call. 'Hallo-o-o!' Conan shouted. 'Here we are!' By that time, Falco was in such pain he could barely croak his own response.

A rider rounded a corner at a quick trot, saw them, and halted so that sand flew up from hooves. Blood-streaked, in tattered garb, it was Daris. She dropped her spear, leaped from her saddle, and pelted down the street with arms wide. 'Conan, oh, Conan!' she caroled through tears and laughter.

He embraced her. She sobbed while she kissed him. But when she saw what he had rested against a plinth in order to free his own arms, she let go. Wonder and worship lighted her. She went to her knees. 'Is this the Ax of Varanghi?' Her voice trembled. Conan nodded. She looked aloft. 'Mitra, we thank you.'

As she rose, eagerness and pride spoke in a rush: 'And you are the Wielder, the Deliverer, you, my dear love!'

He knew he should have savored his triumph and her joy. But – was it just the weariness athrob in his bones? – somehow the anger that battle had cleansed him of was rising afresh. Who was she, to claim him for herself? And what kind of military idiots was he condemned to use for troops? They blithely supposed a single weapon, for which he had risked his life that belonged to Bêlit,

158

made victory certain. The attitude almost guaranteed defeat. He had better stamp it down, at once.

'What are you doing here?' he demanded.

She stepped back, bewildered. 'Why, I – I came in search of you.'

'How fare the men?'

'We destroyed many of the foe, but at fearful cost to ourselves. It did not seem we would survive. Then all at once they collapsed, they lay quiet, they were only harmless corpses – and the storm died away and the sun shone – and I knew you had won, Conan, but you might be hurt or – or anything.' Almost timidly, she touched the slash that the flying beast had given him. 'I must see to this.'

'It's naught,' he snapped. 'The blood has started to clot. What of the men?'

'About half are slain or badly wounded. The hale are worn out, dazed. I thought they should rest a while.'

The Cimmerian scowled. 'And you went off alone, into you knew not what peril, and left them leaderless? Ha, the only woman on earth fit for command is my Bêlit!'

Daris paled as if he had struck her, clenched fists, stood stiff but aquiver.

'Welcome, princess,' Falco gasped. Unsupported, he swayed where he kept weight on his good foot. 'You – you do wrong to chide her, Conan ... this gallant lady.'

He reeled towards her, stumbled, and fell. A groan escaped him.

'You are hurt!' Daris exclaimed. She knelt beside the youth. 'What is it? How bad?' She stroked his brow. 'Poor darling.'

Ire boiled in Conan. He congratulated himself on how well he hid it, saying merely, coldly, 'He damaged his leg. Nothing that won't heal, but why worsen it when there is no need? Give him your horse and ride behind.'

'No, let him ride, indeed, but we can walk together,' she urged, getting up again.

'Do as I say!' Conan barked. 'I want you back where you belong immediately. Get the men moving. Have them care for the injured, make ready for the road. We must be well away from here before dark. Don't you realize that, you witling? I will come after you.'

She gave him a long look, bit her lip, and turned away to bring the horse over. Conan helped Falco into the saddle. She, already there, slid back onto the rump and held the Ophirite's waist. Wordless, they departed.

The barbarian stood sullen among the ruins in the incandescent day. He thought that he hoped Daris enjoyed her ride, the scatterbrained tease. Finally he mumbled an oath, hung the Ax over his shoulder, and trudged after his vanished companions.

For a while he sensed nothing but heat, stillness, faint squeak of sand under his boots. He did not recognize the buildings he passed. Belike he had gotten onto a different route, in this accursed maze. No matter; it sufficed to maintain the right general direction. Ahead of him he noticed a façade that was eroded but otherwise whole. Nearing, he saw that above the doorless entrance was inset a ruby the size of his fist. It smoldered blood-red against jet stone. Why had no one removed it when the city was abandoned? Should he?

A figure appeared in the portal. Conan gasped. He seized the Ax and crouched. Each hair on him stood erect.

Laughter trilled sweet. 'What, is the Wielder frightened? And of a woman, at that. For shame. Be at ease. It is only poor Nehekba.'

She stood aglow with beauty, hand on hip in an insolence of allure. Her eyes, her smile enticed. The garb she wore, woven of golden-brown feathers, form-fitting from bosom to thighs, drew the gaze along every curve of her body.

Her voice sang: 'Behold my throat, my fingers, all of me. See, I wear no talisman. It would be useless, did I want to harm you. Only think what happened to Tothapis. The Ax is potent against all magic that strikes from without at its Wielder. Surely Parasan told you that while you bear the holy weapon you are invulnerable to sorcery as long as you yield nothing of yourself to its blandishments, so that it may strike you from within. I repeat his warning in token of the truth that I wish no hurt on such a *man* as you.'

'What is your aim, then?' he responded hoarsely.

She undulated through a shrug. 'I will not insult you by lying. I came here with Tothapis in hopes of stopping you. But your

160

destiny was too strong; no, you yourself were, Conan the magnificent. You won the Ax, you killed Tothapis after all the centuries he had lived in power, you are going on to a victory that will shake the house of Set to its foundations. The fall of my master has left me stranded. My enchantments fail, my tower is afar in Khemi, my potions are gone, my goddess has forsaken me. If I stay here I shall die most horribly tonight. If I flee into the desert I shall die miserably tomorrow.'

'And you appeal to me – you?'

She straightened. 'I will not beg.' He must needs admire her steadiness. 'You have much to avenge upon me. But I for my part have much to offer in exchange for my life. I am a skilled healer. I kept my knowledge of spells and how to guard against them. I can tell you well-nigh everything about King Mentuphera, his forces and officers and plans, information a thousand spies could not win for you, that will save countless Taian lives when the final engagement comes.'

Conan frowned. 'I know not which I despise more, a witch or a traitor,' he declared; but his words lacked force. How gorgeous she was!

'I gave no pledges, save to the goddess, and she has votaries in many lands,' Nehekba replied. 'Nonetheless I will plight my faith to you if you are merciful, and never break it. Everything I can do, everything I am, shall be yours, wholly yours.'

He stood dumb. His temples pounded.

'And how gladly I will give you myself,' she went on. 'There is no other man in the world like unto you, Conan. Make me your slave, and I shall rejoice.'

She glided forth. Sunlight sent blue ripples across raven locks; heat brought out a fragrance that overwhelmed his senses. She cupped his face between soft palms and purred, 'Come, let me show you. Inside is a pleasant place that was established for those who awaited you. There is water for washing, salve for your hurts, clean cloth for bandages. Afterward – oh, I understand you dare not linger here, but your men will not be ready to go for hours. I have wine and chilled fruits for your refreshment, a bed for your ease, myself for your service.'

161

She kissed him as she had done in Khemi. He hung the Ax again on his shoulder and responded. For minutes they stood straining together, in a cataract of brilliance. At last she slipped free and skipped toward the building, merrily beckoning him on. He followed, an earthquake in his breast.

As she had promised, the interior was cool, dim, well furnished. He could ignore a disturbing frieze that ran below the ceiling.

He must not let this lovely creature perish, he thought. And why should he not take his pleasure of her? If that hurt Daris, why, Daris had brought it on herself. And Nehekba would in truth be an invaluable ally.

Of course, he was no mooncalf like Falco. Conan investigated the room thoroughly. He found nothing that might be magical or a weapon. The inner doorway showed rubble where a section had fallen, so she kept no hidden implements there. All she had were the things she had mentioned: a table bearing ewers, basins, bowls, linens; a couple of chairs; a wide, well-mattressed bed.

He set down the Ax, ready to hand, and took a sip of water. It tasted quite pure, and he hardly supposed she would have thought to bring poisons along when she meant to assist in things far more powerful. 'Ungarb yourself,' she murmured as he quenched his thirst. 'I long to care for you.'

Her fingers aided him to remove his ragged outer garments. While he drew off the hauberk and its underpadding, she knelt to remove his boots. Together they stripped away what was left, and he stood before her naked.

Lust burned high and red in him. Her eyes widened in surprised admiration. He gripped her by the arms. 'Ishtar!' he bellowed. 'Get rid of that feather thing – at once!'

'Conan, you hurt me,' she wailed. He let go. She touched the places he had seized. 'What bruises I shall have.' She smiled, fluttered her lashes, blew him a kiss. 'I will bear them as badges of honor, from the mightiest man on earth.'

'Undress,' he said out of a thick throat.

'Oh, I yearn for you,' she avowed melodiously. 'But you are hurt, beloved. Blood and sweat and dirt hide your splendor. Let me wash you, anoint and bandage you, that you may feel no more pain or tiredness. *Then* we will go to our joy.'

'As you wish,' he yielded, and sat down. Still he kept the Ax in reach.

She wet a cloth and scrubbed him, slow, sensual strokes that brought delicious ease even while they raised desire further yet. Her free fingers combed through his mane.

He almost regretted it when she was done. His gaze followed her hotly as she moved off. Limned against the daylit door, she resembled a golden-edged shadow. He watched her wipe both hands on the bloodstained towel, no doubt to get rid of filth and stray hairs and the like. Yes, she had been right about this. Next she would give him soothing medications in the same playful manner –

'Hoy, where are you going?' he asked in surprise.

She poised at the exit. Her voice fluted mockery: 'Away. I have decided I would rather not travel overland. Farewell, barbarian.'

He surged to his feet. She slipped out. He grabbed the Ax and leaped in pursuit.

The sun dazzled him. For a moment he was nearly blind. When vision returned, he saw that he stood in an empty street.

'Crom!' he muttered. 'The witch made a fool of me after all. What for?'

He bent to seek her tracks in the sand. It gave blurred, shallow footprints, but he possessed a huntsman's eye. The trail went a few yards along the housefront – she had run trippingly – and ended in a whirled confusion that told him only that something strange had happened.

He peered everywhere around. High overhead, a golden eagle was winging west; otherwise heaven, earth, and the hell that was Pteion seemed lifeless.

Had Nehekba simply meant to pique him? Had she nourished hopes of doing him harm, been baffled by his caution, and given up the attempt? Conan did not want to think about such things. They were too eerie. Nor did he want to tell his friends what had occurred; in a way, it was too ridiculous.

Suddenly he laughed, gigantic shouts of mirth that rang off stones and up to the sky. He laughed at himself. He laughed defiance at every foe. He laughed in jubilation that he had truly won the Ax which set men free. He laughed for sheer gusto, in rampant aliveness. It was as if Nehekba had taken with her the foul mood that had plagued him for days, and he was again himself, Conan, wanderer, warrior, lover.

Memory sobered him. He made haste to dress and go on. The ruby glowered behind him, forgotten.

They were busy at the Taian site, under Daris' gentle but firm direction. She spied the Cimmerian, approached him, and reported impersonally: 'Subject to your approval, I have divided the survivors into two groups. One is of the disabled, and enough hale men to escort them home where they can get proper care. It will take our dead as well, to bury tomorrow in the gorge where there are rocks for cairns. We cannot leave them to the ghouls. The second party, of course, consists of those who can still fight. Tyris tells me he can lead us pretty directly to meet Ausar. Both groups should be ready to travel in another hour or so.'

His blue glance sought hers, he laid hands on her waist, he said low, 'You have done splendidly, daughter of kings, and I have been a surly brute. I know not what ailed me, but I see now how I wronged you, and ask your forgiveness.'

'Oh, Conan!' she cried. Regardless of stares, she cast herself into his arms.

XIX

THE BATTLE OF RASHT

The military highway entered that region called Taia at the northwestern corner. A day's march farther on, it passed through a narrow valley. In crags and scaurs and boulder-strewn steeps, hills rose lofty on either side. What red soil was on their slopes and in their gullies bore a growth of shrubs, coarse grass, a few scrub trees. The sky at mid-morning was ultramarine, and already heat baked pungency out of dwarf juniper.

Screened by brush, men on the heights lay prone and peered downward. Distance made tiny the figures on the road, but did not conceal their numbers. Cavalry in the van, chariots rumbling behind, infantry in serried ranks, supply train, rearguard – the army filled two or three miles of paving. Metal flashed, pennons streamed, banners flapped, a ripple as over a grainfield went among lances and spears. Even this remotely, the watchers heard a surf-like noise. It came from marching feet, clacking horseshoes, booming wheels, relentless drumbeat.

Conan whistled. 'Your scouts did not lie,' he said. 'Rather, they understated the matter. That must be the entire cadre of central Stygia, and whatever reserves could be mobilized in a hurry.'

'Well, if Mentuphera himself leads them –' Ausar let his voice trail off.

'Are you certain? You have just the word of those scouts, simple hillmen.'

'They are excellent observers, and I have traveled enough to recognize what they described. None but the king bears the standard of a silver serpent on a black field, staff topped by a bronze vulture. He means to make sure of us, once for all.'

'Aye,' said Conan grimly. His gaze sought behind the host. The road bent around a ridge that hid what lay in its direction, but smoke made a pillar against heaven yonder and no carrion fowl hovered; they were at meat instead. Yesterday the village of Rasht had existed there, amidst fields, orchards, pastures. Ausar's folk had not warned the inhabitants to flee, because he did not expect a massacre; he had supposed the Stygians would hasten to find him. 'He will make sure of the whole country. Maybe afterward his own people will colonize the waste he leaves.'

'It shall not be!' Daris swore. 'This day his reign ends.'

'That is as the fates decree.' Anguish wrenched at Ausar's voice. 'If – in spite of everything – we must lose, remember my vow. I will tell the chiefs to bid their clans lay down arms, and then I will yield myself up, that Taia be not utterly devastated.'

'First,' said Conan dryly, 'suppose we try out our plan. You may have no count of your fighters, but they must outnumber the enemy. If they lack training and proper equipment, why, they do not lack valor; and we are well positioned for the attack. Besides, we have the Ax.'

Ausar and Daris regarded him in an awe that made him uncomfortable. Hang it, he was no incarnation of anything, he was a plain barbarian adventurer.

Yet luck, or destiny, or strife among the gods had made him a symbol, a vital rallying point. Often in the past did rebellion flare across the highlands, but never like this wildfire. Ausar, moving west, had pledged that near the border he would league with the Wielder who had been prophesied. That word flew right and left and before him, borne by runners who passed a war arrow from camp to camp, by the whistled language of herdsmen and hunters, by beacon fires on mountaintops, perhaps by ways more ancient and mysterious than any of these. From end to end of the country, boy, man, hale grandsire, strong maiden took weapons and trail rations and started off to join the head of Clan Varanghi. Theirs was a wild horde. Conan could but hope that, after he arrived, he had succeeded with native help in teaching enough of them the rudiments of organized warfare that the rest would have proper guidance.

Meanwhile General Shuat had moved his detachment un-hindered in such haste that he wrought no havoc on the way. He must have gotten word from his king, by courier or pigeon, to change whatever plans he bore; for he stopped at the provincial border and waited for the royal force to appear. Now he was bound back toward Seyan, part of an army that took time to ravage as it went.

But there was nothing worth its attention in the hills near Rasht; and lowland Stygians would not notice any sign of the thousands who were gathered to ambush them.

'Let's go,' said Conan. He and his companions slithered off until they could safely walk upright.

In a hollow beyond the crest, about a hundred horsemen and as many foot waited. More could not be assembled at one spot without betraying their presence. Few except these were mounted, but groups of comparable size lurked everywhere above the valley. Their scheme was to fall on the Stygians at numerous points, split the column into segments, and, when it was thus in disarray, fight a whole set of simultaneous battles until it was destroyed.

Conan's gang would go first, meeting the enemy head-on; that would give signal and inspiration to the rest. Therefore his men had better gear than their kilted fellows: helmets, breastplates or byrnies, in some cases reinforced gauntlets or greaves or vambraces or other armor. Daris sprang to the saddle, herself wearing naught but tunic and leather cap, bow and quiver, dirk sheathed at the belt she had come to believe was lucky. From a lean gray clansman she took the banner she would carry: woven in the temple of Mitra, hung from a crossarm, a sunburst golden upon heaven-blue.

'About time,' grumbled Sakumbe. 'It's been a weary while, and not a woman for any of us, no, not even much beer. The plunder today had better be good.'

Conan grinned. The Suba were with him partly because he alone could talk to them, through their leader – but partly, too, because he knew their kind for grand fighters, and they would make his band the more conspicuous and fearsome. Their dark hides drank down the upland light, their alien outfits were somehow doubly menacing. 'Well,' said the Cimmerian, 'I daresay the king of Stygia does not travel like a beggar. What would you think of tableware made from precious metals and gems, or rare wines and spices, or

167

silken raiment, or chests of money? Help yourselves!'

Sakumbe gave a villainous chuckle and addressed his followers. They cheered, save for Gonga the witch doctor. That gaunt man stood armed for combat, but he had painted his cicatriced body in eldritch patterns, he wore a necklace of human teeth and fingerbones, a wand and rattle and pouch of magical stuffs hung at his waist.

Falco edged close to Daris. The Ophirite had regained strength, was free of pain, but still rather lame. He insisted this made no difference as long as he sat his fine gray Stygian gelding. Besides cuirass and plumed morion, he had found a flamboyant scarlet cape to hang on his slender frame. The lance in his grasp quivered like an aspen in springtime.

Himself agleam in chainmail and winged helmet, breeks tucked into steel-capped boots with gilt spurs, Conan turned to Ausar. He became as grave as the Taian. 'Now the storm rises,' he said, 'and none may foreknow the wind's path. May we meet again, victorious. If not, then I thank you for your kindness, chieftain, and ask that Mitra take you home to him.'

'My thanks are to you, the thanks of all Taia,' answered Ausar. 'Whatever comes, while this folk live, the memory of you will abide.'

They embraced. The native would lead an assault on the Stygian rearguard, lest it execute a flanking manoeuver. For a moment, father and daughter clasped hands, before he departed.

Conan mounted. For him, the rebels had captured a splendid charger, a great black stallion that whickered and pranced in eagerness. He patted the warm neck. 'So, so,' he murmured, 'you will have your fill of action today, I promise.' Muscles surged under his thighs, and he moved toward his destined hour.

Daris rode her mare on his right, standard rippling above her. Falco was at her other hand. Incredibly to any who did not know him, Sakumbe's swag-bellied form kept easy pace afoot on the left. His tribesmen were close behind, heading up spearmen, axmen, swordsmen, archers, slingers. In front of these, to either side of the Cimmerian, lancers rode in the wedge formation favored by Taians. They would be no match for skilled Stygian cavalry; but they hoped they could keep it busy until reinforcements arrived and then, perhaps, dismount to fight in their customary wise.

Stones rattled. Tawny grass and dusty shrubs rustled. Harness creaked and jingled. The sounds of the enemy grew louder.

Conan had not imagined he could burst upon his foe as if out of nowhere. He had, though, studied a route beforehand over which it was safe to go fast. Without that, his entire company might be picked off by arrows on its way. As he crossed the hillcrest, he broke into a trot.

Downward! In minutes, the army below was no parade of ants seen in entirety; it was troopers whose weapons he mad out, it was sunlight reflected blindingly off a gilt war chariot and coach that must be the king's, it was the royal standard he meant to cast down, it was shouts and trumpeted alarms and a first sinister whistle of missiles.

'Hoy-ah!' he roared. 'Taia and freedom!' Reaching down, he loosed the Ax of Varanghi from its fastenings at his saddlebow. It sang and gleamed as he whirled it aloft. Not every such weapon was suitable for use from horseback, but this one lived in his hands, sharp, agile, terrible.

The valley floor was near. He galloped. His fellow riders came along. The runners fell behind, but they would soon arrive, and meanwhile it was needful to get away from arrows. In yonder crowded space, archers would be well-nigh useless, and no full-scale charge was possible.

A Taian horseman toppled, a shaft in his throat. He struck the ground and rolled on in puffs of dust. Conan saw from the corner of an eye. He knew that man, had hoisted ale and traded jokes with him in camps where coals grew dim beneath midnight stars, had heard about his wife and children and old mother. Well, Crom gave no man more than the strength to die bravely.

And now pavement hardened the clatter of hooves. Conan reined his mount around. His saddlemates joined him. Across yards, they confronted the steeds, cuirasses, helmets, leveled lances of a Stygian cavalry ten times their number.

But the whole ten could not come at him together. If they went much off the highway, they would find themselves stumbling about on the slopes, among treacherous patches of talus, rocks, thornbushes, rodent holes where an animal could easily break a leg. Again he swung the Ax on high. 'In line, advance!' he shouted, and spurred his destrier.

The foe trotted forward to meet him, cantered, galloped. Hoofbeats rolled like the steady drums behind them. Pennons, plumes, cloaks streamed to their speed. Shields lifted, lances took aim. Men and beasts grew huge in vision.

According to his orders, Daris dropped behind Conan. Falco closed the gap, shaft held expertly across the neck of his grey.

In a roar, combat began.

A point sought Conan's mail-clad breast, to unseat him. Before it could strike, the Ax had sheared through wood. The Stygian got no chance to draw blade. Conan smote him under the jaw, and his head flew free. In a lightning flash of thought, the Cimmerian wondered who this man had been who had the honor of being the first in five hundred years to die beneath the Ax of Varanghi.

Falco took an attacker in the throat, dropped his lance, whipped forth saber, positioned shield, and closed with the next nearest foeman. Conan split the skull of a horse; its rider fell under hooves. Falco warded off a sword thrust and removed the fingers that had tried it. There was no more charging, there was affray that milled, pushed, clanged, grunted, yelled, gasped, cursed, sweater, bled, stabbed, slashed, smote.

Tall on a tall steed, Conan got glimpses of how the battle went elsewhere. As expected, the Stygian riders had mostly overrun the Taian; but an unhorsed mountaineer, or one who had purposely jumped to earth, became twice as deadly, and meanwhile his animal encumbered the way. And now warriors, brown and black, bounded off hillsides into combat.

The next division of the royal army, sword-wheeled chariots, rolled forward.

Arrows sleeted from above. Horses, drivers, even heavy-armored fighters fell, transfixed, dead or helpless. Wild, hallooing dirkmen got in among them, hamstringing, leaping up on cartbeds to grapple and slash. The entire Taian host was in onslaught. Conan saw banners sway and go down, he saw the Stygian column writhe along the miles like a broken-backed snake.

'Bêlit, Bêlit!' he shouted, and hewed.

'Senufer!' Falco echoed as his blade scythed.

They cleared a space around themselves, red-running, piled high with mangled corpses and moaning wounded. Hundreds more Taians had sought to the banner of the Sun and the gleam of the Ax. They cut their own way in among the Stygian cavalry. Sakumbe barreled through the tumult, his knobkerrie a blur of violence. He had a trick of hitting a rider on the kneecap or a horse on the nose, then, while pain blinded the victim, sliding in the knife that his left hand gripped.

Suddenly Conan had nobody to fight. He looked around him. Everywhere, Taians swarmed over bodies trampled into shape-lessness. Their wolf-howls exulted, their steel shook off blood in showers. A few succored injured comrades or keened briefly over the dead. More harried Stygian lancers across the hillsides, baying at them, loping faster than exhausted beasts could stumble.

Farther on, abandoned chariots cluttered the road. Some careened empty behind panicked horses. Farther still, chaos ramped, scores of human maelstroms in which rebels closed with infantry, weapon-clink, clangor, shrieking.

In front of this, however, and behind the chariots, a Stygian regiment stood firm inside a low wall of slain Taians. They surrounded the golden coach, and over their heads floated the banner of the Serpent.

Conan gestured his close companions to him, Daris, Falco, and stark Ruma, who had commanded the reinforcements here at the van, and who had his Clan Farazi to avenge. 'Those must be their crack troops,' the Cimmerian said, pointing. 'Of the king's household, I suppose, and doubtless of Shuat's legion, too, who have experience in these parts. They could not be knocked over by surprise.' He frowned. 'In fact, we have won this encounter, but I think mainly because the enemy was light on horse and wheels. He did not foresee much need for them. His foot is hard pressed, aye, but could well rally, pull itself together, and cast our irregulars back.'

'What should we do?' asked Ruma.

171

Conan threw a glance across the swarming hillmen. Laughter growled from his breast. 'Why, attack,' he said. 'Break yonder shield-burg, scatter what soldiers we do not kill, stick Mentuphera's head on a pole and bear it onward. If that doesn't break the will of his army, I know nothing about warfare.'

Falco whooped, tossed his saber glittering through the air, caught and brandished it.

Daris looked troubled. 'If we try and fail,' she said, 'I fear – I know my own folk – I fear the word may fly among them that you do not bear the true Ax, and they will be the ones who flee.'

Faith blazed from Ruma. 'But it *is* the Ax, and Conan the Wielder!' he cried.

The Cimmerian hefted his weapon. 'I have no more doubt, myself,' he said quietly. 'Shall we marshal our warriors?'

That took a while, shouting, horn-blowing, exhorting. The king's men watched stolidly, swords, spears, bows at hand, ranks unshaken. The scattered fights beyond them raged on. Sometimes a Stygian band went under, sometimes it sent its Taian assailants reeling away and joined another group. Conan rode up a hill to oversee the entire business. Yes, he thought, if he had not overwhelmed their lord, soon, his enemies would re-form and the day would become theirs.

Well, that was not going to happen. He returned. No weariness or hurt was in him, though he had taken his share of flesh wounds. He burned with lust of battle; his single wish was to strike down those creatures that stood between him and Bêlit.

He, Daris, and Falco were the last of their company who remained mounted. He supposed his stallion could wreak ample harm while he chopped from above; but if he ended afoot, no matter, as long as the Ax played like a live thing in his hands. Hoy-ah!

The Taians were ready, not a regiment but a pack and perhaps the more terrible for that. Daris' banner lifted proud. Conan took the lead. Ax raised like a torch, he touched spurs to his mount. Hooves banged on stone. Trot became canter. The Stygians lowered pikes and nocked arrows to bowstrings.

Pain swooped upon Conan.

It was as though a million fiery needles pierced skin, flesh, veins. He was burning alive. His guts cramped, wave after wave of agony. His muscles jerked, gone berserk, trying to snap the bones underneath them. Black mists rolled across his eyesight, it thundered in his ears, graveyard stenches assailed his nostrils. His heart skipped crazily in its rib cage, and for the first time in his life he feared his own death.

The Ax clattered to earth. A moment afterward, he himself toppled and sprawled struggling before his men. Horror went through them like a night wind. They stopped in their tracks.

Daris sprang from her stirrups, forgetting the banner of the Sun, which also fell in the dust. Frantic, she knelt beside him, sought to hold him, suffered the buffets of his uncontrolled hands. 'Conan, Conan, what is wrong?' she quavered. 'In Mitra's name, speak to me! This is your own Daris who calls, Daris who loves you –'

He heard her dimly, as if from the far side of a hurricane. He could find no answer for her, in the terror and torment that were his universe.

The Taians wavered. Weapons sank, bodies shuddered, mouths gaped. Ruma shook his spear above his head. 'Stand fast!' he yelled. 'I will kill the first man who runs!'

Falco on his horse lifted saber and said, dry-throated, 'Or I will kill him for you, Ruma.'

The tears of Daris dropped on Conan's contorted face. 'Come back,' she pleaded. 'I call you in – in the name of Bêlit. Combe back to Bêlit.'

In the midst of his hell, he heard. Something awoke in him; somehow he could remember, understand, and speak. The words tore from him one by one, each as mighty an effort as ever he had made: 'My ... folly ... I met ... Nehekba ... in Pteion ... She washed ... me ... and bore away ... a cloth ... full of my blood and –' He could say no more, he could only arch his back and gasp.

A Taian wailed and pelted off. Ruma cast his spear. The man went down. White-faced, Falco rode over to give him the mercy stroke. The clansmen moaned but stayed where they were. The massed Stygians regarded them with satisfaction.

From above the helmets of these, up over the Serpent banner, swept a shining shape. A brazen chariot without wheels or tongue, it bore a woman. Filmy garments and sable tresses fluttered behind her. At her throat glistened a mirror. In her hands was a small waxen image, which she tortured with twisting and a poniard and the flame of a taper as she laughed. High she flew and then downward and forward.

Throughout the slaughterous miles, noise diminished. The Taians at the front quailed. In a minute they would all break and run, fear-crazed.

'*Senufer!*' Falco shrieked.

Conan glimpsed her through the darkness that beset him. She seemed the very Derketa leading a troop of ghost-women in flight across the underworld. 'Nehekba,' he groaned.

Daris grew aware that somebody had joined her beside the Cimmerian. She looked at Sakumbe. 'I hear some,' the Negro said in his atrocious Stygian. Sweat of terror pearled across brow and paunch, but he spoke stoutly. 'I see what. She got body magic on him. Him blood in her doll. She hurt. Soon she kill.'

Daris slumped in despair. 'Then her whole scheme was to lure us into this,' she replied, dull-voiced, 'that our faith and will be crushed forever – oh Conan!' She sought to kiss the stricken man, but he tossed about too wildly.

'Senufer, darling Senufer,' Falco called like a sleepwalker.

He wheeled his gray horse about and struck spurs deep. Across the dead he galloped, in among the wreckage of the chariots, toward where Nehekba hovered. Conan's vision cleared, his pain sank a little, and he saw. Surely the witch wrought that, for him to witness this last betrayal.

She signaled the Stygian archers to hold their fire as Falco came in range. She lowered her vehicle to just above the road, joyful, left hand clasping Conan's image but right held out to welcome the youth who sped her way. When they kissed, that would be the last bite of the adder in the Taian heel. A Stygian soldier would bring the Ax of Varanghi to the altar of Set.

'Falco, welcome!' she sang.

The rider drew rein before her. For a pulsebeat he stared into the luster of her eyes.

His saber flew. She had a moment to see the steel in her bosom, and to scream. Blood ran, impossibly brilliant under the sun, but not much; it was as if a god did not wish her beauty defiled, but found it enough that her heart be pierced. She sank and was suddenly quite small. The chariot boomed to earth.

Falco left his blade where it was. He retrieved the image of Conan and raked his horse's ribs. Back he thundered. 'Here,' he said, and gave the thing into the hand of Daris. Then he rode slowly aside and dismounted.

Sakumbe yelled at Gonga. The witch doctor trod from a rebel band that stood dumbstruck, wonder-smitten. Down the road, the king's soldiers panted and shuddered.

Carefully, carefully, Daris passed the doll to Gonga, and returned to her cherishing of Conan. He lay quiet, breathing hard. The black man squatted. He chanted words, sprinkled powders from his pouch, shook rattle, waved wand. After a minute or two, a smile tinged the sternness of his countenance. His Suba waymates, who had lain prostrate, rose when he did, flourished their weapons, and bawled, *'Wakonga mutusi!'*

Conan's eyes cleared. He sat up. 'I am well,' he marveled, like a man whose fever has broken.

'The witch is dead,' Daris wept. 'You are free.'

Gonga drew knife, nicked his wrist, sprinkled a few drops of blood on the image while he chanted. Conan got to his feet. He felt as if he had slept through a long night and awakened to drink from a mountain spring.

Gonga spoke to Sakumbe, who told Conan in the lingua franca, 'He has given you of his own strength, to heal the harm in you. He cannot fight until he has recovered from that. But he will bear the evil thing away, annul the spell, and destroy it.'

Once more, titanic laughter pealed from the Cimmerian. 'Hai, I have other destruction to do this day!' He hugged Daris and Sakumbe to him. 'O faithful friends, I can never truly thank you, but nor can I ever forget!'

He lifted the Ax and soared to the saddle. 'Forward!' he trumpeted. 'In the name of Jehanan!' His men howled joy. Heedless of arrows, they followed him.

175

Down the length of the embattled highway, word flew of a weapon and a banner once more aloft. Taians rallied for the reaping of men.

It did not fall to the lot of Conan that he slew King Mentuphera, or to that of Ruma that he claimed General Shuat. Those Stygians went down in the ruck, and only the gods knew what warriors took them. Conan was satisfied to slay right and left, and have a crowned head borne before him for a sign, and see the Stygians break.

He did not scorn Falco because the youth sat by the roadside meanwhile and wept.

XX

VENGEANCE FOR BÊLIT

Brought down from its hiding place, the wingboat lay waiting at Seyan. Six people stood on the dock. Though folk moved about their tasks in town, none came near, for these friends wished to be alone when they said their farewells.

The sun was still below the eastern heights, but heaven there was silvery-gold and elsewhere blue. Mists smoked through cool air above the Styx, veiling its murkiness in white. From purple western mountains the Helu dashed in laughter.

Conan felt no chill, though he wore just a tunic. At his hip were sheathed a dirk and a sword. Solemnly he laid the Ax of Varanghi across both hands and held it forth to Ausar. 'Now this is yours,' he said. 'May it ever ward Taia.'

'Mitra willing, we should have no need of it soon,' the chieftain replied.

His confidence appeared well founded. Rather than perish in a hopeless resistance, the Stygian garrison here had surrendered and was trudging home, disarmed and under guard. Fat Governor Wenamon accompanied it, having ransomed himself with all the wealth he had squeezed from the country. After the disaster at Rasht, the royal army would be in no shape to campaign for some time to come. Besides, the new King Ctesphon was known to lack his father's imperial ambitions.

'You or your descendants will have to fight again at last,' Conan warned. 'Luxur will never recognize your independence.'

Ausar took the Ax. 'True,' he agreed, 'but that matters little if we are in fact a free nation. We can find support in Keshan, Punt, and other neighboring realms that have reason to distrust Stygia.'

Parasan the high priest was less happy. 'Alas, I fear that will sever our last ties to civilization,' he said. 'We will become entirely a race of barbarian clansmen.'

Conan shrugged. 'What of it?' he answered. 'No irreverence meant, sir, but is not liberty worth any price? Also, frankly, I do not find that much to be said for civilization.'

'As you will,' the old man murmured. 'I dare hope that at least we will keep the light and the grace of Mitra. His blessing be upon you, my son, for what you have wrought in his cause and ours. May your journey back be safe and your arrival gladsome.'

Sakumbe had partly followed the conversation. Perhaps he misunderstood the last words a trifle, for he grinned, slapped the Cimmerian's back, and boomed in the lingua franca, 'Aye, when I reach the Black Coast I will tell them to prepare a nine-day festival of welcome for you, Amra!' The nickname he and his men had bestowed on Conan meant, in their language, 'Lion.'

'I look forward to that,' the Northerner said. 'Surely Bêlit and I will visit you Suba right often.' He sobered. 'However much I long for her, it is sad to bid the rest of you farewell, belike forever. Daris –'

'Yes?' She turned her face from Falco, with whom she had been conversing.

'I will miss you more than I know how to tell,' Conan said awkwardly. 'Your well-being will always be among my dearest wishes.'

'And yours among mine.' She came to take both his hands in hers. The gaze that she laid upon him was steady, and her lips smiled. The evening before, they had talked together in private; today she must be the daughter of Ausar.

'If only we could live out our lives together,' she went on. 'It cannot be, I know. You have your sworn mate. I – I will marry some man who is strong and good, and rejoice in the children I bear him. He will be honored to name our first son Conan. And our first daughter –' She could not quite hold back tears. 'May we call her Bêlit?'

They embraced.

Further speech was but scant, before Conan and Falco boarded. Silent, their craft slipped out onto the river, soon to be hidden from shore by the mists.

*

The sea sparkled sapphire under a fresh breeze, but *Tigress* moved from the white cliffs of Akhbet isle under oars. That was for manoeuverability. Her captain wanted a close look at the boat that had come over her horizon.

Strange indeed were yonder metallic hull and reptilian figurehead. The spritsail was obviously jury-rigged; but if the vessel had not been intended to carry a mast, where was any provision for rowing? Despite a fifty-foot length, the crew seemed to amount to a pair of men. They showed no alarm as the galley bore down on them. Rather, the big one, astern at an equally improvised rudder, steered as best he was able to meet her.

Big man, black-maned, fair skin bronzed, leonine stance – It was as if the heart in Bêlit would burst out through her ribs. 'Conan!' she shouted. 'Conan, Conan! O Ishtar, there is my love come back!'

She caught herself and ordered her cheering corsairs to withdraw portside oars for the boat to lay alongside. The Cimmerian tossed up a painter, jumped, grabbed the rail, and hauled himself onto the deck. Bêlit entered his arms like a hurricane.

After a long while, they could let go, regard each other in ecstasy, and even look around the ship. Her glance fell on the youth who had followed Conan aboard. She stiffened. A moment passed before she could bring herself to say, 'Then Jehanan is not with you.'

'No,' replied the Cimmerian, softer-toned than was usual for him. 'He is ... wherever those go who die valiantly.'

Bêlit closed her eyes, opened them again, and said, 'You can tell me of him? Let that be enough.' She paused. 'That *you* have returned alive is not enough, it is abundance overflowing.'

'The tale is cruel. Best let it wait until we feel quieter,' Conan advised. 'Meanwhile I wish you to meet my gallant comrade, Falco of Kirjahan in Ophir.'

Bêlit gave the youngster her hand. 'Be very welcome,' she said. 'If I am in your debt for bringing my lord back to me, then I am in your debt for all that is mine.'

Falco blushed. 'You told me she is beautiful, but not how

179

beautiful,' he blurted to Conan. 'You forgot to add she is gracious. May my fortune in love be half as great as yours.'

The Cimmerian smiled. This was a healthy lad, who had soon cast off his grief over the witch.

The smile faded. Bêlit had sorrow ahead of her.

A full moon turned argent the waters and the isle where *Tigress* lay at anchor. Alone on her foredeck, above a ship wherein everybody else slumbered after a riotous celebration, Conan and Bêlit stood side by side.

She had finished weeping. Now she gripped the rail, stared out across the sea, and said in a voice that was like steel being drawn from scabbard: 'Rest well, my brother. You shall be avenged. The halls of Derketa shall be thronged in your honor.'

'Has not the loss of a province, an army, a king, and their two foremost sorcerers appeased Jehanan's spirit?' wondered Conan.

Bêlit nodded. 'Surely. His was ever a gentle soul. But mine is otherwise, and I burn unslaked.'

The barbarian sighed. 'I thought you would feel thus. Well, as long as the gods will have it, let us prey on their shipping and harry their coasts so that the Stygian princes will remember us with a memory that is red.' He paused. 'Yet this may be too slow for you at first. Would you not rather hazard a blow of such force that your woe is eased thereby and you can again fare happily?'

'Yes, oh, yes!' she whispered. Her vision turned to search him.

'Here is my idea,' he began. 'The Stygians ended their blockade as soon as they learned we had escaped upstream, of course. Falco and I passed Khemi in darkness. He had told me the harbor patrol does not usually bother vessels outbound, but I still reckoned it best that nobody see what sort of carrier ours was. Nevertheless we could observe that the fleet lay at its docks. Those ships did not seem to have much of a watch aboard them. The crews were mostly in barracks ashore, I suppose, or in their home villages on leave. Besides, confusion must still prevail after what happened at Rasht; and Stygia never was a really naval-minded country. Yet that fleet would be vital in case of war. Its loss would absolutely kill any plans that may linger for adventures abroad – such as an invasion of Ophir.'

Bêlit seized his arms. Her nails drew blood that neither of them noticed. 'By the gods of death! Our single galley – is it possible?'

'I have a scheme. It's simple and straightforward, but I am not a cunning person. Let us talk about it tomorrow, when you are calmer.' Despite the hurt he saw in his darling, a bit of Conan's rough humor broke free. 'We can begin the task then, too, by scuttling the wingboat. A pity, in a way; but she is no more use to us and we certainly do not want to risk her falling back into the wrong hands. Would you like to do it yourself?'

The Stygians always maintained a picket boat on Khemi Bay. This was a light craft, but extremely fast under oars or lateen sail. Aside from the weapons of her crewmen, she was unarmed, and they did not encumber themselves with mail. Their duty was not to hold off pirates or invaders. Who would dare assault the black city? In case of real trouble, a trumpet blast would summon warships; it had never happened. The picket controlled water traffic, making sure no smugglers landed here, or anyone who lacked official permission.

A while after a certain sundown, the boat on station moved to intercept a stranger bound in from the west. That was a double-ended launch such as was commonly carried on the larger ocean-going ships or towed by the lesser. A stiff breeze filled a square sail and drove the hull smartly in between the headlands, against current and unfavorable tide; the moon would not rise for hours.

'Ahoy!' shouted the Stygian trumpeter. 'Stand to for inspection!'

'Yes, sir,' responded a deep voice in the same language, with an accent. The yard lowered and the boat lost way.

Nearing, the police saw by starlight that about half a dozen men occupied the thwarts. They were Negroes, except for a large fellow at the helm. Albeit muffled in spray-drenched kaftan and burnoose, he appeared to be of white race. 'Please, sirs,' he called, 'we are poor sailors whose ship struck a reef. None but us few got to the lifeboat in time, as fast as she sank. In the name of mercy, give us water, take us ashore, and feed us!'

'You realize you must be detained, pending investigation,' the captain said through his megaphone. 'Where are you from?'

'An Argossean merchantman, whose cheapjack owners hired what crew they could get. These are Kushites. I am from Vanaheim myself.'

The captain had heard only vague rumors of that boreal country, but he knew barbarians sometimes wandered afar in search of adventure or fortune, and he bore the contempt of a civilized person for such tramps. This one had clearly been humbled by his experience, and his companions croaked pitifully for drink. 'In oars,' the officer directed. 'Lay to and make fast.' When this had been done: 'Come over here, the lot of you, and let me have a look at you.'

'Yes, sir, yes, sir.' The big man staggered across joined bulwarks and along the catwalk between rowers' benches to a lantern on the foredeck where the captain and trumpeter waited. His mates trailed him. 'Please, water!'

'In due course, after you have answered my questions,' the Stygian commander said. This might be a chance to learn a little about what was going on abroad. In these chaotic days, when King Ctesphon was still groping, lords of state might pay well for information. Be that as it may, the captain would enjoy watching these monkeys grovel.

'Thank you – thank you, sir,' the big man blubbered as he approached. 'May the gods reward you as you deserve.'

A sword flashed from beneath his garment. The trumpeter fell, skull cloven. That was the last thing the captain ever saw. The black men drew weapons of their own. From under canvas, in the bottom of the lifeboat, swarmed more.

The struggle was not loud, nor was it long. The pirates had every advantage of surprise, skill, and wrathfulness. 'Good,' said Conan. 'Dump the corpses, let us care for any wounded among us, and then you start back, N'Gora.'

Bêlit's first officer, who knew some Stygian, gave orders. The launch raised sail and tacked seaward. Whoever happened to be watching would suppose she had been denied admittance. Bearing a minimal crew, Conan their skipper, the picket boat cruised the bay as always.

Presently a swart galley with a feline figurehead hove in view.

The sentinel craft met her and the two lay side by side for a while. No doubt her presence attracted the attention of shore patrols and men guarding the naval ships. It would be natural that the police took time to make sure of her bona fides. They must have been satisfied at last, for their vessel accompanied the newcomer, both rowing straight toward the royal docks. Did she perhaps bear a foreign diplomat, come to implore the goodwill of mighty Stygia, or did she – a shudder – bring home an agent of wizard-priests?

Aboard *Tigress* again, Bêlit at his side again, Conan looked ahead from the prow. Starlight sheened on darkling waters, ample for eyes from Cimmerian forest, Kushite jungle, or the high seas. To port, beyond the bay, the Styx pierced nighted fields at the end of its long journey past the land where Daris dwelt . . . and dreamed? Forward, the city where he had been captive bulked monstrous, altogether black, save where furtive windows glimmered. Nearby, bone-hued under the mass of the Grand Pyramid, were the quarries where Jehanan had been a slave until his sister's man won him his freedom that he himself made eternal. Conan had an eerie premonition that all this was but the beginning of a long war he must wage against ancient horror, the first of whose names was tyranny.

He forced his attention to what loomed before him. The Stygian galleys were berthed bows to a stone wharf which extended piers between the slips. Their masts stood sharp against star-clouds, but their hulls lay shadowed, a lantern or two gleaming lonely upon each. The barracks beyond must hold many sailors, but these would not rouse to action as fast as a barbarian could.

'We are ready,' he said, and strung his longbow.

Down the raised deck, men uncovered firepots. Coals within glowed, a row of small infernos. The picket boat came back alongside, her skeleton crew abandoned her for *Tigress*, she drifted off. Oars clunked softly, metal clanked, whispers hissed.

Under the foredeck, Falco ignited a cloth-wrapped, oil-soaked arrow. The flamelight brought his young face vivid out of the dark as he handed it up. 'Here, Conan,' he said. 'Yours is the first shot.'

'No,' he answered, 'it is Bêlit's.'

The queen of the Black Coast took the shaft and nocked it to her own bowstring. She drew, she aimed, she let fly a meteor. Thereafter Conan did, and Falco, and a suddenly savagely yelling pirate crew.

Sun-dried, pitchy wood kindled easily. Where an arrow struck, a tiny blaze stood forth, hell-blue, cackled like a new-hatched eaglet, reached out a claw, fed, grew, and spread wings. Upward then it soared, from stern to stem, and the radiance of it made bright that water the Styx poured into the sea, and the crying of it was akin to that of a bird of prey as it swoops upon a snake. From end to end of the royal docks *Tigress* went, while fire streaked from her to scourge the foes of Bêlit. Sparks swarmed on the wind, reached where her lash could not, and sowed more flame.

Stygians hastened frantic to stem the conflagration, but already it was too vast. They could do no better than to save what merchant and fisher craft were in harbor. None dared venture forth against the galley that prowled on the red edge of sight.

Mission completed, *Tigress* stood out to sea. Aft, Khemi Bay resembled a storm-tossed lake of blood. Once on the waves, she brought oars in, hoisted sail, and beat northward.

Conan came down the ladder to Falco. 'Well, lad,' the Cimmerian said gruffly, 'next we take you to Danmarcah, and let you off with enough gold in your purse for an easy trip home.'

Adoration looked back at him. 'After – after I have told my tale and it has reached the palace,' Falco stammered, 'never shall you lack for a friend among the kings of Ophir.'

'Thanks,' replied Conan. 'That may be useful someday – as may my friendships in Taia should I ever want to cross the Stygian realm by myself. Who knows what years unborn may bring? Death on a heath or life on a throne or anything in between; no matter now.' He shrugged. 'All I have done while you knew me has just been in the service of my lady.'

Above them on the foredeck, vengeful and joyful, Bêlit was laughing.